LIKE HERDING THE WIND

AN URUSHALON NOVEL

CINDY KOEPP

RARA AVIS
AN IMPRINT OF PDMI PUBLISHING, LLC
ALBERTVILLE, ALABAMA 35950

Like Herding the Wind: An Urushalon Novel
© Copyright 2015 by Cindy Koepp.

All Rights Reserved. Published in the United States by Rara Avis, an imprint of PDMI PUBLISHING, LLC. No part of this book may be reproduced or transmitted in any form or by any means, electronic or mechanical, including photocopying, recording, or by information storage and retrieval systems without written permission of the Publisher with exceptions as to brief quotes, references, articles, reviews, and certain other noncommercial uses permitted by copyright law.

PERMISSIONS
For permission requests, write to the publisher, addressed "Attention: Permissions Coordinator," at the address below.

PDMI Publishing, LLC
P.O. Box 56
Albertville, Alabama, 35950. USA

Please call 1 855-782-5474 or email us at info@pdmipublishing.com
www.pdmipublishing.com

ORDERING INFORMATION
Quantity sales and special discounts are available on quantity purchases by corporations, associations, and others. For details, contact the publisher.

PRINTING HISTORY
First Trade Paperback Edition, First Printing, January 2016.
1 2 3 4 5

ISBN-10: 194081264X
ISBN-13: 978-1-940812-64-9
Library of Congress Control Number: 2015955341

Hardcover ISBN-13: 978-1-940812-27-4

Rara Avis is a ® registered trademark of PDMI Publishing, LLC.

CREDITS
Cover and Interior Illustrations: Matt Ostrom; Cover Design by: TC McKinney; Interior Format by: Nessa Arcamenel; Edited by: Victoria Adams

PUBLISHER'S NOTE
This book is a work of fiction. The characters, incidents, and dialogues are products of the author's imagination and are not to be construed as real. Any resemblance to actual events or persons, living or dead, is entirely coincidental.

The publisher does not have any control over and does not assume any responsibility for author or third-party Websites or their content.

Unto all the people who've had a hand in shaping this tale and all those who have supplied encouragement, support, and an occasional kick-in-the-complacency ...

Grace be unto you, and peace from God, the Father of our Lord.

Prologue

Amaya shutdown the avicopter and stepped out while Ed hopped out the passenger side. She joined him and started to reach for his hand but stopped herself. Teenage humans, particularly the males, almost universally shunned displaying affection toward their mothers, and Amaya supposed that went for adopted mothers, too.

She smiled, keeping her teeth properly hidden, and gestured for him to lead the way toward the museum's entrance. The rock and glass structure had been in operation for only a handful of weeks, but by now the massive crowds had dwindled enough to allow a proper observation of the exhibits.

Amaya slowed her pace a little as Ed darted ahead to the museum door. He slid it open and held it for her as she walked through.

"Thank you." She paused inside the door to wait for him and accompany him to the docent's counter.

"Grace be unto you." Although Ed lived with his own parents and only visited her on weekends, he spoke flawless Eshuvani.

The docent gasped and studied Ed's broad human physique, curly red hair, and freckled cheeks. She stammered a few syllables. "And-and-and peace from God, the Father of our Lord."

Ed smiled without showing his teeth. "Two passes, please."

Amaya traded the fee for the passes and handed one to Ed.

"So, why not a paper ticket?" He studied the small metal disk with the picture of the old Eshuvani generation ship on one side and the name of the museum on the other.

"Why do you think?"

"Paper takes trees?" he guessed.

"Recycling takes care of that." She shook her head. "Think about the kind of place this is."

He squinted and blew out a breath. "No paper at the time of first contact?"

Amaya leaned closer. "Even humans had paper by 1612."

He studied the coin closer. "It's a part of the ship?"

"No, that was scavenged for parts and building materials long ago. Come back this way." She led him back to the lobby. "When we went to the museum in Lansing last week, what did the museum have there that is lacking here?"

"Don't suppose you'd just tell me," he muttered. He looked around, turning in place and checking high as well as ground level. His eyes widened. "Gift store! There's no gift store!" He held up the metal pass. "This is a souvenir. Paper disintegrates too fast, so it's metal to last."

"Exactly." She nodded toward the entrance to the exhibits. "Shall we?"

The first room had been constructed to look like the main control center of the dying generation ship in which the first settlers had crashed. Lighting was the blue of emergency alerts. Gauzy streamers, suspended from the ceiling to some of the stations, represented smoke. Scents injected into the air smelled of burnt wiring. Mannequins were fashioned to look like typical Eshuvani wearing the historical clothing of the time, a loose tunic over a pair of knee-length pants and ankle boots. The typical, modern-style shirt still had the somewhat looser sleeves of the period gathered at the wrists by wide cuffs. The sleeves on Amaya's uniform were less puffy than modern fashion but still more so than the typical, human style.

They toured the stations checking out the timeline from the historical records recovered from the ship's computer.

"In 1612, Earth calendar, a coolant leak in the engine..." The computerized voice droned on through the speakers overhead.

Amaya tuned it out and studied the detail on the exhibit. She knew the history of the first contact quite well. As a *kiand* specializing in interspecies relations, the detailed analysis of the first contact story had been part of her required education. The coolant leak had led to complete breakdown as one system after another struggled to correct the problem. By the time the computer had awakened the technicians in suspension, there weren't enough systems left online to continue. They'd limped to the nearest habitable planet, which turned out to be Earth.

As the recording recycled, Ed turned to her and frowned. "Why did the computer only wake technicians? I would've thought that with systems going down, it would've gotten everyone up? Why wait until just before the crash landing?"

She nodded slowly. *Such curiosity is a blessing.* "What system would have been most severely taxed with everyone awake and so many other systems collapsing all around?"

"Um, oh wow." He frowned and studied the floor. "Not the engines. They're already dying. Weapons won't matter in that situation. Defenses are pretty useless. Um, I don't see it."

Well, then, let's move the setting to something easier to

LIKE HERDING THE WIND

relate to. "Make the ship a submarine under water. Think about the things you must have for–"

"Air!" His eyes widened. "If the computer had gotten all two thousand people awake at once, they might have run out of air!"

She clapped his shoulder. "Excellent."

The path led to an exhibit in a room with a roof that could be retracted. One wall had been built to resemble the outside of the ship. Hull armor was missing or badly scorched. More gauzy streamers in various shades of gray represented smoke. The odor in the air was the same as the previous exhibit but diluted by the ozone common after a storm and the earthy smell of newly turned soil. The carpet below their feet had been rippled like a plowed field.

In the center of the room, the actual first contact was portrayed. Amaya smiled. The curator had gone for accuracy instead of the usual lopsided depiction that favored showing the humans as overly aggressive. A few dozen Eshuvani mannequins were gathered in a loose group opposite seven humans armed with knives, pitchforks, and smallish swords. The Eshuvani would have appeared unarmed, but the curator had fixed that by showing a couple easing small laser pistols from holsters.

"The damaged ship set down hard on a farmer's field in the Saxony region of Germany." The recorded voice explained. "A group of peasant farmers approached the security expedition party. Both sides were understandably frightened. The human party, armed with primitive farm tools, assumed an aggressive posture, and some members of the Eshuvani security force secretly drew weapons. A human religious leader intervened and convinced the other humans to lower their weapons. To prevent further misunderstanding, the leader of the expedition ordered everyone back on board and waited until after nightfall to scout out the land."

After reading all the plaques and studying the descriptions, Ed followed her into the next chamber. The main lights were off. Reading lamps mounted above each plaque gave enough light for the immediate area. Overhead, a dull, glowing orb resembled a gibbous moon and illuminated the rest of the exhibit.

The mannequins here resembled a handful of foraging Eshuvani and a lone human dressed in a black cassock who was handing one of the Eshuvani a basket of food. While Ed studied the central display, Amaya made a circuit of the room reading all the plaques while the speaker overhead relayed the information about the human minister who had come to the aid of the survivors in the crashed ship.

She'd made half the circuit when Ed joined her.

"Amaya, the museum's version of this second meeting doesn't match what my history book said." He ran his fingers partway through his hair then scratched his head. "The book says there were several Eshuvani, the person they ran into was a monk, and they kidnapped him until he taught them what they wanted to know. That's not what the recording says at all."

She looked down at him. "Well, telling which is right will be hard since so much time has passed and each side could be casting the events in a favorable light. Consider the two accounts. What do they have in common?"

"Um, some Eshuvani left the ship. They found a-a-a clergyman of some kind. When they ran into each other the second time, he went back to the ship with them. After he taught them the language, and religion, and other stuff, he left."

Amaya nodded. "Good, and that's probably all we can say for certain. Everything else is speculation."

The next room was back inside the ship. Eshuvani mannequins stood around a table looking at a projected globe of the Earth. Red dots on the map showed major human civilization centers. Blue dots showed the locations that ended up being the first enclaves, one or two on each continent

LIKE HERDING THE WIND

except Antarctica. Eshuvani mannequins around the perimeter of the room were disassembling systems, and some were carrying pieces away.

"The first enclaves were established in areas away from major human habitations," the recording began. It continued with a description of the division of equipment and personnel.

Ed studied the globe, using his shorter, broader fingers to measure the distances between the dots and comparing them to the scale. "Amaya, why did the Eshuvani hide away, then? Except for treaties and disasters, even now, most of your people stay in their enclaves."

"That was deliberately done to protect humanity." She joined him at the display. "We could have shared our technology, yes, but there are dangers in advancing a civilization too fast. Even with a normal rate of development, the technology reaches potential faster than the wisdom to deal with it. Humans are clever people when they wish to be. We feared that if we shared too much too quickly, people would misuse a technology unintentionally or misuse it for their own purposes to the detriment of others. As humans develop, we will share a bit more."

"Someone at school said that Eshuvani only pick someone to be an *urushalon* to spy on humans." He faced her directly, his smile somewhere between suspicious and amused.

"How would that work?" Amaya mirrored his expression. "You were four. Maybe you don't remember, but you adopted me, *Urushalon*."

His pale blue eyes narrowed for a moment before he chuckled. "Of course, I remember, *Urushalon*. Dad was so mad! 'Most kids who wander off and get lost come back with sticks, bugs, and rocks. Mine adopts a resident-alien police chief.' He never does get your rank right."

"We won't tell the *kiat* about his efforts to give me a promotion." As the recording recycled, Amaya led Ed to the next room.

URUSHALON

As if timed to her movement, her gold collar tabs chimed as she crossed the threshold into the next room.

Ed groaned. "Oh, not again."

"I'm never off duty. You know that."

"Yeah, but..." He sighed.

She tapped the blue crystal on her collar. "Amaya."

"Dispatch. Disturbance at the Marquette Train Depot. Marquette Police Department is requesting back-up."

"On my way. Message received." She tapped the blue crystal again and fished out her souvenir coin. "This will grant us entry for the rest of the day. We can return after the call."

"That's okay." In spite of his polite reassurance, Ed's slight frown spoke of his disappointment. He shrugged. "I like watching you work, too. It's kind of like training."

Amaya led the way back through the exhibits. "Have you decided yet if you want to train in police work or medicine?"

"Thinking more about police work, but still haven't decided for sure." Ed followed close to her left shoulder.

"You have time."

Once they were outside, they jogged to the gray and silver avicopter in the corner of the lot and climbed in. As Amaya powered up the systems, Ed looked at the museum.

"Amaya, will the Eshuvani, the ones here on Earth I mean, ever go back to your home world?" He twisted around toward her.

She finished start-up and extended the wings. "Doubtful. Even if we ever manage to adapt our space flight technology to Earth's available resources, we've built lives here. I'm afraid you're stuck with us, dear one. Do you mind?"

"Not at all." He grinned widely then looked out the window as the avicopter lifted off. "Can I fly the avi on the way back?"

"On the way back, sure." Amaya turned onto the course to

LIKE HERDING THE WIND

the train depot.

The soundproofing in the hull kept the hum and whine of the flapping wings to a minimum.

URUSHALON

Chapter One

Sergeant Ed Osborn finished checking over his report. After scribbling a circle on the corner of a notepad, he signed his name and started the date.

May 25, 196-

The radio on the table behind him clicked. "Car Seven. Officer in need of assistance. Two hostile Eshuvani."

Osborn glanced at the radio. From the strain in Tucker's voice, they'd both be spending the rest of the watch at the hospital. Osborn scrawled the last five on the date, dropped his pen, and bolted to the dispatcher's desk in the next room. She handed him a paper with the address.

He ran for the parking lot and looked at the script on the paper. *What do they want at a sporting goods warehouse?*

He slowed as he reached his car and scorched his fingers on the sun-heated door latch. The inside, even hotter than the door handle, could do double-duty as an oven, and not even the sea breeze off the coast could do much for that.

Osborn started his car and flipped the switches for both lights and sirens before he picked up the radio mic. "Car One. Send me one unit for backup."

The dispatcher relayed the call.

"Car Five. Will handle hostile Eshuvani call with Car One."

Osborn nodded. Out of that pair, at least Mark Hollis had some experience with hostile Eshuvani. He'd nearly gotten his head blown off to get that experience, but he knew to keep his distance.

Most of the civilian drivers Osborn encountered were decent enough to honor his siren and move aside. He accelerated out of a turn and into the industrial district of Las Palomas. Car Seven's reds blinked, and both front doors hung open showing Tucker, paler than usual, slumped at the wheel. Parrish, almost as dark as his black uniform, had one suspect against a stack of empty wooden pallets near the brick building's west wall.

The suspect stood an easy six-foot-four and had the nonhuman, narrow build common to the Eshuvani. He had both hands raised and spindly fingers ended at the wrist with a small bit of webbing near the base to look like a palm.

Parrish pulled out handcuffs.

Don't do it, Parrish. Keep your distance. Osborn parked behind Car Seven and bailed out, gun in hand. "Stay back, Parrish! Wait for backup."

Parrish kept his eyes on the suspect but nodded and tucked the cuffs into his belt.

Checking behind stacks of empty pallets and splintered boards, Osborn crept forward.

A second Eshuvani darted from behind a pile of crates and charged at the other officer. Osborn led the target, but he had no clear line of fire.

Osborn tensed. "Parrish!"

URUSHALON

The newcomer gave him a hard shove. He slammed into the stack of pallets then dropped flat on his back. The pile teetered. The first suspect bared teeth, filed to sharp points no normal Eshuvani would approve of, and turned to pull the stack onto the officer.

Osborn made the mental switch to the Eshuvani language and took aim. "Police! Face down on the ground! Now!"

Both suspects gave him a squint-eyed glare.

Didn't expect me to know your language, huh? Been fluent since I was five. Get serious. You think maybe your kind have been on this world long enough for some humans to learn the language?

They took off running.

Osborn raced after them. He wove among the piles of crates and pallets but couldn't match the suspects' speed. He reached the chain link fence separating the warehouse from the furniture factory next door. A mottled green avicopter sat in the factory's vacant parking lot. Both Eshuvani boarded. The birdlike wings extended with a familiar hydraulic whine, and the avi lifted off. Osborn looked for the ID markings on the tail, but the decals were gone, leaving the paint where they used to be a brighter shade of green than the rest. The pilot turned the avicopter's tail to him and fled.

"Next time." Osborn slapped the palm of his hand into the fence. "Next time for sure."

He jogged back to Parrish. Blood ran from a gash on Parrish's forehead. Osborn pressed his handkerchief on the cut, marveling at the contrast between the white cloth and the officer's dark skin and tightly coiled black hair.

Gravel crunched nearby and two car doors opened. Kirby and Hollis hopped out of Car Five.

Osborn drew a deep breath. "Call an ambulance and see to Tucker."

Hollis darted forward to Car Seven. Kirby sat back in his

LIKE HERDING THE WIND

own car and grabbed the radio mic.

Parrish groaned and quivered in an effort to push himself up.

Osborn pressed on Parrish's shoulder. "Stay still, Parrish."

A siren wailed in the distance.

Parrish lowered himself again. "Tucker's hurt."

Osborn glanced at Car Seven as Hollis slid into the front seat. "Hollis is with Tucker, and an ambulance is on the way."

"Eshuvani." Parrish swallowed hard. "Two of 'em."

Osborn nodded. "I know. Just take it easy."

Parrish squinted up at him. "I thought your Eshuvani mom was workin' on gettin' us help."

"She's trying. There's a lot of resistance from the local leadership." *Three hundred fifty-four years of sharing this world and cooperation is still a matter of small clusters here and there.*

"Well, tell 'er t' speed it up."

Osborn smiled. "First chance I get. Now you stay still."

"Don't you worry. Even thinkin' about movin' hurts."

Kirby jogged over and knelt. "Ambulance should be here soon, Sarge."

Osborn nodded.

Although Kirby spoke fluent English, there was a Mexican cadence in his speech. Osborn hadn't understood why until he'd met the young officer's mother at the hospital after Kirby had been injured in a caper. Kirby didn't have a good tan just because he liked to play outdoors.

Parrish grabbed Kirby's arm. "Tucker?"

Kirby nodded once. "He'll be okay, Parrish. Take it easy."

"Come on, man." Parrish's arm dropped back to his side.

URUSHALON

"He hit that wall awful hard."

Kirby frowned. "He has a bump on his head and says breathing hurts. Probably bruised a couple ribs. How about you?"

Parrish pointed to the handkerchief. "Got a headache."

Osborn peeked under the cloth. The gash still oozed blood but not the same fountain as before.

"Looks like I'm gonna have to skip movie night," Parrish said.

Osborn tried a smile, but it felt too tight. "*Few Dollars More* just came out. We'll catch it some other time."

"Yeah, well, maybe the girls can still go see *Sound of Music*. Dorothy was really lookin' forward to it."

Osborn shrugged. "I'll suggest it and see what she says."

An ambulance siren blared louder, then wound down.

Osborn waved a paramedic over. "I think that's your ride."

"'Bout time. This concrete could cook us breakfast." Parrish chuckled then winced.

Osborn smirked and cleared the way for the ambulance crew. "Hey, at least you're in the shade."

One of the paramedics ran over with what looked like a bright orange tackle box. After asking a million questions, checking Parrish's eyes with a small flashlight, and binding the obvious injury, the paramedic brought a gurney over. Osborn helped lift Parrish onto the gurney and stood back while the experts rolled the injured officer away.

Kirby pointed to the bloodstained wood and whistled. "Eshuvani again. How do you take these guys?"

"With plenty of backup and a lot more training." Osborn looked at the stained handkerchief and sighed. "You and Hollis get the reports going. I have to go call a couple wives and get them to the hospital."

LIKE HERDING THE WIND

He'd been calling too many wives.

***

Amaya Ulonya *Kiand* thanked the courier as she grabbed her jacket and hopped out of the gray and white avicopter. She closed the avi door then detached her cargo pod and stepped away. The courier lifted off as the attendants came out and helped her drag the cargo pod to the limestone wall of the *kiat's* headquarters. The brass plaque near the entrance listed the construction date as 1892.

Fairly new construction.

After the Great Dispersal in 1613 Earth calendar, populations of Eshuvani had scattered to six of the seven continents and established settlements as if they had reached their planned destination. Most of those original buildings still stood and served some function, if not their original one. An essential building such as the *kiat's* headquarters raised questions about what had become of the original.

She stretched her arms through their range of motion, a futile effort to lose the tension across her shoulders. When the door slid open at her approach, the cooler air rushed to drive back the Texas heat. She'd swear the air temperature, so far south of her last home, could fry bugs on the wing.

The door slid shut behind her with the dull hum of the electronic motor. A trio of deep blue-green, squashy leather chairs lined the left wall of the waiting room. The floor, made of sand and shells sealed into clear acrylic, reflected both sunlight from the windows and light from the ceiling. The window curtains hung in long strips of silky, dark green ribbons, twisted to look like a bed of kelp. The air smelled saltier inside than outside.

Did you properly impress your intended audience, Emyrin?

"Grace be unto you," the secretary said.

The woman had given her hair a washable dye to match the brilliant turquoise of her dress. Her excessive cosmetics gave her a gaunt, fish-like look while the web membrane at the base of her thin fingers had been painted to resemble fish scales. Was this dress code or personal preference to blend into the marine decorations?

Amaya strode up to the desk to complete the greeting. "And peace from God, the Father of our Lord."

"In what way may I serve you, *Kiand*?" She flashed a wide grin.

"I am Amaya Ulonya. I am expected."

The secretary's smile turned as genuine as her hair color. "You were told not to come."

Amaya took a folded letter from the pocket of the jacket she carried. "I have the mandate of the king and the approval of the Council of the *Kiati*. Whether Emyrin wants the Buffer Zone station or not, it is there, and I am its *kiand*."

The fake smile faded. "But the *kiat* refused you the position. I typed the letter myself."

"His Magnificence assigned me to this post afterward, when no applicants remained. Emyrin has no choice. Will you inform the *kiat* of my arrival?" Amaya set the letter on the desk.

The secretary heaved a sigh. "He won't be happy."

Amaya looked down the long hall behind the desk. "Show me to his office, and I'll inform him."

"He'll like that even less. Sit down. I'll tell him you're here."

"Thank you." Amaya sank into the padding of a leather chair. *This is supposed to be comfortable?*

She adjusted her position and rested her chin on her steepled fingers. The trip from Marquette had been long, and the weariness dragged at her. After holding back a deep yawn, Amaya closed her eyes.

The air cooling system stuttered through start up. In her

LIKE HERDING THE WIND

mind, the noise became the sound of a human power generator, straining as an old elevator lowered her through the one surviving shaft into the collapsed mine. Endless feet of timber-braced rock walls had slid by at a pace marginally better than a dead stop. She had reached the bottom and stepped out of the cage, and there had lain Essien, twisted, broken, and obviously dead.

Amaya opened her eyes and stood, crossing her arms to ward off a chill and hide an intense tremor in her hands. *You're in enemy territory, foolish one. This is hardly the time for the Rite of Final Memorial, even if you had a counselor available.*

The secretary returned and sat. "He's on the communication net at the moment, and he'll be with you once he's finished."

Amaya nodded. "What can you tell me about the situation here?"

"You mean the human situation, I assume." She spat the word "human" like a curse.

"Of course."

The secretary rolled her eyes. "Annoying creatures. Especially that police sergeant of theirs, Ed something."

"Ed Osborn."

"Yes, him. He's always wanting an appointment." She sniffed and inspected her fingernails. "Such a pest, but at least he has the decency to speak Eshuvani."

If you were ten times the person you are, you still wouldn't measure up to him. "I find his curiosity and determination rather endearing."

The secretary's face scrunched up. "You're the *urushalon* he's always talking about?"

"He adopted me when he was four. I applied for this post because of him." *You'll never learn the other reason I came.*

The secretary shuddered. "I can't believe you let a human

URUSHALON

adopt you."

Amaya frowned. "Adopting an *urushalon* has been a common practice ever since our people arrived on this world."

"I've never understood it. They're so backward." She rolled her eyes.

Amaya uncrossed her arms as the chill finally faded. "They're quite clever, given the chance."

"If you say so. I just don't see what you gain from taking an *urushalon*. I see what they gain: access to our technology, our knowledge, and at least a possibility of rising above their human intellect, but what about you? What do you gain? It's not like we need their help to adapt to this planet anymore."

"Must things be done only for gain? Must gain be measured in the terms you describe? Not all benefits can be categorized in such a way."

She sat back in her chair. "Is having an *urushalon* like owning a pet or something?"

"No, it's like having a very dear friend. He adopted me years ago, and I have not regretted it once. Now, back to my question. Can–"

A red light the size of Amaya's fingernail lit up on the desk.

The secretary pushed a button near the light and turned it off. "The *kiat* is ready for you. Follow me."

The woman's glittery dress clung to her body all the way down to the flare at the knees. Amaya arched an eyebrow. How did the secretary manage to walk in that get up? She stopped at a door with carved images of cavorting dolphins and waved a hand in front of the sensor plate. After the door slid open, the secretary pivoted on her high heeled shoes and strutted back to her desk.

Amaya rolled her eyes and stepped into the office. It had suffered from the same extravagant decorator as the gaudy waiting room. Emyrin Koral *Kiat* rose. He had piercing green

LIKE HERDING THE WIND

eyes and perfectly trimmed gray hair. Copper filigree on his gray shirt collar confirmed his rank, and the gems embedded in the reddish metal detailed his training record. The lines marring his old face suggested he hadn't smiled in years.

She squared her shoulders. "Grace be unto you."

Emyrin threw his pen down on the desk. "I told you not to come. You disobey orders already by crushing the carpet with your boots."

Amaya pulled out another copy of her mandate and set it on his desk. "The king and the Council of the *Kiati* said otherwise, so I'm here to get my key card."

"Do you think I care what the Council thinks? And the king was a mere prince this time last year." Emyrin tore the letter in half, crumbled it, and hurled it into the waste bin. "We can't afford to police the human cities."

"That's not the assignment. Humans are capable of policing themselves with proper training and equipment. That's all they're asking for, and they've been quite reasonable." Amaya hung her jacket off her shoulder.

Emyrin's ears went blood-red. "Let them handle their own problems!"

Amaya kept her voice at a civilized volume. "They can't. They're overmatched. Eshuvani criminals seek easy prey among the humans. Officers are hurt, and civilians are dead. Since the criminals come from our own people, the humans need and deserve our help. They wouldn't be in this crisis if we hadn't come here in the first place. Ever since we formed our enclaves in the 1600s, they've been quite content to keep to themselves until our own attacked them."

"Yes, they kept to themselves because we gave them a show of force to prove how futile coming against us would be, so spare me the 'poor humans' rhetoric. They aren't half as noble as you make them out to be." He planted both fists on his desk and leaned forward. "They have a planet they haven't half-used. We don't impact them so much. Now they want us

URUSHALON

to solve their problems."

"Hardly." Amaya brushed his argument aside with a wave of her hand. "They want our help so they can solve their own. The Buffer Zone stations elsewhere have been successful in accomplishing this."

"And in the meantime, our own crime rates rise."

"The king disagrees, and so does the evidence." She numbered off points on her fingers. "Buffer Zone stations have helped human police and paramedics become more self-sufficient in ninety-four percent of all cases. Crime rates in the adjacent cities and enclaves have declined by eighteen–"

"I've already heard your pathetic arguments from another mouth." He came around the desk and stood close enough she could count pores in his skin.

If Amaya obeyed her instincts, she would move back a step, but she overruled her gut and stood her ground. He would gain no satisfaction from his intimidation tactics.

He growled. "Get out of my office!"

"Not without the key card."

"You're not getting it." He backed off a step.

She turned one hand toward the ceiling. "Then I'll contact the Council for more information on where to obtain the key card."

His eyes narrowed. "Breach of protocol."

"I've been given a mandate to command the new station, and I can't do that without the key card. If you won't supply it, what other options do I have?"

Emyrin gave her a bare-toothed stare, and Amaya squelched a smirk at his almost childish temper tantrum. Emyrin returned to his desk and pressed one of the four blue communication gems on his shirt collar while he tapped a short code on another.

"Teviya," the secretary answered.

LIKE HERDING THE WIND

"Emyrin. Forward Ulonya's budget and information to the new station."

Amaya's fist clenched at her side, but she loosened her fingers again. *Calm down. Referring to me by family name is just a petty insult. Very juvenile, really.* She was more an individual than he could guess.

The secretary groaned. "Message received."

"Don't expect me to support your babysitting service, Ulonya." Emyrin snatched up a key card and flung it at her. "Introduce yourself to the station. I'm busy."

Amaya pocketed the card and painted on as genuine a smile as she could manage. "Serve with diligence."

Once the *kiat's* door closed behind her, Amaya blew out a deep breath. She needed a belligerent supervisor? Amaya straightened her back and strode to the secretary's desk.

Teviya sighed and turned to her computer. "So, *Kiand*, what name will your station go by?"

"*Uloniya Varoosht.*"

She snorted. "Hawk's Nest?"

Amaya nodded and dismissed her annoyance. "The *kiandarai* are protectors and healers, not a military establishment."

"Fitting choice for child care, I suppose." Teviya shrugged and typed the name into the system. "Hawk's Nest it is. All of your equipment was already delivered. I'll have your budget for the rest of the year and your personnel files sent to you by the time you get there."

"Personnel files?" Amaya frowned and stepped back. "Have my people been chosen already?"

"The *kiat* said that with the Consecration Day ceremony only two weeks away, he'd do the new *kiand*, you apparently, the favor of speeding up your readiness by choosing the rest of the personnel and purchasing your equipment." Teviya typed and kept her eyes on the screen. "You're ready for operation

URUSHALON

as soon as your staff arrives. You do want to start as soon as possible, don't you?"

So, Emyrin, did you give me an overabundance of gray hair or a flock of brand new kialai *straight from their apprenticeships?*

Teviya smiled like a predator arming for the kill. "I'm sure they're good people."

Amaya hid her scowl under the veneer of professional stoicism. "I'm sure they are. Thank you."

She stepped into the blast furnace of the Texas afternoon and pressed two of the dark blue gems on her collar.

"Dispatch."

"Amaya Ulonya *Kiand*. I require a courier at this location."

"Cargo?"

"One passenger and a small cargo pod."

"Destination?"

"The Buffer Zone *kiandarai* station, *Uloniya Varoosht*."

"Message received."

A muted click signaled the end of the conversation.

A few minutes later, a gray and white courier avicopter landed nearby. While an attendant hitched Amaya's cargo pod to the undercarriage, she walked around the avi, the latest model. The bird-like wings were folded back against the sleek body. As usual, the pilot's and passengers' compartment occupied the exaggerated head and forward body of the bird. This particular model had space for a pilot and two passengers.

By the time Amaya had finished her circuit of the avicopter, the attendant had secured the cargo pod. Amaya boarded the avi and took the seat next to the pilot. He lifted off and headed out.

The gray-haired pilot was a *kiand*, by the gold filigree on

LIKE HERDING THE WIND

his shirt collar. Heavy scars marred one hand and a metal-hinged brace wrapped around one leg. Wherever he'd worked hadn't been blessed with proper medical facilities.

"Exciting business, opening up a new station." He looked over then returned his attention to the instruments. "I made a lifetime habit of it. Always on the frontier."

Amaya smiled. "Impressive. What was your biggest challenge?"

"I opened my fifth station so far out in the wilds, we couldn't get supplies in regular. When things would break down, we had to find some way to make it all work." He chuckled and shook his head. "Why, I remember how we pieced together lubricant lines with pen barrels and tape, but, y'know, we come through it well enough." The pilot regaled her with stories of some of the more bizarre solutions to their equipment problems. As he wound up the third of his tales, he set down in front of Hawk's Nest. "Just take an old man's advice. Don't fret over what you don't have. Look at what you have and how you can use it. Look for solutions, not problems."

Amaya nodded. "Sound advice all around."

He turned in his seat and offered his right arm. As they clasped arms, he pulled her into an embrace.

"I heard all kinds of rumors about what you've got waiting on the other side of those doors. Find your solutions."

She patted his shoulder and sat back. "I will. I appreciate your service."

"Serve with diligence, *Kiand.*"

Amaya disembarked and detached her cargo pod. Once the old pilot had flown away, she bowed her head and turned both hands toward the sky. *Thank you, God, for the new assignment and the much needed pep talk.* She approached the main door of the station and flashed the key card past the reader. The lock clicked, and the door slid to the left.

URUSHALON

She stepped inside the hot, stuffy room as the smell of sawdust and ancient architecture blasted her in the face. The lights didn't turn on and the windows were in their dark phase, so she held the door open. Perhaps this station had the voice command system instead of the heat sensors. That would make sense, given the ambient temperatures in this part of the world.

"Lights, full! Windows, transparent!"

Dust motes twirled in the shaft of sunlight that remained the only illumination in the foyer. In the dim light coming through the door, Amaya made out a faint reflection off the edge of a dial. She released the door and rushed over. Just as she lost the exterior light, she turned the dial, and the windows became transparent. A pull-chain hung from the ceiling in the middle of the room. When she tugged it, the lights came on.

A handful of mismatched chairs, each with a lifetime of scratches and dents, were lined up near one wall. A couple had once been padded, but the foam had long since deteriorated. The dispatch station consisted of a rusted metal filing cabinet, a rolling chair with one caster missing, and an old table, one leg of which had been splinted together with a gnarled tree branch and some wire. Who in their right mind called this "ready for operation?"

Passages led to the left, right, and straight ahead. A scrawled paper sign labeled the one door leading off the foyer as the briefing room. Similar signage tacked to the walls pointed the way to the medical area, jail, storage, and hangar. The walls themselves were faded, splintered wood-veneer paneling with nail holes left from the previous installation.

I'll need more than paint and a few pictures to make this room presentable.

Amaya followed the left wall around toward the hangar and came to a pitch black room. She felt along the wall for the switch as her footsteps echoed, telling her the room had some size. The switch was three full strides away.

LIKE HERDING THE WIND

When she flipped the small lever down, two-thirds of the room lit. The light panel on the far side of the room showered sparks with a loud pop. Amaya crouched and shielded her head with her arms.

There were four avicopters housed in the hangar as required. Two had cracked canopies. The furthest one had one wing attached with the other on the ground nearby. The next nearest avi had wires hanging out of closed repair bays. The second closest had fuselage sheeting missing, leaving the engine compartment open to the elements. The avicopter in front of Amaya had leaked a puddle of dark, gray-brown goo onto the floor of the bay. All four still had their original, faded, rusted paint from the beginning of the twentieth century, when *kiandarai* colors were blue and red. Until she could look over the engines, she didn't dare start any of them.

From there she went on to find a briefing room crammed with construction debris and then to a storeroom populated with old, damaged, or broken equipment. The kitchen needed a good cleaning, and the pantry had nothing but fifty-pound bags of rice and beans. The medical clinic could handle nothing more severe than first aid, so she'd have to use the portable equipment in her own trauma kit for anything needing more than a gauze patch and tape. The safe room was bereft of all but four walls, ceiling, and floor. The holding cell had been built with the lowest possible technology: steel bars as big around as her wrist.

Was the housing behind the station as bleak as the main building? The dwellings were built offsite and flown in on the massive cargo carrier avicopters. Unless they were gutted after arrival, the *kiandarai* quarters should still be equipped with the voice-recognition systems and other such conveniences.

Upon entering the first cylindrical house, Amaya bared her teeth and shook her head. The basic structure had come straight from the factory, but the furnishings came straight from a junkyard. The couch was a park bench with broken and missing slats, and the two living room chairs were concrete blocks with a board across them. The hammocks in the bedrooms were child-sized and torn. The other five houses were no better.

Amaya returned to the station's storeroom. She grabbed a chewed-on pen and a notepad with three blank pages. Beginning in the entryway, she started making three lists: what needed to be done, what she'd like to do, and what she could sell or trade.

When she'd finished her second tour of the station and *kiandarai* quarters, Amaya went to the computer in the entryway. Protocol demanded the system provided to a station had to function within given parameters. If only the protocol detailed such specificity for everything else. She logged into the system and found the budget waiting for her. A housewife couldn't keep her home running for seven months on the paltry figure. Emyrin's office decorations cost a few orders of magnitude more.

She sighed. Emyrin meant for her to fail, and she planned to disappoint him.

Amaya prioritized her to do list and logged into the local *kiandarai* conversation board to introduce herself and list what she had for barter or sale. She had two weeks to get ready for Consecration Day, and her list wouldn't get any shorter until she got busy on it.

At least the constant work would keep her from thinking about the mine.

Chapter Two

Humming the new Beach Boys tune, Mark Hollis strolled into the Las Palomas police station. The white tile and gray paint in the red brick building made the place comfortable and less like they were in a turn of the century dump that hadn't had the decency to fall over yet.

Outside Sergeant Ed Osborn's open office door, Hollis paused. His former partner leaned over a pile of papers on his scuffed and scarred wooden desk. Hollis eyed Osborn's white-knuckled grip on the pencil and wondered how that thing hadn't snapped yet.

"Good morning, Ed."

Osborn continued reading the report in front of him. "Hi."

Hollis stepped into the office and leaned on the back of a black vinyl chair. "Everything all right?"

Osborn signed the top paper, then set it aside. "Sure."

"Uh-huh. Ed, it's me, Mark. Seriously. What's wrong? The monosyllabic response is not your style."

Osborn leaned back. "A little disappointed, I guess."

Hollis sat and waited for Osborn to go on.

He tossed the pencil on the desk. "You remember when we took the kids to California last year to see where Esther grew up?"

Hollis nodded. "Umhm. Why?"

"Well, we're headed to my old stomping grounds this year, so I sent word to Amaya to see if she could spare some time to visit and show Esther and the kids around the enclave. She wrote back that she won't be in Marquette in August."

"Why not?"

"That's the troubling part. Normally, she would've explained, and the lack of detail worries me. Generally, Eshuvani are talkative about things in their lives, even personal things. The only subject Eshuvani won't talk about is someone's death. They have an official rite where they talk out all their feelings and grief, then they never mention it again. Death of someone close is an emotional crisis for an Eshuvani, and I'm too far away to help. I can only remember one time when she clammed up like that, and it had to do with someone's death."

Hollis held up one hand. "Whoa there. That's quite a jump, pal. Maybe it's nothing that dire. Aren't they always on call? What if she was interrupted? Maybe by the time she got back to the note, she forgot she hadn't explained. With only six officers to a station, I suspect they get a little busy from time to time."

Osborn rubbed his forehead. "Possible, I suppose."

"If it helps, I wouldn't mind swapping weeks with you. Ruth's due any day now, so we're not planning on going anywhere. I can easily sit at home and play with the baby in August or June. In fact, if you put it to the guys, I'm sure many of them would trade."

Osborn managed a smile. "Thanks, Mark. I'll check with Amaya and see if that's the problem."

Hollis shrugged. "Just let me know."

LIKE HERDING THE WIND

"How's Ruth?" Osborn sat back in his chair.

"Anxious to deliver the baby." Hollis grinned and leaned closer. "She's hoping for some time before the temperatures hit triple digits in the shade."

"Ah, the joy of living in Texas."

"You know it." Hollis glanced at the clock. Roll call would start in a couple minutes. "I'm going for some coffee. Want some?"

"No, thanks. I've already had two."

He snorted and shook his head. "You are worried. Try not to let it bug you. I'm sure it's nothing big."

Hollis stopped at the break room and fixed himself a cup of coffee before making his way to the conference room. A chalkboard listed everyone's car assignments for the day. He'd be riding with Robert Kirby. Why did Osborn bother posting the assignments? He never changed things around.

Seven other officers sat there nursing coffee at long wooden tables arranged in a rectangle with a hole in the middle. Gale had his chair flipped around backwards and sat facing the table. His mop of black hair had a gray streak over both ears and framed a round, tanned face.

"And then the fella says, 'But the truck lights were on, weren't they?'" Harry Gale chuckled at his own tale while Clyde Sumner, a sandy-haired, blue-eyed transfer from the big city, laughed.

Nearby, Stevens sat with his fresh-out-of-the-academy partner, who didn't look old enough to be finished with high school yet. Both leaned forward and nodded, hanging on Gale's every word as the next tall tale started.

Hollis traded a wave with the other two pairs and with the poor guys from the previous shift who were pulling another half-day to cover for Parrish and Tucker.

Kirby beckoned from the back table, and Hollis made his way over. The Hispanic officer still kept his dark brown hair

URUSHALON

cut to navy regulation length. His mother's heritage showed in his dark complexion and narrow eyes.

Hollis dropped into a folding chair nearby and faced the desk under the chalkboard. "Good morning, partner. You're here early."

Kirby smiled and pointed to the door. "I was on time. You just missed being late."

"Had a mission of mercy to attempt," Hollis whispered behind his hand.

Osborn entered, his brow furrowed.

Hollis sighed. "Didn't quite get it done."

Osborn sorted the papers on his desk and called out the car assignments for the day. "Only one piece of news before you head out. We received an answer from the chief of police for the Woran Oldue enclave. He is not willing to provide training. He says they don't have the manpower, nor do they have a sufficient number of English-speakers among the *kiandarai* at this time. He told us to wait."

"Wait? Is he serious? Don't he know we just about lost Parrish an' Tucker yesterday?" Gale slapped the table in front of him. "Ain't that like an Eshuvani to leave us in the lurch?"

Ease up there, Gale. You're including Ed's adopted mom, y'know. Hollis winced.

Osborn speared Gale with a stern look.

"Sarge, what about your–your whaddyacallit?" Kirby asked.

"*Urushalon*. Amaya's trying to come down here to teach you what you'll need to know. It'd be a speed course but better than I can do. She just has to secure someone to take over her post for a while."

Gale crossed his arms over his chest. "Way our luck's goin' that'll go bust, too."

Osborn frowned and pointed at Gale with his pencil.

LIKE HERDING THE WIND

"Even if it does go sour, the Eshuvani government purchased all the land between Woran Oldue and Las Palomas to form a buffer between the cities. A new station is going to be built to cover this Buffer Zone, support us as needed, and provide training. That's what we're supposed to wait for."

"When will they go active?" Kirby asked.

"I'm not sure. They need to find a *kiand* and five *kiandarai* qualified and willing to staff the station." Osborn showed the numbers on his fingers.

Gale snorted and rolled his eyes. "Six people? That ain't even enough for a football team. How's that supposed t' help?"

"That's a standard complement. They build more stations, not bigger ones."

"Quantity, not quality, eh?" Sumner nudged his partner in the ribs.

"Jus' you wait." Gale glanced both ways and leaned closer. "I hear tell there are women in the *kiandarai*."

Hollis rolled his eyes. "Obviously, if Ed's adopted mom is a *kiand*. You may have noticed we also have two policewomen. They man the dispatch desk most days. This is the twentieth century, y'know."

"The men may be stronger, but the women still get the job done. I've seen Amaya in action on some really hairy calls." Osborn collected his papers. "That's all. I'll give you updates as I get them. Get out there."

Hollis discarded his paper cup on the way out and joined the file of men headed for the parking lot.

Kirby put his hat on and adjusted it. "Have you ever worked with *kiandarai*?"

Hollis nodded. "Once. When I was riding with Ed, we assisted a *kiandara* with a bust when the suspect tried to hide in an abandoned factory over on Eighth Street. I cornered the suspect, or so I thought. This guy could've played for the

URUSHALON

Lakers. Anyway, he closed the distance between us and decked me. Next thing I knew, I was looking down the barrel of my own gun. Before I could even think, 'Uh-oh,' he tensed one, two, three times. Dropped like a brick. Three little darts from a *kiandarai* pistol were sticking out of the back of his neck. The *kiandara* yelled something from off to my left. Ed answered from somewhere in the distance. They both joined me. The *kiandara* took custody of the suspect, and it was all over."

"Was that *kiandara* a woman?" Kirby asked.

"No, but to hear Osborn talk, underestimating a female *kiandara* would be stupid."

Kirby's jaw set and his eyes narrowed.

Hollis could almost hear the gears grinding, probably about the usual concerns people had dealing with Eshuvani. "No, I don't think they're mind readers."

Kirby chuckled. "Maybe not, but how'd you know I was about to ask that?"

Hollis clapped Kirby on the shoulder. "I've been your partner long enough. Don't get lathered up about the *kiandarai*. Everything I've heard Ed say about his mom is incredible, and the one I met was a good cop. He treated me like I was a kid, but maybe I had that coming, after almost getting blasted by my own gun. Anyway, you'll soon see for yourself, by the sound of things."

***

Amaya secured the last screw scavenged from the avicopter with the fused engine. The new blue and red cover plate made from a piece of the same avi's hull hid the dangling wires in the briefing room. Someday, when she could get the funds, a map projector would go there, but for now, the room was safer and more visually appealing. She climbed down the ladder she'd made out of the pieces of broken chairs and four long pieces of sturdy scrap wood.

Back at the dispatch desk, fashioned out of a broken

LIKE HERDING THE WIND

tabletop and concrete blocks, Amaya looked at her list and crossed out, "Fix hanging wires in the briefing room." She looked through the list for the most important thing, but didn't get very far.

"Get two avicopters functioning." She sighed and thwacked the notepad with her finger. *After spending most of last night on those stupid things, you'd think they'd work reliably.*

The avicopter issue had to be dealt with. The station needed at least two functioning avis, and she couldn't afford to purchase one with the crumbs Emyrin had dropped from his eight-course banquet table.

She bowed her head. *God, my Father, I've done everything I know how to do with this one. I need some help.*

Amaya marched herself to the hangar and stared at the junk heap in bay four. Both the wingless avi and the one with the fused engine occupied the far corner for use as scrap parts until she could get them both hauled away.

The compact courier avicopter was a three-seater, but it would do for police work. After a lot of sweat, cajoling, and tweaking last night, the courier had started up and stayed running. The larger, light-cargo avi could hold six people and a significant number of flat or foldable things. It would be slow for police work, but handy for rescue calls, if she could con the engine into working for more than ten seconds.

Amaya climbed into the pilot's seat and turned the ignition. The motor whined through start up, and the wings extended before the engine groaned and shut down.

No, the repairs didn't take care of themselves while I was busy with the briefing room.

What should she look at next? Did she have any other choice besides spending some of her meager budget on an expert to make the remaining repairs?

Maybe one last try. Amaya opened the engine compartment of the avi and checked connections.

URUSHALON

The bent up silverware she'd hung from the ceiling of the entryway clanged in the distance. Her pulse jumped up, but she smiled.

So, the entry alarm actually worked, but who is it?

Her hand drifted to her pistol. Either her visitor was another *kiand*, or someone had defeated the magnetic lock. She hoped the visitor was a *kiand*. Hawk's Nest was a long way from backup.

"Grace be unto you," a man's voice echoed down the twenty-foot hall.

"And peace from God, the Father of our Lord." Amaya darted to the corner of the doorway and listened for approaching footsteps. Nothing. She made her way toward the foyer. "Whom do I have the pleasure of addressing?"

"Hm? Oh, forgive me. I am Pavwin Vueltu, *Kiand* of *Vueltiya Ens Kiandarai.*"

Falcon's Wing was the next nearest station, and she recognized the name from the message board. That could be the man, or it could be someone who knew his name and post. Amaya kept her pistol handy and slinked down the hall. Unless he had military training, she should be faster, and if he did have military background, she wasn't an expert marksman for nothing.

She came around the corner. A man of her own kind stood at the dispatch desk looking over her to do list. Although about her age, he was bald. Muscles bulged under his uniform shirt, and he had a shorter, stockier build than most men. He wore a gray uniform with the gold filigree and colored gems on his shirt collar to mark him as a *kiand*. She relaxed her guard and holstered her gun. Lying about his identity would've been easy. Coming up with a proper uniform would've been harder.

Pavwin set the notepad aside and pressed his fist to his forehead to apologize. "I didn't mean to startle you, and you were prudent to be cautious."

LIKE HERDING THE WIND

She crossed to him. They clasped right arms and embraced.

He stepped back. "Dispatch tells me they don't have you linked in for call reception."

"Not yet, but at least I can call out when I need to."

"That's good, but we're nearest, and it's a five-minute flight. Five minutes can be a lifetime in a crisis." He tapped the notepad. "You've been busy."

"I'm not getting as far as I'd hoped, but it'll come along."

"When the rest of your staff arrives, you'll be able to delegate, and the work will progress faster."

Would he get to the purpose of his visit already? He could see the sheer magnitude of her to do list.

He looked around the room. "The rumors are true, then. The *kiat* really has complicated your station unnecessarily."

"It hasn't been the easiest transition, but the challenge is not insurmountable. In fact, I made some favorable trades already. The curator of the royal museum paid me rather more than I had hoped for all my old gear. He's setting up a new exhibit and wanted to compare the equipment issued in the south with standard gear in the north. Then he contacted me again and offered a set of paper maps of the region. 'For decoration,' he says. I took them. They're not current, but they'll do for now. A school purchased my magnetic disk maps. By the time I can afford a projector, there will be a new set."

"Those are fortuitous exchanges." Pavwin flipped her notepad to the third page. "So, if I recall, that leaves you with several bags of beans and rice."

"And a box of five hundred dress uniform gloves."

"Yes, I'd forgotten those. Contact a military training base. They use the same gloves we do. See if they'll trade something for your surplus. As for the beans and rice, they may take that, too, but you might want to try the farmer's market on Saturday."

"Farmer's market?"

Pavwin nodded. "My cousin's *urushalon* is a farmer by hobby. He drives into town with the surplus of his farm and sells it in these temporary, open-air markets. He makes a considerable sum, I'm told."

"You think I can set up there?" Amaya glanced toward the kitchen.

"Maybe, but I'm not sure what their protocol is for becoming a vendor. You might be able to trade with the humans for more interesting food than what you have."

"Where is this market?"

Pavwin rubbed his chin. "I'll ask my cousin and send the location to you through the message board. You came from the hangar when I arrived. I assume I interrupted your work on the avicopters?"

"Yes, I'm afraid so." Amaya blew out a breath. "One functions. Another may eventually be coerced to cooperate."

"Three would be better."

"I can only send two units into the field at once." She shook her head. "The *kiat* assigned my personnel before I arrived and gave me four *kialai*."

Pavwin frowned. "He populated your nest with fledglings."

"He certainly did. According to their records, a couple graduated last week."

He winced. "Well, I propose a trade of my own. Introduce me to your station, and I'll see what I can do with your finicky avi. My dad was a mechanic and taught me a few things."

Amaya smiled. "I would be grateful."

She led Pavwin down the first corridor to begin the tour. *Thank you, God, for your constant provision.*

***

Like Herding the Wind

The hard floor pressed into Amaya's hip. With a groan, she sat up and stretched her stiffened body, resolving that sometime today, she'd have to get or make a hammock of some kind. Camping on the floor was for kids.

A warm shower finished loosening her muscles. She dressed and grabbed dried fruit and flatbread for breakfast before slinging her trauma kit over one shoulder and walking the twenty strides to the station's back door.

The foyer light glowed.

Her pulse ratcheted up several clicks. *Now what?*

Amaya crouched in the dark hallway leading past the storeroom to the foyer. The station was quiet except for the drone of the air cooling system. She drew her pistol and rested her thumb on the start-up switch as she slunk down the narrow corridor to the edge of the shadow. The air cooler turned off and left the building in palpable silence until some bird outside filled the void with chirping.

She drew her knife and used the polished surgical steel as a mirror to peek around the corner at an assortment of bright-colored, plastic storage bins piled along the wall next to the dispatch desk. A piece of paper was taped to one of them.

What's this about? Amaya blew out a breath and sheathed her knife.

Still keeping an ear on the sounds around her, she walked over to the crates and pulled the note loose.

"Unto Amaya Ulonya, *Kiand* of *Uloniya Varoosht Kiandarai*. Grace be unto you and peace from God, the Father of our Lord. Greetings from the *kiandai* of Woran Oldue. We are universally ecstatic to hear that you are able to perform the necessary duty of making sense of the humans. We have, however, a favor to request. Our storage rooms are overflowing, and we understand you have ample space, so we humbly ask you to store this surplus equipment. In truth, we have no use for it, but discarding what is still in good repair is such a waste. Serve with diligence."

URUSHALON

Amaya smiled and started up her computer.

May God bless you all for your generosity.

While she waited for the computer, she checked the labels on the sides of the boxes. The *kiandai* had gifted her with medical equipment, voice- and body heat- recognition systems, basic police and medical gear, Model Five pistol ammunition, office supplies, a battery charger for the house and avi batteries, hammocks, and a few pieces of assemble-it-yourself furniture.

The computer chimed to inform her it was ready for service. Amaya logged in and went to the *kiandarai* message board. Her fingers danced over the keys.

"Unto the *kiandai* of Woran Oldue. Grace be unto you and peace from God, the Father of our Lord. I received your message and your surplus items. I am pleased to store your excess equipment since I agree that discarding what is still useful would be shameful waste. I am greatly blessed to have such an opportunity to help the community. Serve with diligence."

After powering down the system again, she grabbed her task list and made new entries under the heading, "Install new equipment."

***

Wylin jogged across the open parking lot, empty at this early hour. The human practice of staying closed most of the morning was ridiculous in terms of business sense but perfect for these equipment runs.

He slowed as he reached the back of the brick building and waved his little brother over. Maran looked left, then right before sprinting across and skidding to a stop. After several fifty-meter sprints and short breaks, Maran still breathed easily. Not bad for a civilian kid barely out of his apprenticeship.

"Keep an eye out for the humans." Wylin pushed Maran toward the corner of the building.

LIKE HERDING THE WIND

Maran leaned against the wall and peeked. "All clear."

Of course it's clear, you idiot. I could see that on the way over. Wylin stepped back and kicked the door with all the force his military training had given him. The door frame splintered, but held on. A second kick cleared the way.

Wylin slapped Maran's shoulder with the back of his hand. "Come on."

"Want me to keep a lookout?" Maran grinned like a child in an amusement park.

"No." He grabbed his brother's arm. "I want you to come with me. We've only got a few minutes." Wylin pulled his brother inside.

Maran stumbled a few steps. "So why didn't we park the avicopter closer?"

"Drew too much attention last time. Now stop asking stupid questions and start looking for what we need." He shoved Maran toward the front of the store.

Rows of shelves clogged up one side, but the other was more open. Racks of balls, odd-shaped sticks, and shoes were arranged in small groups. Pictures of grown humans, mostly men, holding some of the equipment were attached to the wall.

Wylin darted down one aisle and sent his brother down another. Stacks of identical baskets filled the entire shelving unit down the right side. The other side was loaded with small boxes decorated with fish.

Wrong aisle.

"Hey, I found them. How many do we need?" Maran asked.

Wylin rolled his eyes and headed around the corner. "How many can you carry and run at the same time?"

Maran got his arms around a box and stood. He grimaced. "One. Maybe. We should've parked closer."

"Time to be a man." He grabbed a box and stifled a grunt

as he lifted it up to his shoulder. *Just take more breaks on the way back.* "Let's go."

A human's car motor rumbled closer as red light scanned across the store a couple times then disappeared. The sound grew louder from the back of the store, and a second car rumbled closer but parked in front.

Human kiandarai! Wylin tensed and gave Maran a push. "Come on! Out the front!"

He darted to the front door and turned the lock from vertical to horizontal, listening for the bolt to withdraw with a loud clack. Wylin pushed the door open as a pudgy human male, not one of their law enforcers, in brown slacks and a white shirt stepped out of a turquoise blue human vehicle with a white roof.

The man's jaw dropped open before he hollered in English.

Wylin charged at him, grabbing him by the arm and flinging him away from the vehicle. The human landed with a thud like a bag of sand. A human's running steps drew nearer around the corner.

"Drop it and get in, Maran." He shoved the box he carried over the top of the front seat and into the back before sliding into the pilot's chair, really just a long bench across the whole passenger area.

He slammed the pilot's door closed. Maran slid into the front passenger seat, leaving the box on the pavement, as Wylin started the engine.

"Can you–um–fly one of these?" Maran tugged his door closed.

Over the sound of the engine, the shouting human *kiandara* was barely audible.

Wylin threw the car into reverse and backed out of the small parking lot causing other human vehicles to blare their warning horns as the pilots stopped the vehicles or swerved.

LIKE HERDING THE WIND

The human *kiandarai* sirens wailed. Wylin wove his way through the traffic, heading for the park where he'd left the avicopter. The human *kiandarai* vehicle pursued a block behind as most civilians pulled to the side of the road, leaving the center clear.

"Told you we should have landed closer," Maran mumbled.

"Quiet."

A couple blocks ahead, the buildings ended and the park began, but the avicopter was on the far side of the park amongst some trees.

Wylin tapped the steering wheel and frowned. They would have to split up, but could Maran keep his head? He'd have to, and if not he could probably outrun the humans, in any case.

"When I stop the vehicle, get out and head for the avicopter. I'll try to lead the humans away and meet up with you there." He glanced at his brother.

"Should I lift off in the avicopter until you get there?" Maran asked.

That would get you out of their reach. "Good idea."

Wylin cut a sharp left turn, squealing the tires. He stopped long enough for Maran to hop out then continued down the road, checking the mirror. The human *kiandarai* turned the corner and followed him. A second black and white vehicle screeched to a stop at the park, and two men in black uniforms slid out of the car and ran after Maran.

With a bare-tooth snarl, Wylin wrenched his eyes off the mirror. Maran was quick, and he just had to reach the avicopter and lift off. He'd stay ahead of the humans.

***

Ed Osborn pulled into the station parking lot. If only he had some manner of distraction to keep his mind off Amaya. He'd sent her another note suggesting a different date for his

URUSHALON

visit, and her answer had arrived yesterday.

"I won't be in Marquette at that time, either." That was it? No explanation. No suggestion for a different date. Nothing. Something was wrong. The last time she'd been so terse had been the day he'd asked her why she wore a wedding bracelet but had no husband. What kind of tragedy could she not tell him about this time?

No, there had to be a logical reason for Amaya's message. Perhaps, as Hollis had suggested earlier, a more detailed explanation would come when she was less busy, but what could be occupying so much of her time?

Osborn entered the station and slowed, eying his office from the hallway. The wooden wedge braced the door open. Inside, a *kiandara* in the typical dark gray uniform sat reading a newspaper with the headline "19 Burn Draft Cards." He looked at the backpack by the chair, hoping to see an insignia he recognized. What he wouldn't give to see Amaya's bird-and-flower heraldry, but the bag faced the wrong way.

A hand tapped his shoulder, and he looked back.

Stevens held out a report. "The new *kiand* of the Buffer Zone station has been waiting for about twenty minutes. Insists on talking to you personally."

As Osborn took the report, Stevens left again, jogging to catch up with his partner.

Perfect.

At a time like this, he had to play the cordial host to a strange Eshuvani? Osborn blew out a long breath. Yes, his long association with Amaya had taught him plenty about how to interact with her people, and he didn't mind talking to Eshuvani who didn't look down their nose at him, but he was not mentally prepared for a long bout of diplomacy. Only a quarter of all Eshuvani spoke any human language, and he was the only one in the entire Las Palomas police department who could speak theirs. The sense of duty Amaya had instilled in him was too strong for him to delay any longer. Osborn

LIKE HERDING THE WIND

nodded once and strode to his office. Butterflies whizzed around his innards as he reached the office door.

"May the light of God illuminate your path," Osborn began in Eshuvani.

"Such a formal greeting for an old friend?" Amaya set the paper aside and stood.

Osborn gaped. It couldn't be her. "Amaya!"

She offered her hand, but he stepped past it and drew her into a tight embrace. Her warm arms wrapped around him, and he rested his head on her shoulder, listening for a moment to her three-part heartbeat.

She rubbed his back. "Here I was ready to restrain my joy to avoid causing you complications with your men. Instead, I'm blessed with such happiness."

"They know I adopted an Eshuvani mom."

Once he let her go, he pulled his desk chair around, and they both sat.

He clasped both of her hands. "What are you doing here?"

"I came by partly in an official capacity but mostly to see you, dear one."

"No, I mean, what are you doing in Las Palomas? I thought you were busy in Marquette."

"I asked God if I could work nearer to you, and he graciously arranged it. I am the *kiand* of Woran Oldue's newest station. Didn't your man tell you?"

"Guess I thought he was putting me on. Stevens is the joker in my deck. When did this happen?"

"It's been official for only a week. When the post came open, I applied. I was denied at first. The *kiat* is concerned the Las Palomas officers won't accept direction from a woman."

"There's cause to think that."

Amaya turned a hand toward the ceiling. "The Marquette police learned, so will Las Palomas."

URUSHALON

"So what changed the *kiat's* mind?"

"One *kiand* wrote that hiring policies should be based on the interests and qualifications of the applicant, not the prejudices of humans."

Osborn snorted. "That was bold."

"Yes, but that fellow is known for strong opinions. After his statement, the other applicants withdrew, no one else applied for the post, and I never withdrew my application, so I'm the one."

Osborn grimaced. "I'm guessing Emyrin didn't take that mini-mutiny well."

"It took a mandate from the king and Council of the *Kiati*." Amaya shook her head. "You should see the equipment he gave me, and my staff? Under the guise of getting the station operational as quickly as possible, he already chose the rest of my people."

"What, did he load you down with gray hair?"

"Just the opposite. There's me, naturally. There's a data analyst, Orinyay, who is some twenty years younger than me. The rest are about sixty and just out of apprenticeship."

Osborn cringed. "He gave you kids."

"Yes, and when I reminded him that I can't pair *kialai* together, he answered that scheduling was not his job."

"Have you talked to Orinyay to figure out what she did to irritate the ol' piranha?" Osborn sat back.

Amaya shook her head. "Not yet. I have read the record sent to me, but it's rather terse. We'll all meet for the first time tomorrow afternoon."

"So you don't even know if you have personality con–"

The dispatcher rushed in. "I'm sorry to interrupt, sir, but Officers Gale, Sumner, Kirby, and Hollis report that they're chasing down two Eshuvani suspects wanted for breaking and entering and grand theft auto. They're in two separate foot

LIKE HERDING THE WIND

pursuits. They were last seen in the park."

Why didn't I hear that on the radio? He stood and turned to the table behind his desk. *Because I was so happy to see Amaya, I didn't turn the stupid thing on.* "We're on our way."

Amaya grabbed her medical bag and stood. "Can you tell them to stay well back?"

He shook his head and led Amaya out. "Not in a foot pursuit."

"Do they know?"

"Hollis, yes." Osborn paused as they got into his car. "The others? I don't know. Kirby's still pretty new to the job, and the other two haven't had many encounters with Eshuvani." He started the engine. "The park is just down the road. We'll be there in under two minutes." Osborn turned on the lights and siren.

Urushalon

Chapter Three

Mark Hollis considered himself to be fit, but chasing this Eshuvani down in ninety degree weather with similar humidity could wipe out Wilt Chamberlain. They didn't even have the wind off the coast today.

The target sprinted a distance then played hide-and-seek. As soon as anyone got close, he took off again. The suspect was in one of his hide-and-seek modes, holed up somewhere among the picnic tables, trash cans, and brick-enclosed barbecue pits.

Kirby disappeared around the far side of a public restroom while Hollis checked the trash cans and shrubs on the way. A police siren drew nearer from the west. Hollis spared a glance that way at a car rolling across the grass. Parks and Rec would be thrilled.

"Freeze! Face down on the ground and spread 'em," Kirby ordered, a little keyed up so his voice pitched a little higher. "Hollis, I got him!"

Hollis ran harder to catch up with his partner. "Don't get too close!"

He came around the building. A lanky Eshuvani male was

sprawled face down. Kirby had his gun trained on the suspect some five feet away. Hollis suppressed a shudder. The guy he'd cornered five years ago had snatched his gun from twice that distance.

Hollis drew his pistol to cover the Eshuvani. "Back up, Kirby."

When Kirby hazarded a look Hollis' way, the Eshuvani sprang to his feet in a blur. Hollis fired, hitting the barbecue pit beyond where his target used to be. The suspect kicked Kirby's arm. The gun flew from his hand as the Eshuvani got an arm around the younger officer's throat. Kirby grabbed the restraining arm and widened his stance. Left-handed, the suspect drew a knife from a sheath on his belt and drove it into Kirby's chest. Kirby tensed and clenched his jaw. The police car racing across the grass arrived. Osborn bailed out of one side, and a female *kiandara* out the other.

Hauling Kirby around with him, the suspect turned to keep all three of them in view. "Back away, or I kill him!"

Was Eshuvani anatomy that different from humans'? The knife in Kirby's chest was practically a mortal injury already.

The *kiandara* barked an order in Eshuvani.

The suspect pushed Kirby into the *kiandara*'s line of fire, leapt over the barbecue, and took off running. Kirby hit the ground with a pained cry, and Hollis rushed to his partner. The *kiandara* jumped, kicked off from the roof of the car, and flew another five feet straight up. She fired three times. Even after a few years, Hollis knew the whine of the dart pistol. The suspect dropped in his tracks with three darts in his shoulder.

The *kiandara* landed with a gymnast's grace. "Ed, call an ambulance and get my medical bag. Mark, you must not move him nor let him move. The knife may be resting against something critical." She ran past him.

Wait a minute. How did you know my name? My tag says, "Hollis." He recalled all those rumors about Eshuvani mind-readers.

URUSHALON

Hollis knelt beside Kirby. Sweat matted his hair, and he took quick, shallow breaths. The knife was buried to the hilt to the right of the sternum and a little higher.

Kirby blinked hard. "I thought–I thought I was far enough away."

"About any other time, you would have been." Hollis pulled out a handkerchief and mopped Kirby's brow. "Stay still. Don't try to talk. You're going to be okay."

***

Sergeant Ed Osborn dropped the radio mic, grabbed Amaya's backpack, and rushed to the fallen officer. Kirby lay on his side, supported by Hollis' steadying hand to keep him from falling forward onto his chest or rolling onto his back. Blood trickled from the wound. With so many major blood vessels in that area, shouldn't that have been a real gusher?

Osborn sat. "There's an ambulance on the way."

Twenty yards away, Amaya secured the suspect and spoke in Eshuvani to her dispatcher over the comm system on her collar.

He waited for her to finish arranging pick-up for the prisoner. "Amaya, what are you going to need first?"

"Transdermal viewer and the regenerative test kit. Everything is where you'll expect it."

Osborn pulled out the equipment and started the viewer's warm-up cycle.

"That's the legendary Amaya?" Hollis asked.

Osborn nodded. "I had a surprise waiting for me this morning."

"You said she was over a hundred years old. I was expecting a grandma."

"They hold their age well, y'know. She's actually one hundred fifteen chronologically. Physically, closer to forty-five to fifty."

LIKE HERDING THE WIND

"Wow. I'd've guessed younger looking at her." Hollis glanced toward Osborn's adopted mom. "Here for a visit?"

Osborn shook his head. "She's the new Buffer Zone *kiand*, the police captain for that station."

"At least it's someone we know who's sympathetic."

"Yeah. That helps. A lot."

The transdermal viewer chimed.

Amaya carried the suspect over to the car and then joined them.

She knelt and opened the test kit. "Robert, I'm going to do a quick test to see if your blood is compatible with the medication in my kit. While we're waiting for that, I'm going to use a device like a small, portable X-ray to see how much damage has been done."

Kirby nodded. "Yeah, okay."

Amaya used a capillary tube to draw up blood from the wound. Osborn brushed her hand as he took the tube from her. Her hands were ice cold, and she trembled. Something was wrong, but he couldn't ask now, not in public. Amaya picked up the transdermal viewer and held the cylindrical device up to her eye. She leaned over Kirby and turned a wheel on the viewer.

Amaya set the viewer aside. "The wound is not mortal. From the size of the hilt, I expected the blade to be most of a hand-length, but it's two inches, if that much, and almost blunt."

Osborn nodded. "Shellfish knife. Real common around here."

Amaya took the capillary tube and held it up to the light. The column of blood stopped halfway up the tube.

He leaned closer. "No warning colors." A terrific tension in Osborn's chest faded away. *She can heal him.*

"That's fortuitous." Amaya set the capillary tube aside.

URUSHALON

"Robert, I'm going to roll you onto your back. Let me do all the work."

"What can I do?" Hollis asked.

"Come over here. As I turn him, pull that leg across. Try to keep his pelvis aligned with the rest of his body." Amaya glanced at Osborn. "If you'll keep his head aligned."

They rolled him to his back, and Kirby groaned.

Amaya pulled a pair of small, sharp shears off her belt and cut Kirby's shirt open. She grabbed her backpack and pulled out a silver, plastic pouch labeled "Regeneration Salve." Her hands still shook.

"You be careful with that," Osborn said.

"Always, *Urushalon*. Robert, I'm going to remove the knife then apply this gel to the injury. It will feel warm, but it won't hurt you. You need to stay still for a while so the salve can heal the injury."

"Okay," Kirby said.

"It might tickle a bit." Osborn rubbed his arm, the last place he'd been treated with regeneration gel five years ago. That dog bite had hurt, but at least he'd managed to protect a kid.

"You're the only one I know who has ever had that reaction." Amaya picked up the plastic packet and the shears and braced one arm against her knee, which did next to nothing to calm the tremors.

Osborn had seen her react to this stuff once when someone had jostled her and she'd contacted a couple drops of the stuff. Her pale skin had taken on a bluish cast moments after she went from breathing, to wheezing, to choking. One of her other officers had taken care of her in less than a minute, but that was one time more than he wanted to see.

"On second thought, give that to me." He reached for the packet. "That stuff makes your throat close up, and there are no other Eshuvani medics in sight."

LIKE HERDING THE WIND

"Use my comm system. Any *kiandara* could walk you through using my anaphylaxis kit."

"No unnecessary risk."

That old Eshuvani axiom was almost a rule among the *kiandarai*.

She handed him the gel and scissors.

He covered her hand with his. The last time he'd felt such a chill had been the day she'd told him about the murder of her husband and child. She didn't know Kirby well enough for this to be about the possibility of losing him.

She withdrew her hand from his. Amaya jerked the knife free of Kirby's chest. He tensed but made no sound. Blood ran in a constant stream as Osborn cut open the packet and squeezed the gel onto the wound. It disappeared into the injury and sank in through Kirby's skin. The flow of blood dwindled, then stopped.

Amaya picked up the viewer again and scanned the wound. "It's working well. You're going to be all right. Keep still. I'll stay with you."

***

Mark Hollis knelt near his partner, shading the sun from Kirby's eyes with a hand. While Hollis had related the whole caper of how apprehending a pair of burglars had turned into two separate pursuits, Kirby's breathing eased, his color returned, and the pain etched on his face faded. From time to time, Amaya used her eyepiece to check the wound. At least she hadn't interrupted his report. She'd say or do something if Kirby's condition deteriorated.

An ambulance attendant leaned over. "Can we take him yet?"

Amaya shook her head and set the viewer aside. "Not yet. He should be stable in another minute or two. I realize this is time-consuming, but the injury is in a critical location. Avoid risk when possible."

Urushalon

A bulbous-eyed, bird-shaped avicopter landed nearby, and a pair of *kiandarai,* jogged over. The silver filigree tabs on their collars said they were a different rank than Amaya. Hers were gold. The new comers were regular officers, *kiandarai.* Amaya stood, gave each a quick embrace, and spoke Eshuvani with them. Based on the hard stares the prisoner got and the more sympathetic gaze aimed at Kirby, the only thing keeping the prisoner alive until the trial would be the *kiandarai*'s unerring professionalism. They loaded the suspect into the back of the avicopter. After another quick embrace, the *kiandarai* left.

She knelt at Kirby's side. "How are you feeling?"

"Tired and a little sore, but I'm breathing much better, and there's no more pain."

"I'm glad for that. We're going to transport you to the hospital. I'll ride in with you so I can speak with the doctor. I'm going to recommend you be placed under observation for twenty-four hours. The newly regenerated tissue is still fragile, so you mustn't lift anything over five pounds with either hand until this time tomorrow. After that, barring strange complications, you should be back to your normal routine."

"Thanks." Kirby gripped her hand. "I owe you one."

She smiled. "The day may come when I'll need you to take care of me."

The *kiand* slung her backpack over a shoulder and lifted Kirby as if he were a child. She settled him on the ambulance gurney and secured the restraining straps. Hollis stared. He'd heard about how strong Eshuvani were, but a woman lifting a man that easily? True, Kirby had a lean build, but he still had some mass to him. He would have to rethink a lot.

Hollis stepped over to the gurney. "I'll come by later."

"I'll watch for you," Kirby said as the attendants loaded him into the back of the ambulance. "Hey, Hollis?"

"Yeah."

LIKE HERDING THE WIND

"Call Susan for me. Looks like I'll miss that date tonight."

"You got it."

Osborn leaned into the ambulance as Amaya climbed into the back. "I'll meet you at the hospital."

Amaya nodded.

Just as the ambulance left, Sumner and Gale walked up. Sumner's hair was flat against his head, and his clothes clung to him.

Hollis followed Osborn over to them. "What happened to you?"

"Our guy ditched the stolen car and ran." Sumner pointed in the distance with a wave of his hand. "He hit pedestrian traffic, which slowed him down. We'd almost reached him when he whacked a lady on the head and threw her into a pond. By the time we fished her out, he was long gone."

Osborn sighed. "But you got a good description at least."

"Never saw his face, Sarge, but he was over six feet easy, had graying dark hair, and he was fast. Brother, was he fast. We already put out a supplemental to Kirby's description."

"What about the woman he tossed into the pond? Any chance she could give us something?"

"Doubt it. He came up behind her, clobbered her a good one, picked her up by the belt and collar, and gave her a heave. She had an egg on her head as big as my fist, so we sent her on to Daughters of Mercy in an ambulance."

"All right. I'll go check on her and see what she knows. You guys need to get back out there. If you hop in, I'll give you a ride back to your cars."

Gale grabbed Hollis' arm. "Hey, what happened t' Kirby?"

Hollis shook his head. "Took a knife in the chest, but he's okay."

"Okay?" Gale stared wide-eyed and slid into the back

URUSHALON

seat. "How'dya figger?"

Hollis slipped into the front seat and twisted around to give the other two the story.

***

Wylin Leonan darted the remaining twenty strides to the mottled green avicopter, which blended in somewhat with the stand of junipers next to the wet weather creek. The six-seater family avicopter once belonged to some waste of oxygen civilian, but Wylin had commandeered it and made some special modifications. From the outside, it still looked like a stylized bird, and the wings still flapped when it was in the air, but the motor was much better than anything from the factory. Gunshots from human or Eshuvani pistols could cause damage but only with great difficulty or unusual precision.

He slowed as he drew near. Where was Maran? He should have been here by now and gotten the avicopter into the air. Surely he'd kept ahead of the humans. He wouldn't have been stupid enough to try to engage the human *kiandarai*.

A gray and silver *kiandarai* avicopter whirred overhead. The humming motor gained then lost pitch as they passed and headed in the direction of Woran Oldue. Wylin shielded his eyes with his hands and squinted up at the retreating avicopter. What were they doing here?

The back of Wylin's neck tensed. Why else would *kiandarai* have been here except to take custody of Maran?

Wylin growled and climbed into the pilot seat. Even in the shade of the junipers at such an early hour, the air inside of the avi was hot enough to make breathing uncomfortable. He powered up the systems and engaged the air cooler. Chilly air blasted from the vents, bringing blessed relief to Wylin's sweat-drenched body.

Once all the systems were up to speed, Wylin lifted off, but chasing the gray and silver avicopter would be stupid. The more recent models had the technology to force a hostile avicopter down from a distance, and Wylin had no offensive

LIKE HERDING THE WIND

equipment or countermeasures of his own. He meant to fix that, but in the meantime, he kept his distance from *kiandarai*.

There was a remote possibility that the avi had been in the area on another errand. Maran might still be out there. Wylin lifted off and projected a course along the most likely route Maran would have taken.

About halfway to the point where he and Maran had split off, Wylin spotted a human *kiandarai* vehicle driving across the grass. One of their ambulances was some distance ahead, turning onto one of the major roads.

Wylin didn't believe in coincidence. Apparently Maran had been stupid enough to attack the humans. He may have injured or killed one, but got himself caught in the process. If one of the human *kiandarai* had been injured, the law explicitly detailed the punishment. Wylin clenched his jaw. He had friends in high places, and those friends had better come through for him. He turned the avicopter toward the coast.

***

Amaya perched on Ed's police car and waited.

She sighed. He'd noticed. He'd been decent enough not to ask about the chill and tremors in the presence of others, but alone, he might work up the courage. He meant well enough, always had, but sometimes that human curiosity was not a blessing.

How could she answer him? Robert's injury hadn't been mortal, yet he'd been lying on the ground in the park like Essien had at the bottom of that mine shaft. Sooner or later, she would have to deal with the loss of her partner, but there was no time for it. Ed and the other officers in Las Palomas needed her. Her own problems would have to wait.

The sun beat down on the black hood of the car. Amaya escaped the heat by standing inside the hospital door. The chemical smell of artificial clean permeated the air. She watched people enter and leave, and most of them kept their eyes riveted straight forward as they hurried past. Ed stepped

URUSHALON

off the elevator and walked toward her.

She fell in step with him. "How's the woman?"

Ed smiled. "They'll keep an eye on her tonight, but the doctor says she's fine." His grin faded. "She never saw the suspect."

"The one who got away? He'll be trouble. His partner made rash choices, but not that one."

"Yeah. We'll have to watch for him." His face brightened. "I have good news, though. Nigel and Frank, the last two hurt tangling with Eshuvani, were released today. They'll be on dispatch or desk duty until the doctor clears them, but they'll be back in action soon."

"Good. Maybe I can bring you my back-up comm system. If something comes up between now and Consecration Day, you or your dispatcher can contact me."

Ed shook his head. "You'd be responding alone."

"Not the most prudent, but a *kiand* is permitted to, and I wouldn't be entirely alone. I would be backing up your people."

"I'll suggest it to the captain."

You say that, but you are too worried about me and will not, at least until my staff arrives. She slid into the front passenger seat.

Ed started the car and put it in gear then shifted back to park. "Your hands were cold, and you were shaking."

"You have always been observant, dear one." She clasped his hand. "I'll be fine."

"But you're not now?"

She hoped her smile didn't look as fake as it felt. "My plate is full. When all has been dealt with, I'll be fine."

"I'm not sure I like that answer, but okay." He put the car in gear and drove back toward the station. "So, Emyrin gave you old equipment and young kids."

LIKE HERDING THE WIND

"Yes, but the *kiand* of Falcon's Wing recruited the other stations, and they have greatly relieved the first problem. I think what I lack at this point is reasonable furniture for the *kiandarai* quarters."

"You could go garage sailing. You may find at least some of your missing furniture."

Was he joking? She twisted in the seat and studied his face. "How does one sail a garage?"

He chuckled. "No, not s-a-i-l, like a boat. S-a-l-e. On Saturdays, people sometimes sell things they don't want. They set up a sort of impromptu shop in their garages."

She nodded. "Ah, I see. Is there a map or listing of such things?"

"Not really. You kind of drive around and look for signs. Esther and Ruth, she's Mark's wife, often go to the farmers market on Saturday morning then hit the garage sales. You could go with them. Ruth is looking for baby things."

"She's expecting?"

"Any day now."

"That's wonderful." Even as she said it, her own heart twinged for the memory of her lost child.

"Both Mark and Ruth are getting anxious." He turned into the station's lot. "Really, though, you should go out with Ruth and Esther tomorrow."

"Among your people, it's rude to invite oneself."

"Enh, Esther will be thrilled to see you." Ed found a place for the car. "I'll call her, clear it with her, and then introduce you to the station."

She nodded. "Good. Then I'll show you my antique avicopter."

He snorted. "Can't wait."

Amaya stepped inside while he held the door. The cooler air promised relief. "You get used to the heat down here, I

URUSHALON

hope."

"That's what they tell me, but I haven't yet. Just wait. August is worse."

During the station tour, they wandered into the break room. Ed fished a dime from his pocket and placed a call to his house while Amaya got some water from the fountain.

The door creaked open.

"–like six-foot-two and skinny as a post, but strong. Picked up the Eshuvani suspect like it was nothing."

Amaya turned as Mark, clutching a paper cup, led in another officer.

"There she is." Mark's face flushed. "Officer Mike Stevens, this is *Kiand* Amaya–I'm sorry, but I don't remember your last name."

She crossed to the officers and shook Mike's hand. "Amaya Ulonya *Kiand*, but among my people, never address someone by last name. Amaya is fine."

"Pleased t'meetcha." Mike smiled broadly. "So, when does the station go active?"

"In about one week." She pointed to the date on a desk calendar tacked to the wall. "In the meantime, I can give my backup comm system to your dispatcher if your captain is agreeable."

"That'd help. Excuse me. I'd better get to the pile of paperwork." He poured himself a cup of coffee, waved, and left.

Amaya turned to Mark. "When I left the hospital, Robert was resting comfortably. He's had no adverse reaction to the regenerative."

His facial muscles relaxed. "Thanks. I was about to call up there before I went back out on the streets."

"So you'll be responding alone?"

"Yeah, but the dispatcher knows that." Mark refilled his

LIKE HERDING THE WIND

paper cup from a coffee pot. "She'll send me on things not likely to turn ugly, and I can always call for backup if I need it."

"I understand. Be careful."

"Sure will." Mark opened the door and paused. "Glad you're the one heading up the new station. We were on pins and needles wondering who the *kiat* would put in charge." He left.

Ed hung up the phone. "You're all set. Esther and Ruth will meet you at the farmers market in the morning, then take you along on their garage sale adventures. Esther invited you over for dinner tomorrow evening."

Amaya thought through tomorrow's schedule. "Unfortunately, my staff arrives tomorrow evening. We'll have to make that another time."

"I'm sure we can work it out." Ed continued the tour of the station.

When they got back to the door they'd entered through, Amaya walked outside. Hot, humid air gusted into her face. Any more humidity and she'd consider taking out her water breather.

"So, where'd you park it?" Ed looked around.

"On the roof."

"The roof?"

"It's flat, and I wouldn't be in anyone's way."

"On the roof." He shook his head. "We'll have to designate a heliport at ground level or rig a ladder somewhere."

"I'll bring it down. It's a courier ship. Where can I put it for now?"

"The back corner over there." He pointed.

She jumped up, catching the overhang in front of the door, and hoisted herself up. Another quick jump got her to

URUSHALON

the roof.

She opened the avi's door and fanned her face. *I could cook lunch in here.*

Next time, she'd leave a window open, but for now, she could take advantage of the courier's overzealous cooling system. Amaya started the avi. The engine stuttered a few times, but after she growled at it, the avi came up to speed. The wings unfolded, and Amaya flipped the cooling system switches. In seconds, arctic air streamed from the vents. The avi lifted off with a lurch but handled the short flight to the back corner of the station's parking lot. She landed, folded the wings into standby mode, and stepped out.

Ed joined her, smiling. "Love the paint job."

Amaya chuckled and ran a hand along the mismatched hull plates she'd scavenged off one of the dead avis. "Unique, is it not?"

"That's one word for it." Ed shook his head.

"I traded my extreme surplus of dress gloves for the paint needed to bring them both up to protocol."

"And the other one's worse?"

Amaya nodded. "The light cargo hauler looks better, but I don't trust the engine as well."

His cheeks puffed as he blew out a breath. "This one doesn't exactly purr like a kitten. I don't know about this, Amaya."

"It will have to do, dear one. I'll repair them until I can replace them."

"I guess."

She wrapped her arm across his back and rested her hand on his shoulder. "You mustn't worry, *Urushalon*. God sees all things and works all things for good, even this."

He covered her hand with his. "As much as we need help, I'd rather you take longer to get Hawk's Nest really ready than

LIKE HERDING THE WIND

activate too soon and lose someone due to a lack of preparation."

"Neither of us has control over that."

"Yeah." He looked over his shoulder at the station. "I should get back to it."

She nodded. "I've kept you from your duties too long, but I am greatly blessed to see you again."

"I'm the one who's blessed. I wasn't sure what to think with all your completely uninformative notes."

She smiled. "It wouldn't have been much of a surprise if I'd told you up front."

Ed turned toward her. "Yeah, but you could've given a guy a hint or something."

"I'm sorry I worried you, dear one."

"Glad you're here." He gave her a quick hug and stepped away. "I'll see you later."

"Undoubtedly."

Chapter Four

Amaya landed at the edge of the lot at Daughters of Mercy, walked in, and took the elevator to the floor where Robert stayed.

A handful of people moved around, but most stared at her, and the rest became engrossed in the patterns in the wood grain or floor tiles the moment they saw her. Amaya greeted an orderly with a smile and continued on her way.

On the third floor, she stopped at the nurse's station. "Good morning."

The nurse looked up from the record in front of her, startled. "Uh, good morning."

"I am Amaya Ulonya of the Hawk's Nest *Kiandarai* station. Yesterday, I brought in Officer Robert Kirby after field-treating a knife wound. Is he well?"

"Offic-officer Kirby? Oh, yes. You're the Eshuvani medic who took care of him?" the nurse asked.

A little higher ranked than a medic, but you're close enough for now. "That's right."

"Oh, not a peep out of him all night. They'll release him this morning."

"Wonderful. May I see him?"

The nurse shook her head. "Oh, no. Against regulations. No visitors before ten a.m., and he'll be going home before that. I'll tell him you were here."

"Thank you." Amaya headed back to the avicopter.

According to Pavwin, the farmer's market was in the same park where Robert had fallen. She found an open space to park the avi where a tree would provide some shade and walked over to the free-standing pavilions. Vendors set up various tables arrayed with bushel baskets of tomatoes, peppers, onions, and small squashes. Brightly colored signs named particular farms for some booths, but others had little more than a bare table and a sparse sample of vegetables. A few had homemade jellies or breads, and a couple sold crafts that were decorative but frivolous.

"Amaya!"

She turned and spotted Esther waving to her. Esther stood a shade over five feet tall and had her blond hair tied up in a bun. The pregnant woman with shoulder-length brown hair and sky-blue eyes standing nearby had to be Mark's wife, Ruth.

Amaya wove her way through the crowd and embraced the wife of her *urushalon*.

Esther kept a hold on Amaya's arm. "Ruth Hollis, this is Amaya Ulonya."

Ruth's eyes widened. "You're the Eshuvani mom Ed adopted?"

"Yes, when he was four." Amaya nodded, recalling the hunt for the lost child. "Congratulations, Mrs. Hollis. Do you hope for a boy or a girl?"

"I'll be happy either way, but Mark wants a boy. We have a daughter already."

Esther smiled. "Ed is just beside himself with joy that you're heading up the new station."

URUSHALON

"I feel greatly blessed to be near ones I love again." A chill settled on Amaya. "How are your children, Esther?"

"Both doing well and growing taller every second. I swear. Sometimes I think they could eat the whole grocery store, bricks and all." Esther sidestepped to avoid a woman hurrying past. "Y'know, I've been thinking about who to sell your excess beans and rice to. There's a Mexican fellow, Miguel, who often sets up here selling empanadas and fresh salsa. He runs a Tex-Mex restaurant in town. He might take some or all of it."

"Empanadas? Salsa?" Amaya asked.

"Mexican pastries and spicy tomato dip for corn chips. Those empanadas are the best you'll ever have. You've just got to try one. Let's find him before the market gets busy."

Ruth pointed. "He's usually in the corner near the main entrance."

Amaya followed the two ladies back through the market to a pavilion draped in canvas sheets painted like the Mexican flag.

A dark-complexioned, gray-haired man stacked jars of red and green concoctions on a table. A second table had trays of what looked like folded flat bread.

He turned around and smiled, showing a full set of teeth. Amaya restrained her instinctive response. Among humans, baring the teeth wasn't necessarily aggressive.

"Well, if it isn't Mrs. Officer Mark Hollis." Miguel kissed the back of Ruth's hand. "How is the family of my favorite police officer?"

Ruth blushed. "Very well, thank you."

Esther leaned closer to Amaya. "Mark and Ruth stopped for dinner at the restaurant week before last, and Mark disarmed a man who tried to rob Miguel."

Amaya nodded.

"What can I help you with? Empanadas? Salsa?" Miguel

LIKE HERDING THE WIND

brought a chair around from behind the tables, set it in front of Ruth, and conducted her to it.

Ruth settled in the chair. "Actually, I need your help."

"Watch her go. You've never seen anyone haggle like Ruth," Esther whispered.

Amaya smiled.

Miguel sat on the corner of a table. "Anything I can do."

"I'm sure you've heard on the news about all the Eshuvani criminals striking at area businesses," Ruth said.

"Oh, terrible, terrible. And officers being hurt in the line of duty. One just yesterday!"

"Yes, Mark's partner, but the doctor says he'll be fine."

"Excellent."

"My friend here, Amaya, is a policewoman at the station that is going to help put these bandits where they belong. Only some bureaucratic paper-pusher mixed up their food order. Would you believe they sent her four hundred pounds each of dried beans and rice? One bag of each is as much as they can use in a reasonable time, but that leaves three hundred fifty pounds of rice and three hundred fifty pounds of–" She looked back at Amaya. "What kind?"

"Black beans."

Miguel whistled. "That's a lot of *frijoles*."

Ruth nodded. "Isn't it? We were hoping you might know someone she could trade with or sell the excess to so they can get what they need."

"I go through many bags with my restaurant. I'll buy them for two dollars per bag."

"Oh, well, she can't afford to give it away. Eight dollars each would be reasonable, don't you think? Still under the going rate."

"I don't buy from the grocery store and can't afford to be nearly that generous. Let us say three-and-a-quarter."

URUSHALON

"I understand, but this station will help my husband protect all of Las Palomas from Eshuvani criminals. Would you consider six-and-a-half?"

"I suppose I could consider this an investment. Let us say four-and-a-half."

"Five-and-a-half perhaps?"

Miguel rubbed his chin and considered the tarp over his head. "Hmm. You bargain shrewdly, but I will agree to five per bag."

Amaya stepped forward and shook the man's hand to solidify the deal after the human custom. "Thank you. I have them in my avicopter. I can bring them to you now or deliver them to your shop."

"I have my truck. Here is good."

She nodded and left.

Amaya flew the avicopter in as near as she could and made multiple trips to cart the bags in while Miguel handled his growing number of customers. By the time Amaya had finished with the last load, sweat poured from her body, she struggled to take a deep breath, and her vision blurred. When her knees threatened to buckle, she sat under the edge of the pavilion. She needed to get a nutrition bar out of her kit before her vision clouded completely.

Esther crouched nearby. "Too much too soon?"

Amaya nodded. "I need my trauma kit from the avi."

"What you need is something to eat."

"Yes. In the side pocket of my kit–"

"I'll get it, but for now, try one of these empanadas." Esther tore off a piece, handed it to Amaya, and put the rest on her knee. "The rest is there if you want it."

She jogged away.

Amaya popped the piece of pastry into her mouth. It was mostly bread with some cinnamon and what she supposed was

LIKE HERDING THE WIND

either pumpkin or sweet potato cooked inside. In other circumstances, she would have enjoyed it, but it lacked what her body needed to restore her equilibrium.

A shadow fell over her, and Amaya looked up at Ruth.

"Are you okay?" Ruth asked.

"I'll be all right." Amaya managed a smile to put the woman at ease. "For Eshuvani, too much exertion too quickly is wearying. I need to eat, rest for a little while, then get some water."

"I hope it's okay that I told him you were a policewoman instead of the captain. He wouldn't have accepted the idea that you're in command."

Esther returned with a nutrition bar.

"Thank you." Amaya returned her attention to Ruth. "You did an excellent job. I trust your judgment. I have little experience with the southern cultures, and I appreciate the way you handled the negotiation."

Esther tore open the package. "Eat."

Amaya nodded. "Yes, dear one."

The honey, apple, and nut bar chased off the muscle weakness, blurry sight, and labored breathing.

Esther pressed her hand to Amaya's forehead. "Do we need to take you home?"

"You do look awfully tired," Ruth added.

Amaya shook her head. "No, no. I will rest in the avi while you two finish your shopping. When you're ready, come get me, and we'll see about these garage sales Ed told me about."

Esther frowned. "Only if you're well enough."

"I'll be fine."

Esther helped her up and held onto her all the way back to the avi. Amaya climbed in and opened both doors to let the breeze blow through. She leaned back and dozed off while the

URUSHALON

others went about their shopping.

Giggly kids coming nearer woke her up again. Amaya sat up and waved at the two boys chasing each other around nearby, but they took one good look at her and ran off.

Amaya sat in the open door of the avi, finished the empanada Esther had given her earlier, and looked around for a source of drinkable water.

Where do they hide water fountains in this park?

Esther and Ruth appeared in the crowd. Amaya grabbed her trauma kit, secured the avi, and went to join them.

"Oh! You're awake already." Esther handed Amaya a paper cup. "Ice water. That dumb soda vendor insisted on putting ice in it after I told him not to. I was hoping it'd melt by the time you needed it."

Amaya sipped the water. The chill was enough to cramp muscles. "It'll be fine. Thank you."

"It won't be too cold?"

"Not if I drink it slowly." She wrapped both hands around the cup to warm it up faster.

"Are you feeling better?" Ruth asked.

"I am, thank you. Rest and food were excellent, and the water will finish my recovery. I should pace myself better in weather like this. Up north, moving those bags that distance wouldn't have been a problem. They're not that heavy, and I wasn't moving that quickly. I've learned my lesson for the next time."

Ruth tilted her head to one side.

Esther turned to Ruth. "Eshuvani believe all failures are learning experiences."

Amaya shrugged. "How else do you grow?"

"Oh, um, should we go look for furniture and baby things?" Ruth asked.

Amaya gestured for them to lead the way. If she couldn't

LIKE HERDING THE WIND

find the furniture she needed, she might find substitutes that would serve the function well enough.

***

Wylin paced the length of the depression in the sand, a natural dip in the terrain he and Maran had spent weeks widening to accommodate their camp on the edges of the deserted ruins of Woran Juvay. As he completed another circuit, he touched the silver *kiandarai* collar tabs. The dark blue crystals had better light up soon with an incoming call, or else that old barracuda and his partner were–

A soft chime sounded from the collar tabs and dull, blue light radiated from the four crystals.

Wylin tapped one of the glowing crystals. "Well?"

"Yes, he was captured." The woman's voice included a built-in sneer. "He's being held on charges of breaking and entering and intentionally injuring a peace officer. If there's a reliable witness, he's as good as–"

"Get him out!" Wylin clenched his jaw and bared his teeth.

"Not possible." She tossed off the comment as if answering a request for buttered toast.

"Make it possible. You're supposed to have enough power to handle these things."

"I told you it's not possible! Now don't compound one burst of idiocy with another," she hollered, her voice turning shriller than usual. "You have a job to do."

Wylin blew out a shuddering breath. "What about Maran? I can't just leave him there."

"Aren't you the same guy who described him as 'a dumb, scrawny kid with more brawn than brains'?"

"That doesn't mean I want him dead. He's my brother!"

The woman huffed. "I'll see what I can do. In the meantime, how is the equipment collection going?"

URUSHALON

"We were interrupted before we could collect what we needed." He pressed his fist to his forehead.

"You're holding up the process, y'know." She growled.

"Hey! The humans must have had some kind of silent alarm in place or a sentry stationed. We weren't in the building two minutes before the *kiandar*–"

"Police. In English, they're called police."

"I don't care what they're called. They were there not two minutes after we arrived."

The line stayed silent for long enough. Wylin began to wonder if she'd disconnected.

Finally, she drew a deep breath. "Go at night. Raid places at the edge of the town, land your avi in close, and be quick."

Wylin paused in his pacing. To do a night raid, he would need to pick his target out during the daytime. Then at night he'd need gear to compensate for the poor nocturnal vision that plagued all Eshuvani. Flashlights would be too obvious. He might as well redecorate the avicopter in phosphorescent paint and advertise his intentions.

"I'll need infrared gear to fly and maneuver in the dark." He resumed his restless movement.

"Hmm. I'll see what I can do and contact you later."

"With news about Maran."

"Sure." Her tone was like a kid being told to go do chores. "But don't get your hopes up."

The lights on the silver collar tabs went dark. Wylin paced a few more circuits before he flopped down next to the campfire and groaned. He never should have let Maran go off alone.

***

Nurinyan entered the open hangar to escape the late afternoon sun and shook his head. If this was *Uloniya Varoosht*, he had to be hallucinating. A junk heap of two

LIKE HERDING THE WIND

wrecked avicopters occupied the back half of Bay Four, and the other two avis belonged there, too. The ancient specimens were cobbled together from parts of more than one model. The courier avi had hull plates from one of the junked ones in the corner. Was this the norm for the station, or was the *kiand* taping this practical joke for future amusement?

The loud bangs of a vigorous hammer led him down the long corridor to the entryway. A woman, the *kiand* perhaps, nailed slats scavenged from the remains of crates onto an old park bench. Five other makeshift benches and a dozen chairs littered the room along with five hip-high piles of cushions and pillows in clashing colors and patterns.

So, was the *kiand* the formal sort? He'd best assume so until she proved otherwise.

Nurinyan waited for the construction project to end. "May the light of God illuminate your path."

She faced him and started to pick her way through the debris. The gold filigree on her collar confirmed her rank. She had gray eyes and dark brown hair, which she wore at the length of her collar. The *kiand* stood a little over average height and had a somewhat more muscular build. She wasn't hard to look at, but she'd never make it as a model. The level of fitness required for *kiandarai* made the model's heavier build all but impossible to maintain.

The *kiand* had to be old enough to be his mother. The jewels in her collar tab bore her certifications in all the usual skills and three human languages. The swirls of metal around the opal told him she was an interspecies relations specialist, and the pearl ring around a white stone showed her teaching credentials in marksmanship. An extra loop of gold removed from the rest of the insignia marked her as one of those unfortunates who reacted badly to regeneratives.

One more teaching credential and a little more medical training, and she'll make kiat.

Nurinyan's guts sank into his boots. He might be one

more misunderstood action away from a boring life. Hopefully this *kiand* was more grace than law.

She stopped within arm's reach, clasped his right arm, and embraced him. "Walk only on the path he provides. Nurinyan Tano *Kiala*?"

"Almost. Whether or not I make journeyman is up to you."

"It's equally your choice, and I've already made my decision. Your collar tabs and basic gear are in the briefing room. You're welcome to claim them, but I'd suggest you wait to hear what we're up against. If you decide this isn't the challenge you had in mind, I'll release you without prejudice, and it won't count as your third rejection."

He frowned. Of course she'd know about his catastrophic mistake. Half his record detailed his stupidity. Would he ever live that down?

She gripped his arm. "Peace, Nurinyan. I reviewed the actions against you. What you did was against protocol, but with the level of training you had at the time, I understand how you came to that point. You have potential, but you are young."

How was he supposed to answer that thwack on the ear? At least she hadn't turned him away as a matter of course. Two other *kiandai* had.

"The others are in the briefing room." She gestured to the door. "We're waiting for one more. Then we'll begin."

He nodded and entered the room. One *kiandara* and two other near-*kialai* sat on chairs that looked as contrived as the avicopters. Their gear and collar tabs were arrayed on a makeshift table constructed from concrete blocks and a weather-beaten wooden slab. Apparently the *kiand* had given all the *kialai* the same warning.

He eyed the *kiandara*. She was an average height woman with dark green eyes and brown hair, which she'd braided then put up in a bun. She looked about thirty years his senior. Her

LIKE HERDING THE WIND

collar tab showed gems for the basic skills and the human language, English. The metal swirls around the gem for data analysis showed her specialization.

The two *kialai* didn't look old enough to be through their apprenticeships. The boy had short light brown hair and green eyes. His stiff, perfect posture suggested he came from the upper echelons of society. The girl fidgeted with the cuff of her shirt, then with her black hair. She looked up at Nurinyan with dark blue eyes and a goofy grin.

Nurinyan walked further into the room. "Grace be unto you."

The one *kiandara* stood. "And peace from God, the Father of our Lord." She came over and embraced him. "I am Orinyay Midorin *Kiandara*."

How had such a soft-spoken woman managed as a *kiandara*?

She indicated first the boy then the girl with her hand. "This is Vadin Tara and Ishe Danyon."

After greeting the kids, Nurinyan found a seat to wait for the last member of their group. He tuned out Vadin's litany of useless information. That one didn't understand the value of silence.

The door opened.

"I'll be there directly," the *kiand* called.

Nurinyan glanced up and scowled. "Jevon Nuri."

The perpetual whiner had the same spiky black hair and dwarfed all but the tallest men.

Jevon sneered. "I'm surprised to see you haven't been shipped off to the wilds yet."

Nurinyan started to bare his teeth then recomposed himself. "Hey, you're on your last chance, too."

Orinyay interceded and introduced herself and the two youngsters. She'd no sooner finished than the *kiand* entered

URUSHALON

and sat on the edge of the concrete and wood table. Nurinyan waited for it to shift and dump her on her head, but the improvised structure held.

"I am Amaya Ulonya *Kiand*, and this is *Uloniya Varoosht Kiandarai*. Once you've decided whether to join the station, I'll introduce you properly, but first I want you to know what this station is for and what we're up against."

Nurinyan leaned forward with his elbows on his knees and listened. He'd heard news reports about human police being injured by Eshuvani crooks, but the details he heard turned his stomach crossways. The humans weren't just getting hurt, the criminals were tossing them around like children's toys and leaving them half-dead.

If that weren't enough to keep him awake nights, Nurinyan's hackles raised to hear about how this station had been crippled. The *kiand* didn't say as much, but the outrage had to be the *kiat*'s doing. Nurinyan had heard of the *kiat*'s hatred of humanity years ago. Couldn't the old man see that his actions were encouraging criminal activity? Was his prejudice worth so much to him? Ludicrous.

Jevon crossed his arms over his chest. "So, ultimately, our job is to babysit the human police with outmoded, damaged, ill-functioning gear."

Amaya propped her hand on her hip and glared at Jevon. "No. Our job is to assist the human police, train them to safely take Eshuvani suspects into custody, and transport Eshuvani suspects to the courthouse prison. We have additional responsibilities of attending to rescue, emergency medical, and police work in the Buffer Zone. We'll have to handle those responsibilities with inadequate equipment until our budget can afford replacements."

"We have to cover the whole Buffer Zone?" Ishe's eyes went wide. "That's a lot of territory."

"Yes, it is, and we have additional complications. Four of you are *kialai*, or will be if you pick up your collar tabs. We

LIKE HERDING THE WIND

can only field two units, and Orinyay and I will be busy. That's just as well. You saw our two functioning avicopters when you came in, and it took some real effort to get them running. They both have idiosyncrasies I'll teach you about later. The other two avis we were assigned are not reparable."

Nurinyan frowned. "All this because the *kiat* hates humans?"

"That's likely." Vadin gestured in the direction of Woran Oldue. "He was very vocal at a party thrown by my parents' friends."

Amaya shook her head. "Regardless, to assist the human police is our mandate."

"Straight from His Magnificence." Vadin turned both hands outward and bowed his head.

Ishe gasped. "From the king? Really?"

Amaya nodded. "Really."

"This is never going to work." Jevon rolled his eyes. "The Buffer Zone is big enough to be covered by three stations. Five by the time you factor in Las Palomas."

Nurinyan scowled. *The door operates in both directions, Jevon.*

"I intend to succeed in spite of the *kiat*'s efforts." Amaya stood and made eye contact with each of them. "However, if we can't overcome the obstacles, and this station fails, the collapse will count as a strike on your record. That doesn't mean terribly much for Orinyay or me, since we have a more extensive file, but to a couple of you, you'll lose the freedom to choose your posts and spend the next several years, if not the rest of your career, in some unpleasant duty assignments. That's why I cautioned you to hold off on taking your equipment. You are now informed. It is entirely your decision. For those who choose to remain, the introduction to the station will begin in the entry in five minutes." She turned to leave.

"*Kiand*," Vadin called.

URUSHALON

She stopped and looked back at him. "Yes, Vadin."

"If I contact my family, they might be able to help us with the equipment issues."

Nurinyan raised an eyebrow. If Vadin's family had that kind of money, how had he gotten assigned to this station?

"That's against protocol." Amaya smiled and came back to level ground. "If your family wishes to equip you with things for your personal use, you are their child, and they have that right, but if you loan that gear out or in any way make it available to others, then we are violating protocol. Such donations have to go through the *kiat*. He clearly intends our failure. If he can shut us down for breach of protocol, our own actions will serve his purpose."

"Plenty of evidence for a sabotage charge." Nurinyan pointed to the creatively engineered table, the red and blue plate on the ceiling, and the half-disintegrated chairs.

"The investigation would temporarily shut the station down. The human police are being decimated, and we need to help them deal with that. In a couple of years, they should be properly trained and equipped. I'll file the charge then. In the meantime, do continue to think of ways to solve our problems. Join me in the foyer if you wish." She stepped out.

Orinyay picked up her equipment and left a few seconds before Vadin collected his gear and walked out.

Ishe approached the table next and picked up a Model Five pistol. "I, uh, I've never seen this kind."

"A Model Five. Not too different from a Six." Nurinyan took it from her and checked the sights. "It aims differently, but it's not hard. The *kiand* can show you. She's a certified marksmanship instructor."

"Is she really?"

Jevon rolled his eyes. "That is what the pearl around the white crystal means."

Ishe giggled. "Oh, right."

LIKE HERDING THE WIND

She grabbed her equipment and skipped out of the room.

Jevon waited for the door to close and tapped Nurinyan's shoulder. "Are you sure she's old enough to be here?"

"No. Same for Vadin."

"Yeah, but at least he acts like he's out of basic school." Jevon sighed and picked up his collar tabs. "Would we be stupid to pick these up? This is an impossible job, and a station collapse could mean we get shipped off to Antarctica or worse."

"This *kiand* is willing to try us. Any guarantee we'd get the same if we go elsewhere?"

"Not the way my luck runs."

Nurinyan extended his right arm. "Truce?"

Jevon clasped his arm and embraced him. "As long as you don't assume you know it all."

"If you'll stop complaining about everything."

"No promises."

"Likewise."

They gathered their equipment and joined the *kiand* in the foyer.

URUSHALON

Chapter Five

When the tour of the station ended, Amaya stopped in the middle of the field between the main building and the houses. "For housing assignments, going from the right end of the arc and around, it'll be Ishe, Vadin, Nurinyan, me, Jevon, and Orinyay."

Orinyay turned to look at the largest of the houses, then spun back to stare at Amaya.

Yes, Orinyay. I did that on purpose. "Take your choice of a bench, two chairs and one pile of cushions. I'll give you this afternoon to get settled. I have a court appearance in the morning. Upon my return, I'll expect to see everyone whittling down our list of unfinished tasks. Partner assignments have not been solidified, and won't be until we have six *kiandarai*, so make no assumptions. I will be working around the station if you need me. Serve with diligence."

The new *kialai* headed for the station.

Now, let's see what else I can strike off the list today. Amaya headed for the foyer.

Orinyay caught her arm. "Please wait."

You won't let that housing incongruity go without

explanation, hmm? "There is a question in your eyes. Let's get out of this sun and answer it." Amaya entered the briefing room and drew two chairs together.

Orinyay secured the door.

A private meeting because you don't understand the housing situation? Amaya sat in one of the chairs. "This is serious, then."

"It could get that way." Orinyay held onto one of the haphazard chairs until she'd settled into it.

"Fire when ready."

"What?"

Amaya smiled. "A human idiom. Bring it into the open."

"Did you mean to take the smaller house?"

"Yes. You have a family. I don't. You'll need more space."

Orinyay reached into Amaya's right sleeve and pulled the wedding bracelet out of her cuff.

Amaya maintained eye contact and slipped the bracelet back into her sleeve. "I commend your powers of observation, but you've made a poor assumption. My previous statement stands." She crossed her arms over her chest to hide the developing tremor.

"Forgive my impertinence." Orinyay shifted in her seat. "How are we going to handle having four *kialai?*"

"I'll give you my idea. If you like it, we'll make it the standing order. If you have another idea, we'll discuss it."

Orinyay nodded.

"Nurinyan and Jevon are nearest to their ascension to *kiandarai*. I suggest you take one. I'll take the other. Once they pass the required mastery tests, I'll take Vadin, and you can continue to work with both of the others to increase their experience. Once Vadin graduates, I'll take Ishe, and you can choose your partner. Once all four have the silver collar tabs,

URUSHALON

we'll establish more stable partnerships."

"That's probably the best way to do it." Orinyay looked away for a moment. "You know Nurinyan and Jevon have some tense history between them."

Amaya frowned. "How tense?"

"Before you entered, they were civil. Barely."

Amaya shook her head. "Either they'll be professional, or they'll be up for diplomacy training. Which would you rather be partnered with for now?"

"Nurinyan will need a strong hand. I'm not sure he'll hear me. It looks to me like Jevon's biggest problem is his pessimism. That I think I can handle."

"Fair enough. I'll take Nurinyan. Jevon would get a sore ear the number of times I'd have to thwack him, so if you can counter his perpetual lamentation, I'll leave him to you."

"What will Ishe and Vadin be doing?" Orinyay nodded toward the foyer.

"They'll be on permanent dispatch duty, unless something happens to one of the others. Not ideal, but our options are limited."

Orinyay nodded. "Perhaps by the time Ishe's turn comes to be partnered with you, she'll have matured some."

"She does seem awfully young, doesn't she?" Amaya winced and shook her head. "She'll learn. Do you have other concerns?"

"No, nothing."

"Then let's go see what the kids have left for us."

Amaya gestured for Orinyay to go through the door first.

The creatively engineered furniture had all vanished leaving a pile of cushions and the construction flotsam of tools and leftover wood.

Orinyay looked around. "Maybe they took the furniture to our houses?"

LIKE HERDING THE WIND

Amaya smiled. "I'm glad they're being so helpful."

"There don't seem to be enough cushions."

Amaya shook her head. "I haven't made mine yet. These are all yours."

I don't even have the materials for mine yet. Minor detail.

***

Wylin set his avicopter down near a cluster of short, scraggly yaupons in the Buffer Zone. He left the avi in standby mode and climbed out, grumbling. All this hide-and-seek nonsense had gotten well past ridiculous. What purpose did it serve? So what if he went to the headquarters now and then? There were legitimate reasons for civilians to go there. Sneaking out to this random stand of trees to leave a bizarre assortment of materials was supposed to be more covert? Insane.

"Whatever," Wylin mumbled.

He picked his way through the trees and crouched next to the burlap sack. When he pulled it open, the reflection off the infrared goggles beamed up at him. Wylin lifted the eyewear out of the sack, bringing a white, paper envelope along. He tugged the paper loose and set it on the bag.

The goggles had two glass disks that fit over the eyes and a heavy canvas hood that blocked out natural light. An adjustable strap wrapped around the wearer's head to keep the goggles in place. Small wheels on the sides of the lenses adjusted the focusing depth and the resolution. Not the latest model, but they'd do the job well enough. Wylin slid the strap over his arm and snatched the paper.

His heart beat faster. Was this news about Maran? Wylin tore open the envelope and tugged out the slip of paper inside.

There's nothing we can do. I was hoping that the only witnesses would have been the other humans. I could have argued that humans are unreliable witnesses, or that the accusation was a human conspiracy to blame all the recent

URUSHALON

injuries on a helpless, innocent Eshuvani, but there was no chance for that. He was foolish enough to make his error in the presence of a kiand. Kiandarai *are considered by the court to be the ultimate witness, and with the corroborating testimony of a ranking, human policeman, the sentence was a foregone conclusion. The sentence was carried out immediately. When you seek a counselor for the Rite, I suggest you find one outside the immediate area.*

There was no signature, but the tight, narrow script was easily recognizable.

Wylin read the letter again, looking for some indication that he'd misunderstood, but no. The sentence had already been carried out, and the only sentence for intentional injury of a peace officer was execution.

He clenched his jaw and crushed the letter and envelope in his hand as a fierce chill settled on him in spite of the hot sun beating down on the terrain. Wylin returned to his avicopter and headed for his camp on the barrier island. A little checking through public court records would show who was involved in Maran's death.

***

Mark Hollis stowed the rest of his belongings in his locker and stopped humming "Ticket to Ride," the latest tune to get stuck in his head. Humming and whistling to himself was one thing. Driving everyone else crazy with it was another.

He grabbed the mess of sticks and ribbons he'd found on his porch that morning and hustled to Osborn's office where his boss and former partner leaned over his desk working on some papers.

Hollis knocked on the door frame. "Can I talk to you for a minute, Ed?"

"Sure. Come on in." Osborn looked up and set his pencil aside. "What's on your mind?"

He glanced at the pair of sticks tied together with red and

LIKE HERDING THE WIND

gray ribbons. "I found this on my porch this morning. There's Eshuvani writing on one of the ribbons."

"You, too, huh? I wonder if yours has the same message."

"Me, too?"

"Mmhmm. Gale, Sumner, your partner, and I also got one." Osborn took the twigs and looked at the writing. "Yeah. Same words. 'An alert dog barks.'"

"What does it mean?"

"I have no idea. Probably an old Eshuvani idiom. I've found more meaningful messages in a bowl of alphabet soup. Amaya is coming in this morning to brief you guys on how the new station will be available to help us. We'll ask her about this and see what she thinks."

Hollis nodded. "Okay. I'll see you there."

"I'll be right with you."

As Hollis entered the conference room, scattered laughter faded.

Kirby pointed at Gale. "I'm telling you, if you judge a female *kiandara* by her anatomy, you're going to be making a huge mistake."

Hollis took the seat next to Kirby. "The one we saw got a clear line of fire by kicking off from the roof of Osborn's car and going another five feet straight up. She shot a retreating target three times before she gracefully landed on her feet. Then she carried not only the male Eshuvani suspect but also Kirby, as easily as I can pick up my own kid."

"It's true, and it wasn't a real effort for her."

Parrish waved a dismissive hand. "Ah, you're a beanpole, Kirby."

"Maybe, but I doubt you could pick me up as easily."

"I could arrange a demonstration." Amaya led Osborn in.

Osborn chuckled. "Maybe after watch. I'm a little short-handed today, with two guys on light duty."

URUSHALON

Amaya shrugged and set her backpack on the front desk. "I wouldn't hurt any of them."

"Next time." Osborn set his papers on the desk and stepped forward. "Gentlemen, some of you have already met Amaya Ulonya *Kiand*. She's the new captain of the Buffer Zone station. She's here to provide you with a quick overview of the *kiandarai* station's duties."

He stepped back, and the *kiand* stood in front of the desk.

Amaya turned the palms of both hands toward them and bowed. "Good morning. Hawk's Nest will officially go active in five days. The Consecration Day ceremony is a public event, so you are all welcome to join us. Starting today, if you need *kiandarai* advice or assistance, your dispatcher has the means to contact me. If all goes well, eventually, you'll all have the means to contact the Hawk's Nest dispatch desk. In addition to providing training and assistance, we will serve as the intermediary between the Las Palomas police and Woran Oldue's *kiandarai*. Any questions?"

"Let's deal with the one everyone's wondering about." Osborn stepped forward. "Are women in the *kiandarai* really as effective as men at field work?"

"Yes, in general, our men are stronger but our women are faster. Although they use strategies that play to their particular strengths and take advantage of available equipment, both men and women accomplish the job effectively."

Hollis leaned forward. "You mean, if the guy we chased down in the park last week had been a woman, he'd've been faster?"

"Likely. But, remember Eshuvani are capable of full speed or strength for only a short burst of time."

"So that's why he kept sprinting a distance and then hiding for a while." Kirby exchanged a look with Hollis. "I'd wondered why he didn't take off and keep going."

Amaya nodded. "One of the things you can do to gain advantage over a hostile Eshuvani is to use your greater

LIKE HERDING THE WIND

endurance. Don't let them take a rest."

Gale clicked his ball point pen and set it down on his notepad. "You said men're stronger'n women. Put some real numbers on 'at."

"Sure. I have three men and three women including me at Hawk's Nest. On average, the women can lift and carry a maximum of two hundred pounds. The men, about seventy-five more than that, but bear in mind, *kiandarai* are expected to maintain a higher level of physical fitness. For the general population, reduce both numbers by about fifty to seventy-five pounds."

Gale snorted. "You're puttin' me on."

Amaya shook her head. "Have you not had enough demonstrations of Eshuvani throwing humans around lately?"

"A man doin' that, sure. A little far-fetched, but like you say, we got proof." Gale leaned forward in his seat. "But a woman? Liftin' two hundred pounds? Ain't gonna happen. You're all sticks and rubber bands."

Amaya turned to Osborn.

He cocked a half-smile. "All right. All right. Show him."

"Officer Gale?" Amaya asked.

"Tha's right."

Amaya stepped into the open space in front of the tables and beckoned Gale forward.

Hollis exchanged a smile with his partner.

"I'd guess you weigh around one hundred eighty pounds," Amaya said.

Gale nodded. "'Bout that."

"I'm going to pick you up and hold you over my head for at least fifteen seconds."

Gale smirked at the rest of the watch. "Oh really? Am I supposed t' try an' stop you?"

URUSHALON

Amaya turned a hand toward the ceiling. "Try if you wish, but for the sake of Ed's anxiety level, let's not turn this into a full-contact sparring incident. I'm not a specialist, and in these tight quarters, my lack of precision might hurt one of us."

"Don't you worry, missy. My daddy taught me better'n to take a swing at a lady."

"Fair enough. Ready?"

Gale shrugged. "As ever."

Amaya's hand shot forward. Gale swung an arm across to parry, but Amaya deflected the effort and caught Gale by the front of the shirt. A second later, Gale was suspended parallel to the ground over Amaya's head. She brought her other hand up to steady him and took a step back to brace. He stared down at her, wide-eyed, and held onto her arms.

Hollis looked between the second hand on his watch and the demonstration. "Five seconds. Ten seconds."

Amaya's arms shook.

"Fifteen seconds."

Perspiration glittered on her forehead.

"Twenty. Twenty-five."

Her breathing came heavier.

Osborn took a step toward them. "Amaya. Enough."

"Thirty seconds," Hollis said.

She set Gale down. He landed, slack-jawed, as Amaya staggered. The entire watch applauded the demonstration.

Gale steadied her. "You all right, missy?"

She nodded. "Overexertion. As I said, our strength and speed are short-lived."

Gale returned to his seat as Amaya rejoined Osborn at the front desk. By the time she reached him, Osborn had taken a sealed foil packet out of her backpack and unwrapped what

LIKE HERDING THE WIND

looked like a bar-shaped cookie.

Sumner whistled. "If you can all do like that, then no wrestling matches with an Eshuvani."

"We'll train you on ways you can employ leverage to either pin an Eshuvani or break a hold if you become pinned." Amaya tossed the food wrapper into a trash bin near the door. "You have other questions. Bring them into the open. Be as blunt as you need to be. I'd rather have an honest question than a festering lament."

"Are you readin' minds?" Parrish asked.

"No, Officer Parrish. I can read your posture and facial expressions, but not your mind. Other questions?"

Kirby looked down at the table and absently rubbed his chest below the right collarbone.

Hollis nodded. *Yeah, I'd have questions about the incident in the park, too.*

Kirby's brow furrowed.

"Ask her already." Hollis used the back of his fingers to hit Kirby's arm.

"I will," Kirby whispered.

Amaya studied Kirby. "It's about the park?"

Parrish smiled. "You sure you don't read minds?"

"In his place, I would have many questions, and I haven't had a chance to speak to him since the incident. I tried to visit him in the hospital, but they wouldn't let me in."

Kirby blew out a breath. "All right. If a guy's holding a hostage, why try to kill the hostage before securing an escape route?"

"You were hit before he had a way out?" Tucker asked.

Hollis nodded.

Tucker shook his head. "Yep. That's pretty stupid."

Amaya walked over to Kirby and leaned on the back of a

URUSHALON

nearby chair. "He wasn't trying to kill you, Robert."

Gale tipped back and laced his fingers behind his head. "I dunno, missy. Some mighty important anatomy near the sternum."

"In a human," Osborn said.

Amaya nodded. "As we were drawing nearer, I thought I saw you adjusting your balance. You were getting ready to throw him over your shoulder?"

"If I could, yeah," Kirby said.

She looked toward the corner of the room. "His apparent balance, your relative heights and masses. Your leverage against him would have been about right." She returned to eye contact with him. "He couldn't have that. Had you thrown him and taken a few steps away while he recovered, Mark would have had a clear shot." She pressed her hand below her collar bones. "This area on an Eshuvani holds the majority of the pulley system that operates both shoulders, independently of course."

Kirby squinted. "Pulley system?"

"You are familiar with using a multiple pulley arrangement to increase force?"

"Yeah, like a chain hoist."

"Right. Most major joints on an Eshuvani have tendons and ligaments that loop around bony structures to form something like pulley systems."

Gale slapped the table with his hand. "That's why you can look like sticks and rubber bands and still pick up a guy like me?"

Amaya glanced back at him. "Exactly. And that's why I can't maintain the effort for long. My muscles weary quickly. He wasn't trying to kill you, Robert. He was trying to immobilize one or both arms so you couldn't throw him off. He apparently didn't know human anatomy."

Kirby studied the wood grain of the table. Hollis couldn't

LIKE HERDING THE WIND

blame his partner for being a little rattled. Most guys wouldn't have survived that afternoon.

Amaya's long spindly fingers gripped Kirby's shoulder. "We can speak more of the incident later if you wish."

He nodded.

She returned to the front desk and perched on it. Her hands quivered.

Osborn looked at her hands, then her face, and stepped in front of her. "That's all we have time for today. There will be other opportunities for questions. I need Officers Gale, Sumner, Hollis, and Kirby. The rest of you are dismissed."

Hollis waited for the others to file out and then joined the sergeant in the front of the room.

"This about those twigs?" Sumner asked.

"Twigs?" Amaya's hands were steady again.

Hollis handed her the ribbons and sticks he'd found on his porch that morning.

"All five of us found one this morning," Osborn said.

Amaya turned the bundle over in her hands. "A remembrance token."

Hollis tilted his head to one side. "Remembrance token?"

"They were popular some fifty years ago. If you wanted someone to remember something, you'd buy a pre-made token or make your own with ribbons and sticks or rocks or whatever you could find. On the ribbon, you'd write what it was you wanted the other person to remember and sign it. This looks like a remembrance token, but there's no signature, and the vague reminder doesn't do much to help. This one says, 'An alert dog barks,' an old expression meaning, 'Look out' or 'Keep your eyes open.' Is it possible you all received a different part of a larger message?"

Osborn shook his head. "They're all identical."

"Have all five of you been involved in the same case

recently?"

Gale shrugged. "The only Eshuvani I ever tangled with was that fella in the park last week."

"That might be it. His partner was tried, convicted, and executed yesterday."

Gale whistled. "That was fast."

Osborn nodded. "Eshuvani law is swift, when the case is that obvious."

"Intentionally injuring a peace officer closed his options." Amaya looked at Kirby. "I was called to testify about Robert's injury."

Kirby tapped the twigs. "But you didn't get one of these?"

"Don't rule out your theory yet." She held the bundle up. "I won't have an official place for him to put this for a few more days. May I keep this one?"

Hollis shrugged. "Go ahead."

"My data analyst may see something we missed."

"All right. Get out there." Osborn aimed a thumb over his shoulder at the door. "When I hear something, I'll let you know."

"Be watchful." Amaya tucked the sticks into her backpack. "Have your dispatcher contact me if there's need."

Hollis nodded and followed Kirby out.

* * *

Amaya finished her welcome and stood toward the back of the stage while the crowd of humans and Eshuvani sweltered under the midmorning sun. The prayers and litanies continued.

All the pomp and foolishness of the usual Consecration Day Ceremony could finish right that moment, and it still wouldn't be soon enough. Why couldn't they gather everyone involved, pray for guidance and blessing on their endeavor, and get to work? Would God bless them more for all the

LIKE HERDING THE WIND

verbose, false-praise speeches and artificial joy? Hardly. These ridiculous ceremonies allowed the powerful and egotistical an opportunity to build more monuments to their own supposed greatness.

Even the priest leading the service wore heavy, expensive robes boasting his wealth and glory. The rich layers of embroidery and beadwork bulking him out would be hot in the temperatures she'd come to associate with late Texas springs. Only divine intervention would keep him from heat prostration.

When the chanting and prayers ended, Amaya left the temporary platform to rejoin Ed, her own people, and the small contingent of officers from Las Palomas. The *kiat* hovered over the master of ceremonies and all but shoved the man out of the way after being introduced.

Emyrin drew a deep breath. "Coexistence on dis planet has been a noble goal from de beginning, and I am pleased to see dis station operational to..."

With his dense accent in English, an interpreter might have been better, but that would have dragged the festivities out even longer.

Amaya hid an eye-roll behind an effort to wipe sweat from her forehead as the *kiat* droned on and on about the virtues of her new station and its staff. Politics and posturing were the two greatest evils in her job, next to the sick-minded people who made half her occupation necessary.

At the last Consecration Day Ceremony she had attended up in Marquette, she'd had her husband with her, and his presence had made the whole farce tolerable. A couple short years later, a sniper aiming at her had stolen much more than her life.

I still need you, dear one. I always will.

Amaya caught herself rubbing the links of her wedding bracelet again and tucked it back into her sleeve. She was supposed to be restarting her life far away from the growing pain associated with her last station, yet she kept rehashing all of what she was trying to escape. There was no time for her own problems right now, the old ones or the new, and there wouldn't be until the station stabilized.

Aware of eyes on her, she turned. Ed studied her. She spared him a smile he wouldn't believe.

He leaned closer. "Windy ol' boy, y'know?"

She nodded. "Enamored of his own voice, I think."

The sun was approaching its zenith when speeches ended. No doubt the timing had more to do with the onslaught of Texas heat than with the speakers' desire to finish their lectures.

The crowd dispersed. Many went to their vehicles. Others headed for Hawk's Nest to take a self-guided tour of the facility.

Amaya surveyed the station from the distance. Her brow furrowed. "Something's not right."

Ed scanned the dwindling crowd. "Where did Sumner and Gale go?"

Mark shrugged. "Probably went searching for the men's room."

"Perhaps." Amaya scowled. "Wait. The hangar door is down. I left it open."

"Is that a problem?" Robert asked.

The comm system on her collar beeped for attention.

She tapped one of the dark blue crystals. "Amaya."

"Orinyay. I'm in the hangar. There are two humans in here. One is lying on the floor. His eyes are open, but he's unable to move or speak. There are small, purple crystals on his face, and a definite, foul odor. The other is hanging from the rafters by a rope wrapped around him. He's tightly bound, but alive."

Ed translated for the others.

LIKE HERDING THE WIND

Amaya ran for the station with the human officers behind her. "I'm on my way. Take care of the one in the rafters."

"Message received," Orinyay said.

URUSHALON

Chapter Six

Amaya entered through the main doors and turned down the left corridor. The door into the hangar stood open.

Harry Gale lay less than a stride inside the hangar. He made no movement beyond shallow breathing, but his eyes were wide open. A purplish sheen sparkled on one side of his face like child's glitter. Ten strides away, Orinyay stood under Clyde Sumner, who hung from the rafters. The rope bound his ankles and wrapped around his legs. It pinned his left arm to his side and wound around his chest. His right hand was caught between the rope and his neck. The other end of the rope was looped over a rafter and secured to the rear door of the hangar. Nurinyan, knife in hand, stood on top of the cargo avi and hurled the knife at the rope with expert precision.

Amaya knelt by Harry. His physical symptoms, the purple crystals, and a distinct aroma like a garlic-scented skunk all pointed to the old paralytic. Could that be? All but two of those were supposed to have been confiscated forty-odd years ago. Had one of the last two shown up after so many years, or was someone making them again?

Amaya lifted Harry, a tricky task with his stiffened, immobile joints. "Ed, look for physical evidence of their attacker. It's unlikely either saw him."

Ed nodded and directed his men to spread out.

Amaya hurried down the corridor, through the entryway, and into the clinic. The awkwardness of her hold on Harry tired her own muscles. She set him on the floor, dragged him to the center of a depressed area, and reached up to turn on the emergency shower. Cold water rained down on them. She crouched next to Gale and kept him turned on his side to keep his airway clear. The spray washed off the chemicals, but it was a long while after all visible traces were gone before his breathing returned to normal.

He rubbed his face with his hand. "What happened?"

She reached up and turned off the shower before she helped him up. Once he was steady, she retrieved a towel for him from a repainted storage cabinet. "How do you feel?"

"Like a drenched cat." He sluiced the water off.

"I'm sorry, but there was nothing for that." Amaya touched her fist to her forehead.

Harry grabbed the towel and applied it to his bare skin. "That's all right. I'm glad enough I c'n breathe 'n' move."

"You didn't happen to see the fellow who hit you, did you?"

"Not at all. Me 'n' Sumner got tired o' gettin' cooked out there listenin' to ol' windbags so we decided to go inside and get some water from the kitchen. After we set a spell, we went on the nickel tour. When we walked into the hangar, Sumner got knocked silly, and I got stung in the face by somethin' that smelled like rotten garlic. I ain't never smelled anythin' so foul in all my life. The next thing I knew, I was fallin', and I heard some ruckus behind me. It weren't half a minute later when one o' yours came in, took in the whole scene, and called you." He took a few steps toward the hangar. "Is there some way you c'n see how Sumner is?"

"They should have him down by now."

URUSHALON

Amaya led the way back to the hangar. Robert stood at the door from the main station while Ishe and Vadin barred entry from the front. Ed, Mark, and the other two *kialai* searched the place. Orinyay sat with Clyde. She beckoned Amaya over.

"Where'd you find the pool?" Clyde asked.

Harry shook his head. "No pool, but a pretty handy shower. My turn. You went swimmin' las' time."

Amaya crouched nearby. "How do you feel, Clyde?"

"A little banged up, but I'll live."

Orinyay handed Amaya a capillary tube. "He will have plenty of bruises and a few rope burns. Not'ing dangerous. He says we got to him less dan a minute after he was hit."

Pretty heavy accent in English. We'll have to work on that, when we find time. None of the humans seemed confused, though.

She held the tube up to the light. A bright green stripe appeared above the column of blood. "No regenerative salve for you, Clyde. Your reaction is almost as bad as mine."

She returned the tube to Orinyay, left Harry in her care, and went to Ed.

"Find anything?" Amaya asked.

"Not much."

He led her to the avicopter nearest the door to the main station. He knelt next to one of the rear landing struts and pointed to a cylinder as big around as her finger and most of the length of her hand. "We left it where we found it. Orinyay had your guy Nurinyan check the part he could see for prints, but he found nothing."

Amaya picked it up. "Paralytic canister. I haven't seen one of these in forty-five years."

"Sumner says all he saw was gray, the same gray as your uniform. Are there *kiandarai* who don't like this alliance

LIKE HERDING THE WIND

enough to go so far as to take two of us out?"

Amaya shook her head. "Just the *kiat*, and he was on the dais the whole time. Let's shoo out our extra guests, lock the place up, and go have a general debriefing."

***

After helping Amaya oust the last of the visitors, Osborn followed her to join the rest of their people. The door to the briefing room slid open as she approached. Her other five *kiandarai* and his four officers were already seated around the room. Gale, with a towel still draped around his shoulders, looked a little less waterlogged. Kirby had taken the bold step of crossing over into the Eshuvani side of the room to have a seat next to the *kiala* whose collar showed the grass green crystal marking him as a Spanish-speaker, but not the red crystal for an English-speaker. Kirby's half-Hispanic heritage bridged that gap.

Osborn smiled.

He waited for Amaya to find a seat and then took one near her.

Amaya made eye contact with Ishe. "Could you translate for Jevon?"

Kirby waved. "I've got that covered."

"Excellent."

Orinyay pointed at Gale and Sumner. "And I have already asked de two officers who were attacked to tell us everyt'ing dat happened."

"Good." Amaya held up the cylinder they'd found under the avicopter's landing strut. "This is a paralytic canister. It's harmless now. I dissolved what remained of the chemical, but it once contained the toxin you were hit with, Harry. It was standard *kiandarai* equipment about forty-five years ago. They were in use for only five years, because the chemical is unstable. It decomposes into a slightly different compound that still paralyzes, but could be fatal. Efforts to stabilize the paralytic failed, so the canisters were confiscated. Two were never accounted for."

As she spoke, she paused now and again for Kirby to give Jevon a translation.

Gale snorted. "Found one of 'em. Same guy probably has the other."

"Likely, but not necessarily." Amaya passed the empty cylinder around.

"Same guy who left us the memory tokens?" Hollis asked.

"That sounds plausible." Osborn nodded.

"So then, it's not the guy from the park? Or is the guy from the park a *kiandara,* of any rank, who went bad?"

Amaya shook her head. "If the attacker is *kiandarai,* he's hidden the paralytic for forty-five years. There were some *kiandarai* who tried to hold onto their canisters for souvenirs, but they were written up for insubordination, which meant a loss of pay until there was compliance. The canisters could only be kept without penalty if they were neutralized."

Gale ran his fingers through his short hair. "What 'bout a *kiandara* who left the job an' took 'is gear?"

"That doesn't happen." Amaya grimaced and shook her head. "Apprenticeship takes fifteen to twenty years to make sure you're committed. Once you become a *kiala,* a journeyman, the only way to leave is through death. Apprentices are not issued gear."

Nurinyan leaned forward. "Den most likely, de attacker is de relative of one who died forty-five years ago, and somehow dis relative got away wit' not returning de equipment?"

Hollis nodded. "And he's a martial arts specialist."

"No. Dat is my specialization. From de injuries our friend received, dis one counts on power, not skill."

Sumner rubbed the back of his head. "Could have fooled me."

LIKE HERDING THE WIND

"An' bold as brass t' walk into a station to attack us," Gale said.

"Well, maybe not. On Consecration Day, with so many people coming and going, what's one more uniform?" Osborn asked.

Gale shook his head. "Still purty gutsy, I say. Someone coulda heard 'n' caught 'im at it. Almost did. He weren't gone half a minute 'fore Orinyay come in."

Osborn took the paralytic cylinder from Jevon and gave it back to Amaya. "What other hazards will he have in a forty-five-year-old kit?"

Amaya closed her eyes. "What was standard issue back then? Two paralytic canisters, a knife, a Model Four tranquilizer gun and maintenance kit, a couple flashlights, infrared goggles, handcuffs, all the necessary uniform parts, and climbing equipment. A *kiala* does not receive a medical kit. A *kiandara*, a regular officer, would have a first aid medical kit with few medications. A *kiand* or *kiat*, captain or chief, would have a full medical kit with all sorts of medications, some of which would be dangerous if misused. That about covers it."

Osborn blew out a breath. "What if it's a history expert who makes equipment that looks forty-five years old?"

"That's possible, I suppose. There's a number on the canister." She leaned closer and pointed it out to him. "I can look it up to make sure it was legitimate."

"What's our next move?" Hollis asked.

"I will ask around." Orinyay took a small notepad and pen from a pocket and jotted a note. "I might find a historian wit' de information on *kiandarai* of forty-five years ago, particularly dose who died but de families did not return de equipment."

Amaya fidgeted with her wedding bracelet. "That will help. Do be careful, all of you. I believe he meant to do much worse than simply frighten you."

URUSHALON

Osborn checked his watch. "Shift change will happen soon. Let's get back."

She pushed the bracelet back under the cuff of her sleeve.

He watched her for a moment while waiting for his men to file out. Was she thinking about the sniper who'd killed her family? He clasped Amaya's hand as she walked out with him.

Her eyes were narrow and her jaw was tight. Once they were alone, he could try asking her, but should he? The last time she'd talked about the sniper, she'd collapsed into some kind of seizure. He couldn't risk causing another one, but he had to do something.

When they reached his car, she pulled him into an embrace. "I'll let you know what we find."

He sat in his car. "Yeah. Stay safe."

She closed the door and stepped away.

***

Amaya watched until Ed was out of sight.

She never should have come to Las Palomas. The fellow who had attacked Clyde and Harry could go after Ed next. She'd lose him, as she'd lost everyone else who meant so much to her.

Quit that already. Events can occur simultaneously and not be related.

Her arrival happened to coincide with the chase through the park. Even if she'd stayed in Michigan, there was no guarantee Ed wouldn't have been involved. He was, after all, the only one in the Las Palomas department who had any experience with the Eshuvani. The one real, predictable difference would have been Robert. There was a decent chance he would have died. Her arrival had preserved him, at least.

With that settled for the moment, Amaya returned to the briefing room where her people were still assembled. "Some of you didn't have much to contribute to our discussion. If I'd wanted my own thoughts, I'd've had that meeting with a recorder."

Jevon snorted. "Opening my mouth at the wrong time is how I got myself gifted with this assignment in the first place."

"Hmm. Anyone else?" She glared at him. "Get it out of your head and into the open. I took care of my own self-pity on the way in. No? Then, I think that will about cover it for the whining. If any of you have somewhere else you'd rather be, then you can pack your gear and go be there without any prejudice from me. I'd rather run short-staffed than with people who don't want to be here."

Nurinyan leaned over and thwacked Jevon on the ear. "And how many *kialai* are still awaiting an assignment?"

Jevon glared at Nurinyan and rubbed his ear. "I'm sorry, Kiand. You don't know why we all got this post."

"You think I haven't read your records? If I read what wasn't said properly, Orinyay corrected the *kiat*'s bad math in a report, and he didn't appreciate being shown an error. Nurinyan broke protocol in a crisis and someone got hurt. Ishe had the lowest passing score on the final exam. Vadin's parents tried to influence his first assignment location, which pleased the *kiat* not at all, and Jevon, you were turned down by two other *kiandai* because they didn't care for your attitude. For the record, I'm here because the other *kiandai* forced the *kiat*'s choice. You were all given to me for our mutual punishment because the *kiat* considers this a childcare assignment rather than real police and rescue work. Lives depend on our ability to get to the truth behind these assaults. In my experience, if the attacker doesn't get some satisfaction against his targets, he'll likely escalate. Any one of you could join his list of viable targets."

Ishe shuddered. "You're serious? We're all targets?"

"Yes. The admonition to remain alert was not just for the humans."

URUSHALON

Orinyay glanced in the direction of her house. "*Kiand,* are my husband and children in any danger?"

Amaya nodded. "Possibly. If you want to move them to the station's safe room until the present storm passes, you may do so. If you need time to remove them to a relative or some other location, we can arrange something." *Maybe if I'd done more, I wouldn't be a widow.* "Anything else?" Amaya looked at each of them. "We're officially ready to take calls. Remember that all calls will require either Orinyay or me until further notice. Be about your work with diligence."

She waited until they'd all left, then returned to the hangar to give it a look herself. She wouldn't rest until she'd confirmed no other clues waited to be found.

***

Mark Hollis shifted into park and idled in front of the darkened sporting goods store. The place had been closed for hours, but someone had reported seeing suspicious activity inside. As they got out of the car, Hollis gestured for Kirby to check around the back. With a hand on his revolver, Hollis approached the front of the store and peered in through the windows. Racks of sweatshirts, shoes, and game equipment waited for the next day's paying patrons. The suspects had either left or hidden somewhere.

"Police! Stop where you are. Face down on the ground with your hands out to the sides!" Kirby ordered.

Hollis ran to back up his partner. A distinctive hydraulic hum preceded the sound of an avicopter lifting off.

Kirby came running back the other way. "Eshuvani male. Carrying a large box. Couldn't see his face. Wearing dark goggles. Took off in a green avicopter."

Hollis turned and ran back to the car. He let Kirby handle the radio and kept himself focused first on locating the avicopter, and then keeping it in sight in spite of ground traffic. He spotted the running lights first. There wasn't much

LIKE HERDING THE WIND

of a moon, but with the running lights as a guide, Hollis made out the silhouette of the avi.

"Hollis," Kirby said.

"Yeah?"

"Did you hear me?"

Hollis glanced at his partner. "Sorry, no."

"Orinyay and Jevon are in the area and moving to intercept."

"Good. We're going to run out of road pretty soon."

"There." Kirby pointed. "A second set of lights."

Hollis looked where Kirby pointed, and then slowed down. The second avi had to be the *kiandarai*. They turned to pursue the first. Hollis pulled onto a county road that paralleled the course the two avis took toward the coast. They were outdistancing him when the *kiandarai* ship spewed a plume of fire from the side. The flame dwindled back to glowing smoke.

God, please help him land that thing in one piece.

He accelerated to catch up.

"Think we should call in the fire department?" Kirby asked.

"Might not be a bad idea." Hollis' guts turned remembering the casualties and damage from the last brush fire. "Even if he can land it intact, if he puts down in the grass..."

"Brush fire, dry as it's been."

Kirby took care of that as Hollis kept an eye on the descending avi. He pulled to a stop near enough to see the last few feet in the patrol car's headlights. Orinyay had the controls. Her jaw was clenched. Jevon, sitting shotgun, held a bright orange cylinder with a short nozzle. Both wore heavy, opaque-looking goggles. A missing panel on the near side of their ship billowed smoke that still glowed.

URUSHALON

The avicopter plummeted about five feet, then jumped up about a foot before Orinyay got the landing gear on the ground in the right lane of the county road. Jevon hopped out and aimed the cylinder in his hand at the gaping wound in the avi's side. Heavy white fog engulfed the opening. He struck the side of the ship and hurled an Eshuvani insult at it.

Hollis looked at Kirby and stepped out of the car. "I think that would roughly translate to, 'Stupid piece of machinery.'"

Orinyay came around the front. "Dat is de right idea, actually. De more direct words would be, 'Condemned piece of trash.'"

Kirby nodded toward the car. "I'll cancel the fire department."

"Are you guys okay?" Hollis asked.

Orinyay translated for Jevon, then answered. "We are unhurt."

"Is there anything we can do?"

"Actually, if you can keep de lights on your car aimed dis way, dat will help."

Hollis went back to the car and turned on the brights.

Orinyay smiled. "Oh, much better."

He went to the trunk and took out a handful of road flares. This road didn't see much traffic, but between the damaged avi and the patrol car, they had most of the road blocked.

Kirby jogged over. "That was some flying. When we saw the fire, I thought for sure you were going to crack up."

She scowled for a moment. "Oh, you mean, crash? Part of de standard training involves how to handle a damaged avicopter."

"Handy."

By the time Hollis had put out the road flares, Jevon was head and shoulders inside the avi's compartment looking around. Orinyay held both pairs of goggles.

LIKE HERDING THE WIND

"What happened up there? You were pulling away from us when we saw the fire." Hollis rejoined his partner. "Did he shoot you down?"

Orinyay's brow furrowed while she considered the idea. "I do not t'ink so. We were at an oblique angle to him at dat point, so hitting de side of de avi would have been possible, but de avi lurched and went to half power den started to overheat. It didn't feel like an external impact."

Jevon came out of the avi's compartment with a broken belt and two pieces of a rubber tube. He and Orinyay spoke for a couple minutes, then Jevon went around to the other side.

"The timing belt snapped and broke a fuel line?" Kirby asked.

"Fuel? What is—?" Orinyay stared at him for a moment. "Oh, no fuel. Avicopters are powered by a battery and a generator. De belt goes from de generator to de motor. De hose is a coolant line. When de system overheated, wiring and a circuit board caught fire. Jevon is not too optimistic, but he t'inks he can get us operational at least long enough to get back to de station. What was our fugitive wanted for?"

"He broke into a sporting goods store again and made off with a box. We aren't sure what was in it."

Jevon came back around with a small toolkit, a taped belt, and the coolant tube patched together with a hard plastic, narrow tube. As he leaned into the compartment, Kirby went over to talk to him.

Hollis listened for a moment, then shook his head. He never could follow Spanish-speakers. "What about the circuit board and wiring?"

"Jevon says dey operated de air exchange fans, a noncritical system. Critical systems have better shielding. We will make it back," Orinyay said.

The repairs were soon finished. Orinyay and Jevon donned the heavy goggles again and climbed into the

URUSHALON

avicopter. The avi started, lifted off, dropped half a foot, then got into the air and headed back toward Hawk's Nest.

Hollis watched until he couldn't see the avi. "I sure hope they make it back okay."

LIKE HERDING THE WIND

Chapter Seven

The avicopter set down on the helipad at the human police academy.

Nurinyan sighed and ran his fingers through his hair.

Amaya smiled. "You'll do fine. You're working with Ed's watch first. They've been hit pretty hard by recent events, so they're willing to learn whatever you can teach them. The only one who might give you some guff is Harry, but most of that's for show."

"I know, but..." He slumped forward, leaning his elbows on his knees. "I'm not sure I can communicate well enough. Speaking English is more than knowing the vocabulary and syntax."

"Umhm, but your English is better than Orinyay's, and the humans understand her fine."

"You'll be there to help me, right?"

"Unless I get a call, but if I didn't think you could handle this, I would've made other arrangements."

"All right. Let's go." Nurinyan hopped out and waited for her to come around from the other side so they could walk in together.

Every step tightened the muscles on the back of his neck. In spite of Amaya's encouragement, he couldn't shake the feeling that she should have given someone else this assignment.

The police academy's gym was a huge room with concrete walls and a wooden floor. Boxes and circles were painted on the floor in several places. Ed and the eight guys from his watch sat around the edge of a thick, blue mat.

Nurinyan stopped at the edge dreading the next step that would take him from spectator and student to teacher.

Amaya embraced her *urushalon* and walked to the middle. "Good afternoon. My martial arts specialist is going to teach you how to use what you already know against an Eshuvani suspect, and then he'll show you a few ways to break loose if you get pinned. This will be the first of several sessions, so don't feel like you have to master everything today." She walked off the mat and sat next to Ed.

Nurinyan leaned closer to Amaya. "I don't suppose there's any way you'd take over."

"Consider this practice for your instructor's credential test."

He winced. He couldn't be a specialist unless he could teach the skills.

Nurinyan stepped onto the mat. If his guts twisted any further around, he'd lose them. Where could he even start? They had some knowledge of self-defense, so he didn't want to insult their intelligence by assuming they were complete novices, but he didn't want to assume more than they had, either. How had his instructor started with him?

"You can't teach someone something until you know where they're starting."

"Okay. De first t'ing I need to do is find out what you already know."

Nigel slapped Robert's shoulder. "Go on, beanpole."

LIKE HERDING THE WIND

"All right." Robert stood up and walked to the middle of the mat.

After his near-death experience, Robert was willing to be the first? Nurinyan would have hung back and watched for a while.

"We will go half-speed at most." Nurinyan squared off with him. "Just react to what I do."

Robert nodded. He stood with his right side forward. His right hand was up at shoulder level but the left was lower and closer to his chest. Both hands were closed in loose fists, which wasn't too bad. There wasn't a whole lot of target to aim for.

Nurinyan threw a slow motion punch at Robert's chest. The human swung his arm across to deflect the shot and stepped to the right. A punch to the abdomen was also met with a parry and a step aside. A kick at the leg was dodged. Nurinyan nodded. He had the pattern.

"Okay, good. Now, you attack."

Amaya's comm system beeped. "Amaya."

Nurinyan held up a hand and turned to face her.

"Ishe. I'm sorry to interrupt." His youngest colleague said in Eshuvani. "Orinyay and Jevon are handling a bank robbery. Two human kids and a dog went for a hike this morning. They're supposed to be back by now. The mother says they may have gone into the Buffer Zone. One of them is supposed to be taking some medication called insulin, whatever that is. Anyway, can you take this or should I call Wolf's Teeth?"

Nurinyan winced. He recalled this "diabetes" from his basic human medical course.

"I have it." Amaya stood and tossed her trauma kit onto one shoulder then explained in English. "Medical emergency. A diabetic kid wandered off."

Ed got up. "I'll go with you. You may need extra eyes."

The two of them left at a run.

URUSHALON

Nurinyan's guts twisted a couple new knots. *I hope I don't make too big a mess of this.*

"Ready?" Robert asked.

Nurinyan turned back to him. "Yes. Go ahead."

After blocking Robert's first punch to the face, Nurinyan stepped in closer, and Robert stepped back. Nurinyan blocked a second punch to the chest and a third to the abdomen, each time stepping closer, which made Robert retreat.

Nurinyan nodded. "I understand now. Dere are many t'ings in common. Really, de biggest differences are where to aim and how to deflect a kick."

Harry smiled. "Awright, teach, where d'we start?"

His own instructor always began with a physical skill, then, when everyone needed a break, he went on with the knowledge skills. "We should start wit' protecting yourself from a kick. Dis is a common attack you will see from Eshuvani."

He used Robert for the demonstration and once certain the human had the basics of the skill, Robert taught his partner and Nurinyan worked with Nigel. That progression continued until all the humans were half-speed sparring and gradually picking up the pace. That gave Nurinyan a chance to walk around and correct errors in form.

Harry stepped away from the group. He held one hand vertically and the other horizontally, tapping the palm of the horizontal hand on the fingertips of the vertical hand. "Time out. I need a breather."

So there is a limit to their endurance. "I am sorry. I did not t'ink about taking a break."

"Don't fret over it, son. I ain't worked out like 'at in a long while. It's supposed t' be good fer me, I guess."

While they all went to get water from the fountain in the corner of the room, Nurinyan pulled a nutrition bar from his pocket. How could they drink water so soon after exertion?

LIKE HERDING THE WIND

Didn't they get terrific headaches that way?

The humans returned about the time Nurinyan finished his snack.

Mark pointed to the corner of the room. "There's a water fountain over there."

"T'ank you, but water must come later." He waited until everyone had settled. "You all learned dat quickly."

Mark smiled. "Wasn't all that hard, once I saw how it worked."

"Good. While you rest, I can tell you ot'er t'ings." Nurinyan stuffed his snack wrapper in his pocket. "Robert, when you attacked me, you aimed de first punch at my head. Is dis a common attack?"

Robert nodded. "If you can ring the guy's bell, he's disoriented, and you can subdue him easier. Not a good idea?"

"Not against an Eshuvani. De bones in de face are dense. Your hand will come apart first. You instead aim for de lower chest and de abdomen. A hit on de lower chest takes his air. A hit on de abdomen hurts very much."

"What about the upper chest, where all the pulley mechanisms are?"

"Wit' a weapon, yes. You will disable de arms. Wit' your hand, you gain little."

"Where d'ya hide the pulleys fer yer legs?" Harry asked.

Nurinyan pressed his hands against the top edge of his pelvic bone. "Here."

"'Bout what I figgered."

"You ask good questions, but are you ready to go on?"

"Yep. Tell ya what. I'll be your guinea pig this round." Harry stood and tugged his loose, gray pants.

"Guinea pig?" *What does a small furry rodent– No, it's an idiom.* "Oh. My demonstration student."

URUSHALON

"Right."

Nurinyan stood and beckoned Harry forward. He walked behind Harry and wrapped an arm around Harry's neck. "Amaya tells me dat de way you break dis hold is de same on humans and Eshuvani."

"So I jus' grab yer arm, lean forward, and hurl ya over." Harry matched his words to his description.

Nurinyan flew over Harry's shoulder and smacked flat on the mat hard enough to see a burst of light.

Mark winced. "Careful, Gale. Don't hurt the kid."

Harry leaned over. "Sorry, son. Tall as ya are, I figured you to weigh more."

Nurinyan tucked his legs in, rolled up to a crouch, and stood. "Eshuvani bones are hollow. I only weigh one hundred t'irty pounds."

"Good to know."

"Yes. Try again. Dis time, I will show you what can happen if your opponent is ready for you."

Harry frowned. "You wouldn't be tryin' for a little payback, wouldja?"

Nurinyan shook his head. "No, no. Not'ing like dat. I want you to know what can happen. I will not hurt you."

"Awright."

Nurinyan stood behind Harry and wrapped an arm around his throat. "T'row me off, but den I will continue."

As soon as Nurinyan left the ground, he twisted midair and pulled Harry with him. Harry landed face down on the mat with one arm under him. Nurinyan landed in a crouch and pinned Harry with a hand on his head and a knee in the small of his back.

Mark's eyes widened. "Wow, I didn't even see that."

"You kiddin'? I didn't see that." Harry's voice was muffled by the mat. "Awright, so now what do I do?"

LIKE HERDING THE WIND

"Before my weight is completely settled, you have to use de hand you have free to grab my belt and pull. My motion is in dat direction already, so you are only forcing me to continue dis way."

Harry flailed back with his free hand, but reached no further than Nurinyan's thigh. "Ain't happenin'."

Nurinyan tried to guide Harry's hand. "Harry, for dis to work, you must put dis hand back here."

"Son, to get my hand back there, I'd have t' have g'rilla arms or three extra joints."

Nurinyan checked his position. Nothing wrong there. He was in the right place, and Harry was where he should be. Why couldn't he reach? Nurinyan let Harry go.

Harry sat up. "Kirby, you try it. Mebbe my ol' joints jus' ain't limber enough."

Robert shrugged and traded places. He blew out a breath and shook out his arms and legs.

Nurinyan stood behind Robert with an arm around his throat. Like before, Nurinyan twisted as he flew over and pulled Robert around. They landed exactly the same way Harry had been pinned moments before. Without waiting for instruction, Robert reached back with his available arm but couldn't get far enough no matter how he stretched.

Robert strained. "Nope, I can't get there, either."

Nurinyan released Robert and sat. "I do not understand. If dere is one of you who cannot do dis, I t'ink it is you, but bot' of you cannot. Yet, dis is de way I am taught. Except for de hands, you have all de same joints I do."

Robert sat cross-legged on the mat. "Do Eshuvani have more range of motion in their joints?"

"I do not t'ink so. Amaya speaks of your better endurance, not movement limitations."

Mark scratched his head. "Are the moves you're trying to teach us dependent on strength? None of us can get near you

URUSHALON

on that level."

"No, no." Nurinyan thought back through the comparative anatomy lesson Amaya had given them. "It is all leverage. Balance, not power."

Harry shrugged. "Mebbe humans jus' cain't do it."

"That's not it." Mark sat still for a moment then drew a breath. "Ed told me Amaya taught him the whole thing in one afternoon. He says it would've gone quicker, but she'd just recovered from a shoulder injury, and he was afraid he'd hurt her."

Clyde looked past them all. "Here they come. She might be able to figure this out."

Nurinyan rolled back onto his shoulders and then pushed himself up into a handstand and dropped down onto his feet. He ran to meet Amaya and Ed as they entered the gym.

"Taking a break?" Ed asked.

"Dey cannot learn it." Nurinyan skidded to a stop near them. "As Harry puts it, to break de hold as I tell him, he must have de arms of a monkey or extra joints."

"I don't get it." Ed turned to Amaya. "You taught me when I was eighteen. These guys are a lot smarter than I was then."

Amaya studied the humans and then smiled and shook her head. "On average, how tall are they?"

Nurinyan turned one hand toward the ceiling. "Mark is de tallest, but even he is only six fe—Oh."

Mark was short. They were all short. Nurinyan struck his forehead with his fist.

"I'll bet you're teaching them, um, men's strategies. Aren't you?" Amaya mimed thwacking his ear.

"Yes." He rubbed his ear.

She chuckled. "Foolish one."

"Fill me in on the revelation," Ed said.

LIKE HERDING THE WIND

"Come along, and I'll fill in everyone."

Nurinyan followed her and Ed back to the others.

"Did you figure it out?" Mark asked.

Nurinyan cringed. "Yes, and it is not your fault."

Amaya dropped her trauma kit and walked onto the mat. "The normal height for an Eshuvani ranges from about five-foot-ten for an average woman to about six-foot-six for an average man. Center of gravity and available leverage are different on the ends of the range, so there are two different sets of techniques. Which is taught is determined by the height of the student, but because, as with humans, men are generally taller than women, some incorrectly call them men's and women's techniques."

Harry snorted. "An' so Nurinyan was showin' us the techniques fer taller folk cuz we're men."

Nurinyan's ears got warm. *And this is my specialization. I should know better.* "Yes, and dat was my fault. I do not know de wom-, I mean, short people techniques well enough to teach dem yet."

Amaya smiled. "Being in the middle of the range, I was taught both, so I will teach you the one you need."

Nurinyan sat back and watched the lessons begin anew.

***

Amaya yawned, picked up her backpack, and walked to the station. After a full day of helping Nurinyan train officers on basic self-defense, dinner with Ed and Esther, and a full night of chasing calls in Las Palomas and the Buffer Zone, Amaya felt like she could sleep for two days straight. Her mid-morning nap had helped some, but she had too many things to do to sleep the day away.

The cargo hauler rumbled through start up.

Ishe came out of the kitchen with a blue ceramic bowl of grapes. "Aren't you going with him? He said he'd collect you on the way out."

URUSHALON

"Who? Nurinyan?" Amaya asked.

Ishe nodded. "Dispatch says there's a human drowning in a pond about two miles southwest of here."

Amaya ran to the hangar, arriving as the cargo avi started to climb. She sprinted the remaining distance and jumped, catching the exterior handhold with one hand and the door latch with the other.

Don't come apart now.

Throwing the door open, she swung herself into the seat, slammed the door closed, and then took her backpack off and set it behind her chair.

Amaya leaned across and thwacked Nurinyan on the ear. "What brand of foolishness are you about?"

"Well, you and Orinyay were out on emergencies all night." Nurinyan rubbed his ear. "I can handle this one. I'm as highly rated in water rescue as you are."

"As of two days ago. And how many real water rescue calls have you been on? Even one? You listen to me closely, *Kiala.* I haven't been in the *kiandarai* for most of sixty years without having to deal with a light sleep schedule a time or two. You do not determine my readiness. I determine yours. Second, only a *kiand* can go on a rescue alone, and I've only done it a cupful of times when there was great need. Third, the dispatch information said the victim is a human. You are not rated for human medicine. Fourth, I won't have anyone else dying on my staff for extreme foolishness if it can be helped. Finally, I gave explicit orders that either Orinyay or I would go on every run. The protocol requires it that way for a reason. I should suspend you from active service until you learn professional discipline. Whether or not I suspend you upon our return will be determined by how much professional discipline you show on the remainder of this mission. Do you hear me, Ess–" She frowned. Essien? This was Nurinyan acting like a fool, not Essien. She shoved all that aside. "Do you hear me, *Kiala?*"

LIKE HERDING THE WIND

Was she angry at Nurinyan for his foolish act, at Essien for getting himself killed, or at herself for driving Essien to go off alone? Fatigue. That had to be the answer. If she were more alert, she wouldn't have slipped like that. She blew out a deep breath.

Nurinyan had one eye on the skies and terrain and the other on her. "I'm sorry, *Kiand*."

She rubbed her eyes. "Forgiveness will be granted when I see the degree of your repentance."

The landscape passed below them for several hundred meters.

Nurinyan gave the battery gauge a solid tap. "That can't be right. Amaya, this battery gauge reads zero, but if that were true, the wings would lock and we'd glide, right?"

She nodded. "Decrease our altitude, in case we are running low on battery power. We'll check it once we land and rescue the human."

They approached a pond. A broad, human figure in a green and gray camouflage shirt and blue jeans floated face down in the water. What was this? Sports hunters did their work in the late fall, not June. Nurinyan landed the avicopter nearby. They both exited and jogged to the water's edge.

"I don't see any movement." She gave Nurinyan a tap on the shoulder and pointed. "You'd better be quick."

His eyebrow shot up. "Me?"

"You claim equal rating with me. You could use some real experience."

Nurinyan waded a couple steps in, then jumped, landing horizontally on the surface of the water and swimming at a good, consistent speed.

About three strides from the victim, Nurinyan came up short, turning vertical to tread water while he swiped at something below the surface. Whatever it was jerked him under.

URUSHALON

Amaya tensed. A bitter chill settled on her. "Nurinyan!" *That was stupid. Even if he can hear me underwater, he'll never be able to get a response back.*

She scrambled to get her water-breather out of its pouch, but her hands trembled too much to get a firm hold on it. Images of Essien's body kept floating up in her mind, but the face was Nurinyan's.

She growled and closed her eyes. "Stop it! He's not dead, but he will be if I don't get out there. God, help me, please. I can't lose another partner. He's just a kid."

Again, Amaya tried to pull out her water breather, with only slightly steadier hands. She fitted it into her nose and waded into the water. Amaya took the collapsible underwater goggles from another pouch and slipped those on a moment before she went underwater and started weaving a path through the waterlogged tree skeletons. She couldn't see more than an arm length ahead and threaded her way forward at a speed that ate away at her nerves. If she went any faster, she might get herself tangled in the debris, and then what help would she be to Nurinyan? The water churned ahead of her and became murky with silt rising up from the bottom.

She found him with one wrist and one ankle pinned against rocks by some unseen agent. He flailed and pulled, but whatever held him was too strong. He had not put on his goggles or water breather.

As Amaya came within range, Nurinyan took a blind swing at her. The water slowed both his attack and her evasion, but she managed to duck under his punch. She came in behind him and pinned his free arm and then used her other hand to get his water breather and insert it into his nose. She held onto him until he stopped fighting her and an intermittent stream of bubbles rose from him to the surface.

Amaya went down to the rock pinning his wrist and found some kind of reel bolted to the substrate rock and loaded with a fine, clear wire. She slid the point of her knife against the clear wire and cut through it, then did the same with the one

LIKE HERDING THE WIND

pinning his ankle.

Wrapping an arm around Nurinyan's chest, Amaya swam upward toward the shore. When they broke the surface, he coughed and sputtered.

Thank you, God, for sparing him.

Upon reaching the shallows, she lifted him, carried him onto dry land, and then reentered the water to go back for the victim. From the complete lack of motion, this would be a corpse-retrieval rather than a rescue.

She got to the area where Nurinyan had run afoul, dove for the bottom, and pulled her way forward, sweeping a hand back and forth in front of her. She found several more reels. Each had a strong, thin, all but invisible wire ending in an open slipknot. Amaya threaded her way through the snares. A wire was anchored to a rock at one end and secured the corpse at the other. Was this murder? If so, why the elaborate trap around the body?

Following the wire back to the surface, she found no murder victim, but rather a pair of balloons wrapped in human clothes topped with a wig. Given the detailed set-up in the rest of the pond, she supposed these balloons weren't filled with simple air. Her guess was something either poisonous or explosive. She'd have to disarm one trap before she figured out the other.

Nurinyan first. Weird balloons later.

Amaya dove to the bottom, then found a way back through the ring of wire loops and returned to shore.

URUSHALON

Chapter Eight

Amaya crawled out of the water and took off her breather and goggles.

Nurinyan sat, breathing hard but evenly. His water breather was no longer in his nose, and a length of the clear wire sat in the grass next to him, while he tried to free the one around his wrist. A line of blood marked where the filament had cut into his skin. His efforts to get a fingernail under the wire tore up his arm.

Amaya crouched next to him. "Stop, stop. There's another way."

She found the loose end and pushed on it. The loop around his wrist opened enough to allow him to pull the wire off.

"Your hands are like ice," he said.

Naturally. I'm so exhausted I keep taking you for Essien. "I had to dive all the way to the bottom. That water is cold down there."

"It wasn't that cold, and you weren't down there that long."

"It felt that cold to me."

The intense chill permeating her had nothing to do with the brief swim to the bottom of the pond. Nurinyan wasn't stupid enough to fall for that excuse for long, but she hoped he'd be kind enough not to bring his suspicions up. They were taking too many calls for her to become incoherent for most of eight hours, so for now, she put her grief out of mind again and focused on her task.

"Wait here. I'll get my kit."

He caught her arm as she stood. "What about him?"

"Clothing and a wig wrapped around balloons. Probably as dangerous as the rest of what you found." She ran to the avicopter and grabbed her backpack then returned.

He hugged his knees to his chest and put his head down. "Do y–do you mean I nearly drowned because of someone's stupid prank?"

"I don't think it was a joke, and I don't think you were the intended victim."

Amaya gave him the tube of regenerative and an applicator. "What happened out there?"

"As I was swimming, I thought I felt something in the water. I stopped to figure it out what it was, and it cinched tightly around my wrist and ankle and pulled me under."

"And then?"

"I was dragged all the way to the bottom and–" He sighed and closed his eyes. "I panicked. All I could think about was getting loose to get back to the surface. I didn't even remember to put my breather on."

How can I fault you for panicking? I did. "Personally, I don't do any water rescue, surface or submerged, without both goggles and breather. The protocol doesn't require it that way, but I would much sooner deal with the discomfort than be in the middle of a particularly difficult rescue and have to pause and put them on."

"After this, that sounds like excellent advice." He pressed

URUSHALON

his fist to his forehead.

She took the tube of regenerative back from him and put it away. "Did this event teach you anything else?"

"I am not ready to go alone. I would have died if you hadn't been here."

"That's why I don't go out alone unless I have to. You never know when a situation is going to turn on you. I've seen many supposedly easy rescues become dangerous. Anticipating every contingency is all but impossible."

"I also learned that experience means more than test scores."

"Knowledge is good. Knowledge with experience is better."

Nurinyan nodded.

"How's your wrist?" she asked.

He looked at the pink line, which was all that remained of the wound. "It will serve."

"Good." She clapped his shoulder. "I'll begin disarming the trap. Put my bag back in the avicopter and contact our resident chemist for advice on dealing with potentially hazardous balloons."

Nurinyan waved a hand at the balloons. "What if they're just air?"

"Then we'll take a great deal of precaution for nothing." Amaya stood up and stretched. "That's better than the alternative."

"I understand. Once I have an answer, I'll come help you. Be careful."

She nodded. After retrieving a tool from the avi's repair kit, she donned her water gear again.

The water felt warm, a testament to how chilled she'd become. Amaya skimmed along the bottom of the pond to the weighted reels. She spotted another a few feet away, and a

LIKE HERDING THE WIND

third a short distance from that all the way around in a ring. Amaya came full circle and then swept her hand above a reel to find the wire. When she gave it a quick tug, the thin wire retracted into the reel with a high-pitched whir. She sought out the next and gave it the same treatment, but when the third one didn't react, she wrapped the wire around the reel.

She'd gotten about two-thirds of the way around when the remaining wires swayed. The water pushed her from side to side. She turned. The vague shadow in the water had Nurinyan's shape. She worked her way around the rest of the snares as he disarmed them from the other end of the arc. After a careful search turned up no more, they removed the bolts, made several trips to the shore, and generated a large pile of reels. Her muscles ached with exertion and her breathing sped up, but she kept her pace slow to conserve strength long enough to finish the job. On her fifth trip into the pond, she encountered Nurinyan on his way out with one reel in hand. He shook his head and waved her back to shore.

Amaya waded onto the dry grass and lay back. She removed her water gear and set it on her belly while the warm sun chased away the cold. Weariness from both the lack of sleep and from the exertion dragged at her consciousness. Taking a nap right here would be far too easy.

Nurinyan tapped on her shoulder. "Here. You'll want one of these."

Eyes still closed, she extended a hand toward his voice until the foil-wrapped nutrition bar slapped against her palm. "Thank you."

She propped herself up on her elbows and tore open the wrapper. He'd given her a berry-flavored bar, but she was too tired to go swap it for an apple one in her kit. An old instructor had once told her that if she was too tired to go get the one she wanted, she needed what she was eating too desperately to be picky.

Amaya choked down the last of the too-salty snack. "What did Ishe have to say about the balloons?"

URUSHALON

"Hm? Oh, um, she said to shoot the balloons from the distance." Nurinyan rolled his eyes.

Amaya snorted. "That's it?"

He nodded. "The beginning and the end."

"Even I'm not too tired to come up with that idea. I was hoping for something a little more technical, like a way to test what's in there. We don't want to release toxins into the air." Amaya sighed and rubbed her forehead. "She may not know better."

She could contact Ishe and insist on a more comprehensive plan, but did she have either the patience or the endurance to deal with their most immature, most inexperienced colleague? Essien would have–

Her hands trembled and an intense chill shook her. Amaya bolted to her feet and took several steps away. Why had he come to mind? Essien hadn't even been a chemistry specialist. That had been Adri's job.

"Are you okay?" Nurinyan asked.

"Yes, yes, I'm-I'm fine. I'm fine." Now she needed an excuse to jump up like that. Amaya looked out over the pond. "I'm going to have a look at our problem from another angle. Wait here."

Amaya walked around to the other side of the pond and crouched. Sure enough. The "corpse" looked like clothing wrapped around balloons from this angle, too. She ran her fingers through her damp hair and then pressed and held two of the dark blue crystals on her collar.

"Dispatch."

"Amaya Ulonya *Kiand*. Connect me through to the fire suppression service, please."

"Message received."

Relays clicked.

"Fire suppression dispatch. How can we be of service,

LIKE HERDING THE WIND

Kiand?"

Amaya stood and paced. "We received a bogus water-rescue call. There was an elaborate trap arranged for us. The greater part has been disarmed, but there are balloons wrapped in human clothing. It could be nothing, but we suspect toxins or explosive gas. Do you have a station available to assist?"

"Yes, *Kiand*. We have a station specializing in hazardous materials. We'll dispatch them to your location."

"Excellent. Thank you."

Amaya gave the dispatcher the coordinates and then returned to Nurinyan. "A hazardous materials team is on the way." She flopped down next to him and rubbed her forehead.

"Are you okay?" he asked.

She nodded. "I need to sleep."

"I won't tell anyone if you to take a nap."

She shook her head. "When we get home, I plan to sleep until the next call, and I pray it's a while coming."

After a few minutes, a huge avicopter's bass rumble rattled their little avi. She looked toward Woran Oldue at the looming brilliant yellow fire suppression avi. It settled on its landing struts almost a quarter mile back from the pond before a half-dozen Eshuvani, all dressed in the yellow uniforms of the fire service, exited the avi and followed the ranking officer over. Amaya rose and went to meet the leader, a man who towered a full hand-length over her and sported the gold filigree on his collar. The leader had graying blond hair and a tanned, weathered face.

He embraced her. "Grace be unto you."

"And peace from God, the Father of Our Lord. I am Amaya Ulonya."

"Havrin Tonsi. So, what makes you think those balloons are more than they seem?"

"The elaborate set up in the rest of the pond and a

URUSHALON

persistent adversary." She pointed to the pile of reels.

Havrin looked out over the water. "Better safe than not. You have everything cleared except those balloons, right?"

"Yes. That we know of. I suggest you make entry along the path we used. That I can vouch for with some certainty."

"All right. Let's start by getting a reading on the gas in those balloons." He turned and pointed to one of his people. "Get breathing gear and syringes and get me a sample from each balloon."

"If you pierce the balloon, it'll explode, won't it?" Nurinyan asked.

"Depends on where you pierce it." Havrin mimed slowly popping a balloon. "Go in where the plastic is most dense, where it ties, and no problem. If you're careful, that is."

The yellow-clad fireman swam out to the balloons and disappeared under the water for a few moments before swimming back to shore. Havrin took a brown plastic syringe, picked up a stoppered vial containing a small slip of paper, and drove the needle through the cork. Both syringes expelled a yellowish green gas.

"Chlorine?" Amaya asked.

Havrin nodded. "Sure enough. Not flammable. Heavier than air. Likely to react with the water to make hydrochloric or hypochlorous acid. 'Bout how deep is that pond?"

"Three to four strides where the balloons are, but it gets shallow quickly toward the edges."

He compared the size of the syringe to the vial. "Not too dense, by the look of things. We're an easy thirty, forty strides away. Plenty far enough. Not much wind today. Think you can shoot 'em from here?" He looked up at her collar and smiled. "Dumb question, marksmanship instructor."

She clapped Nurinyan's shoulder. "Go ahead."

Nurinyan shrugged and drew his pistol. "Easier than breathing."

LIKE HERDING THE WIND

His pistol whined through start-up before he took a one-handed stance and fired twice. The heavy, wet cloth surrounding the balloons muted the mini-explosions. A faint greenish cloud formed around the site as the material faded a shade or two.

"That's the way," Havrin said. "The rest is clean-up. If you've got other things to do, we'll handle this."

"Thank you for your help," Amaya said.

Havrin smiled. "Serve with diligence."

Nurinyan grabbed her arm and pointed. "Amaya. Green avicopter."

She followed his hand and saw the mottled green ship flying in from the south.

"Is it him?" Nurinyan asked.

"Perhaps." She shaded the sun from her eyes. "If not, he shouldn't be here anyway. Let's go."

She ran back to their avi and climbed into the pilot's seat. While Nurinyan settled in the passenger seat, Amaya flipped the switch to power up the avi. The engine made a dull groan, but didn't start. She turned everything off then tried again, getting nothing at all.

Nurinyan spewed a stream of venomous words at the avicopter and stepped out.

Amaya pressed one dark blue crystal and tapped Vadin's ID code on another.

"Vadin."

"Amaya. Where's Orinyay?"

"In Las Palomas. A couple West Division officers needed help on a call. Is everything okay?"

The green avicopter hovered for a few moments, then turned back to the south.

"The cargo hauler's battery appears to be dead, but we'll get it started off the fire suppression avi. We're returning to

URUSHALON

station, soon."

She signed off.

***

Clyde Sumner pulled into his driveway and turned off the car in the middle of a report about the Cassius Clay-Sonny Liston fight. Normally, he would have listened to the rest of the report, but after the day he'd had, he could go to sleep right there with the steering wheel for a pillow. He'd wake up with a terrible crick in the neck that way.

With a heavy groan, Sumner rolled out of his car and trudged to the door.

Sorry, Jane, but I won't be joining you at the lock-in tonight after all.

As much as he loved his family, the shift change plus a long day of wild calls equaled sleep, not boisterous kids and games.

He opened the door and stepped in. When a cross-draft slammed it shut, he spun toward the door.

A strong arm wrapped around his throat and hauled him off balance. He tucked his feet up. Within seconds, the attacker's arm quivered. Sumner slammed his heel onto his captor's foot then drove his elbow twice into the intruder's ribcage, eliciting a grunt from the man. Sumner hit the linoleum floor, scrambled away, and went for the gun in the off-duty holster near his hip. He pivoted and fired. Something sharp struck him between the collarbones.

***

Mark Hollis slid into the driver's seat and started the engine as Kirby radioed in and changed their status to available.

Hollis took one last look at the dilapidated, pier-and-beam house before he checked for traffic and drove away. "I hate those kinds of calls. Never know what you'll get."

"Yeah. So, how long do you think it'll be before they're

throwing dishes around again?" Kirby asked.

Hollis checked his watch. "Oh, three and a half hours, I hope. Then it'll be someone else's problem."

"And if they don't find someone to take the other half of the shift?"

Hollis shot his partner a mock stern look. "Don't even think that. I can handle a shift and a half when I have to, but a double shift—"

"Car Five, Car Five. Shots fired," the dispatcher reported. "Seven-two-two Raintree. Seven-two-two Raintree. Code three authorized."

Kirby acknowledged the call.

Hollis flipped the switches for the lights and sirens and accelerated, weaving a way through those cars that didn't honor his request for right of way.

Why do I know that address?

"Car Five, Car Five," the dispatcher said. "Additional on your call, Seven-two-two Raintree. An avicopter was seen leaving the vicinity. *Kiandarai* are responding."

"Car Five, ten-four." Kirby hung up the mic. "Going after residences now? That's new."

"Hopefully it's a fluke."

Hollis turned onto Raintree and checked the address on the corner house: seven-ten.

Kirby grabbed Hollis' arm. "Sumner."

"Sumner what?"

"Six houses from the corner on Raintree. That's Sumner's house."

Hollis felt a sympathetic pain in his chest. He recognized the house when he pulled up to the curb. "All right. By the numbers. Go around back. I'll go in the front."

Kirby nodded.

Urushalon

With his gun in hand, Hollis darted to the door, leaned against the wall, and listened. A mockingbird sang its heart out in a nearby tree and an air conditioner hummed, but no noise came from inside. Hollis reached across the door and turned the knob. He pushed the door halfway open before something blocked it. A splatter of red dots discolored the wall inside.

He slipped sideways through the door. Sumner lay on his side near a puddle of blood covering half the foyer floor. A bundle of sticks bound with a ribbon sat on the side of his head. His gun was still clutched in his hand. Sumner was too still, too pale, but Hollis crouched and pressed his fingers against Sumner's throat above a hand's width cut between his collarbones.

Kirby stopped at the edge of the foyer. "Is he—"

"Call the coroner." Hollis sighed and looked up at his partner. "Did you find Jane and the kids?"

Kirby shook his head. "There's a lock-in at our church tonight."

"Probably best they weren't home."

"Yeah." Kirby slipped out the door.

Hollis stood and wrenched his gaze away from his friend's body.

Fall apart later. Think like a cop now.

The little table near the wall had been shoved out of place and now sat at an angle. A picture with broken glass lay next to a table leg. The spots on the wall formed a half-ring around a bullet hole.

So you did get a shot off and at least grazed the guy.

He walked through the rest of the house looking for evidence of Sumner's killer. When he reached the kitchen, splintered wood on the door frame showed how the suspect had entered.

The drone of an avicopter grew louder. Hollis opened the

LIKE HERDING THE WIND

door as Amaya landed Hawk's Nest's courier in the backyard and powered down. Amaya stepped out as Nurinyan came around from the other side. Hollis waved them in.

***

Amaya stood next to her avi at the edge of the Catholic Church's extensive yard. Scrawny yaupon trees and statues of angels and people in ancient-style clothing dotted the landscape around the stone structure of the church.

The funeral for Clyde Sumner had ended more than an hour ago, and the gathering had already started to wind down as officers left to go on watch and mourners paid their final respects before departing.

Amaya looked at her hands. The tremors had increased in frequency over the last week, but didn't seem much worse than usual.

See? There's still time, but next week I'll definitely find a guide for the rite. Next week.

Once most of the mourners had left, Harry and Ed escorted Clyde's wife and children to a brown car. Harry drove the family away, leaving Ed alone.

Amaya hopped over the low stone wall and waved to get Ed's attention.

Ed met her halfway. "I didn't expect to see you here."

"We decided someone should be here in case our adversary tried to interfere."

They walked among the statues, shrubs, and scraggly trees. A tranquilizer pistol whined through its warm up. Amaya swept Ed's feet out from under him, catching his wrist as he fell. A dart struck a nearby statue, shaving off a few rock chips. Amaya searched the trees and statues for a half-hidden gunman. A second shot flew past her hip.

Ed pulled her down on top of him and rolled between her and the shooter. "Are you crazy?"

A dart bit into the ground near his hand.

URUSHALON

She shook her head. "I couldn't see him."

"Let's get over there. Behind that shrine."

She craned her neck and spotted the large rock structure some five strides away. Amaya drew her own pistol and flipped the switch to prime it. It whined through start up as the shooter hit a statue of an angel.

She lay prone and aimed toward the gunman. "I'll cover you."

Ed bolted for the shrine. Amaya toggled her gun to auto-repeating fire and maximum range. She crouched behind the nearest statue and fired a seemingly endless stream of darts in the direction the attacker's shots had come from. Her magazine was empty by the time Ed reached his destination.

Keeping the gun in hand, Amaya sprinted toward the structure. Something sharp grazed her leg, and she stumbled, rolling to a stop next to Ed. He grabbed her under the arms and pulled her behind their shelter. A dart blasted a piece off the corner. Amaya shut her pistol down and ejected the empty magazine.

"Where were you hit?" Ed asked.

She pulled her second magazine off her belt and slid it into place. "How did you know?"

"I've never seen you trip on level ground," he said.

Amaya showed him the thin cut in the leg of her pants and the crease on her left thigh.

"How do you feel?" he asked.

"Fine. Better than I ought to, actually."

"You're shak—"

Amaya held up her hand to stall his next comment.

"He stopped shooting." Ed turned his head away. "Did he give up, or is he going for a better angle?"

Amaya counted the shots she could remember. "If that's our friend with the old gear, he's out of shots. The Model Four

LIKE HERDING THE WIND

is a six-dart revolver. He's reloading. Do you have your gun?"

"Yes, but not much for extra rounds."

"All right. I have the magazine I just loaded and one more. I'll go straight in. You try to get around him."

"I wish your gun sounded different, so I could count his shots."

"Nothing for it, dear one." She gave him a push. "Go on."

He ran off around the other side of their shelter.

URUSHALON

Chapter Nine

Amaya toggled back to single-fire and turned the power level down to half. She leaned around the edge of the shrine, and fired at where the shooter had last been. A dart struck the stone facade from a different angle. She projected the angle back and frowned. He had moved most of ninety degrees clockwise from his previous position, and she had no way to update Ed without giving away his intention. Amaya sprinted to a statue and fired off a couple of shots. She pressed and held two of the dark blue crystals on her collar as another dart blasted rock bits across her shoulder. She pulled the dart loose and examined it as another struck a nearby tree.

"Dispatch."

"Amaya Ulonya *Kiand*. I'm with Ed Osborn Sergeant at St. P—" No, St. Peter's was in Marquette. Where was she again? "At St. John Catholic Church. We're being fired upon by an unseen gunman with a Model Four dart pistol." She bolted for the next bit of cover. "Contact Mar—" She frowned. No, she was not in Marquette. "Contact Las Palomas Dispatch and have them declare, 'Officer in need of assistance. Shots fired,' and provide our location. Additional *kiandarai* not needed at this time."

"Message received."

She popped up and fired a couple more shots as one whistled past her ear. After shooting a few more his way, she ran to a boulder half her height decorating a flower garden. Before she'd settled, a dart tore through the sleeve of her shirt, missing her arm. A second one buried itself in the stone.

That was six shots from him. Even at her fastest, Amaya needed thirty seconds to reload a Model Four.

"Go. I'll cover you."

"All right. Be careful, Ess—"

Just a minute. That couldn't have been Essien, but the voice was definitely his. Who had told her to go on? Later. She could figure that out later.

She popped up and ran straight in the direction the shots had come from. Police sirens wailed from several directions.

Her quarry, clad in a faded *kiandarai* uniform, sprinted down a low hill. She followed. He climbed into a mottled green avicopter. Keeping her breathing even by force of will, Amaya took quick aim and fired three times, but her hands shook, ruining her aim. Two shots struck his leg above the ankle while the third stuck in the door. Raising her aim, she hit the toggle to repeating fire and increased power then squeezed the trigger. The shots hit, but none got through the canopy.

Two police cars rolled up from different directions. Four officers emptied their rounds as the avicopter lifted off. The avi's hull sported new dents and holes but flew away trailing smoke.

Amaya pressed one dark blue crystal and tapped a code on the other as she tried to catch her breath.

"Border Guard Dispatch."

"Amaya Ulonya *Kiand*. A mottled green avicopter is heading for L—" She shook her head. No, not Lake Superior. "–for the coast from Las Palomas. Pilot is wanted in connection with multiple crimes. Can you intercept?"

URUSHALON

"We can't cross into human space except in active pursuit, but if he crosses into Eshuvani space, we'll be ready for him. Have you contacted Hawk's Nest?"

"They'd come from too far inland to catch him," she said.

"I apologize, *Kiand*, but we have no jurisdiction unless we're pursuing when he crosses the border."

"Message received." She growled and shook her head. Even if she had the stamina to race back to her own avi, she had the light cargo hauler, and that ponderous behemoth wouldn't be able to catch up.

Ed spoke to his officers before coming over to her.

She blew out a sigh. "Almost had him. I got him twice in the ankle."

Ed nodded. "Yeah, what's that canopy made out of? Bullet proof glass?"

"No, but similar. If I could have hit it enough times in the same place, I could've gotten through."

He whistled. "That's one tough avicopter."

"I think it has some minor armor plating." She shut down her gun, ejected the spent magazine, and inserted a new one.

"How did you ever know he was there in the first place?"

Amaya primed her gun. "I heard the distinctive wind up of the weapon."

Ed smiled. "Nothing wrong with your hearing. Now about that hole in your leg."

"Honestly, it stings a bit, but I'm fine." She looked at the hole in her pants and shrugged.

"So the tranquilizer used forty-five years ago doesn't decompose to something else?"

She frowned. *I should've thought of that.* "I don't know. I'll contact my chemist."

Amaya pressed and held one of the dark blue crystals and

LIKE HERDING THE WIND

tapped a quick code on the other.

"Ishe."

"Amaya. Ishe, does the chemical used in forty-five year old tranq darts change over time into something more interesting?"

"Uh, *Kiand,* I-I don't know. Were you hit?"

"Glancing shot across the left thigh about one hand-length above my knee. I feel fine, but there is concern."

Ishe stammered through a few useless syllables. "Orinyay is on a call. Should I contact another station?"

"Unnecessary. Could you look it up for me and call me back? In the meantime, I'll use my toxin test kit and see what that can turn up."

"Yes, yes, of course. Message received."

The connection terminated.

Ed shook his head. "I know. I know. She's new, and she's got potential." He pulled Amaya's arm across his shoulder and stood.

She smiled. "I'm not that pitiful, dear one."

"Then humor me and let me feel useful."

She powered her gun down and holstered it. "Very well. Lead on."

They started across the cemetery when everything took a slight spin leftward. She needed food.

When they reached the avi, Amaya perched on the seat and retrieved the toxin kit from her backpack. She used her shears to make the hole in her pants a little wider. For such a small cut, too much blood flowed. Although smeared by contact with her pants, red streaked past her knee, and the wound still bled freely.

Ed pulled out his handkerchief and pressed it against the injury.

URUSHALON

Amaya broke the seal on a test vial then used one of the sterile paper strips to swab some of the blood from the wound. She dropped the thin paper into the vial. While she waited, Amaya ate a nutrition bar.

Her comm chimed, and she tapped a blue crystal. "Amaya."

"Ishe. Did I call you too soon?"

Amaya held the vial up toward the clouded sky and shook her head. "No, *Kiala*. Your timing was impeccable. My test shows no reaction at all. What did you find?"

"'The Model Four pistol was the second magnetic propulsion gun. It was used by *kiandarai* during the earliest portion of the second dynasty. The pistol was designed by–'"

Amaya smiled and shook her head. "Stop. I don't need the history lesson. I was there. Skip to the section entitled 'Pharmacological Changes over Time.'"

"Um, yes, *Kiand*. Please wait."

Amaya listened as Ishe read off the subheadings. "You'll find it three-quarters of the way down."

"Oh, there it is. 'The chemicals used in the darts for a Model Four pistol have a twelve-year half-life. Upon decay, the resulting products are water-soluble and have a mild anticoagulant effect. The wound will stop bleeding and heal properly with application of regenerative salve. No further medical treatment should be necessary.' Is that what you need?"

"Keep reading, Ishe. Regenerative salve is potentially fatal to me. The protocol will continue with instructions for sensitive patients."

"Yes, I–Here, I've got it. 'For patients who are sensitive to regenerative salve, use the following procedure. First, irrigate the wound to clean out any remaining traces of the tranquilizer or the product of decomposition. Second, apply a sterile dressing. An antiseptic may be applied if desired. No

LIKE HERDING THE WIND

further medical treatment should be necessary.'"

"I will comply with the protocol and return to station. Thank you, Ishe. Message received."

Ed smiled and shook his head. "I'm not going to say it."

Amaya shrugged. "At least she doesn't give me a lot of attitude."

Ed pulled a sterile water packet out of her backpack. Once she cleaned out the injury, she applied a bandage.

"Well, I think I used up my excitement quota for the day." Ed leaned against the side of the avi. "And I'm on the next watch."

Amaya smiled and stowed her medical gear. "Who wants boring routine?"

"There are definitely times when I'd rather." He pulled her into an embrace.

"We'll catch this one. In the meantime, try not to worry about me so much."

"I'll try if you will, but I think that's like herding the wind."

"Be careful, dear one."

"Always."

She watched him until he drove away.

Amaya flipped the generator and hydraulics switches. The gauges and dials in the dash blurred. She closed her eyes and rubbed her forehead. When she looked again, the control panel was normal.

I must be more tired than I thought.

The flight to Hawk's Nest wasn't too long. She'd be home soon. Amaya grabbed another nutrition bar from her backpack and ate it in a few quick bites. There, that should hold her until she got back home. Then, after a quick nap, she'd be ready to confront the day again.

URUSHALON

She lifted off and set a course home.

The blood-darkened patch on her pants caught her eye. She shivered and reached for the switch to disable the cooling system. Her hand twitched, and she missed, brushing the panel next to the switch. The avicopter drifted off course. She snapped her hand back to the control stick, corrected the trajectory, and tried again. With a broad sweeping motion, she pushed the switch off and scraped her fingers on the altimeter.

"Careful, darling."

"Essien, I told you not to call me that."

Wait a minute. Essien? She turned in her seat. *It can't be him. He was–he was–*

"I'm right here, dear."

"No, no. I-I found you at the bottom of that mine shaft. You—"

"Yes, at the bottom of the shaft where you left me to die!"

"I didn't leave you! You were already–"

"But you weren't happy with just abandoning me, were you? No. You came down here. Ed's next, isn't he? First your son and your husband. Then me. Now Ed? How long before you get him killed?"

She shook her head. "No, Essien. I never–"

"You're the death of everyone who matters. Only thinking of your own happiness, while people around you pay with their l—"

Her comm chimed, and her partner's voice broke off. She shivered with the glacial cold that had settled on her and blinked several times to clear her head. She looked around the cockpit. "Essien? Essien, where are you?"

He was gone. He'd been gone for weeks. She had to get control again, or the guy in the green avi would destroy Ed. He counted on her to keep him safe.

The chime sounded a second time.

LIKE HERDING THE WIND

With a trembling hand, she tapped one blue crystal. "Amaya."

"Orinyay. What is your position?"

She checked the terrain below her. When had she taken off? She'd seen Ed walk back to his car and leave, and she'd climbed into the avi to start up the systems, but when had she lifted off?

"Amaya, can you hear me? What is your position?"

Good question. She checked for landmarks. "Just passing the outer edge of Las Palomas. ETA at station, about two minutes."

"Do you require assistance?"

She shook her head. "No, I'm fine."

"You sound a little distracted."

"This isn't exactly the easiest bird to keep in the air sometimes. I'm coming in for a landing shortly." *Now leave it alone.*

"Message received."

The hangar door was already up when Amaya arrived, and the rest of her personnel gathered nearby. Ishe had her hands clasped in front of her chest.

If Amaya could divert attention away from herself, she might get away without anyone noticing. She landed, kicked in the ventilation fan, and climbed out, shutting the fan back off as she exited with her backpack on one shoulder.

"Nurinyan, how was your test?" she asked.

He pointed to the single purple crystal newly added to his collar. "One more to go, and I can be a *kiandara*."

"Excellent." Amaya crossed her arms in front of her chest.

"Do I need to call in a replacement?" Orinyay asked.

"Hardly." Amaya adjusted her backpack in hopes that the

Urushalon

quivering in her hands was less noticeable as she moved. "I need to reload two magazines and put on an intact uniform. I'm fine."

Ishe ran over and embraced Amaya, nearly knocking her flat. "Oh! I was so worried." She recoiled. "You're frozen."

Amaya shrugged. "You know how that avi is. The air cooler is either off or full speed. Thank you for being concerned, but I'm fine. I'll be in my quarters changing."

She strode away.

***

Wylin's eyes drifted closed but snapped open again to find the avicopter's nose aimed for the waves below. He gasped and pulled up. Once he had the avi leveled, he blew out a deep breath and shook his head. The barrier island was only a few dozen strides ahead, but that irksome pins-and-needles sensation had radiated from his ankle up through his leg.

His head lolled onto his shoulder, but the sudden change in position jolted him awake again.

"Gotta stay 'wake for Mar'n." The slur in his voice made him sound like a drunkard. A brutal chill shook him and the shivering of his whole upper body sent fatigue into the background. Wylin smiled. "Those *kiand'rai*, they're gonna die f'r wha' they did to you, Mar'n."

The shiver intensified, and he tightened his hold on the controls. The beach at the edge of the Woran Juvay ruins passed beneath him. Once he passed the line of plants, weathered bark, and shells marking the high tide, Wylin brought the avicopter down. The landing jolted him, and the avicopter's landing struts creaked in protest.

After throwing open the door, Wylin stumbled out, dragging his numb leg. He collapsed onto the warm sand in the shadow of the avicopter and faded off to sleep with thoughts of justice, real justice, for Maran.

LIKE HERDING THE WIND

***

Nurinyan sat across from Vadin at the dispatch desk and dealt out another round of coins, tails side up. Sometimes the only thing interesting about dispatch duty on a Tuesday night was trying to find something to pass the time for several hours. On nights like this, he almost hoped for the call volume to increase so he could have something to do.

The computer played its short "New Mail" tune. He swiveled the chair to look at the screen.

Vadin stood and leaned over the monitor to look. "Anything interesting?"

Nurinyan shrugged. "Maybe. It's for Orinyay from a *kiand* named Talin Elka and marked 'Immediate Action Item.'"

Vadin came around the desk to look more closely. "For Orinyay, not Amaya? That's odd. Talin worked with Amaya in Marquette. He took over as *kiand* after she left."

He sent a sidelong look Vadin's way. "Thanks. Now the curiosity will bleed all the neutrons out of my mental reactor."

Vadin chuckled. "Sorry."

The hangar doors rolled up.

Orinyay strolled down the hall with Jevon. "You did fine. Your actions were reasonable and well within protocol. Don't let that bitter, old man disturb you."

Nurinyan turned the chair to face them. "Orinyay, you have an immediate action item."

She squinted. "Me?"

"Umhm. From Talin Elka *Kiand* up north." He vacated the chair for her and stepped away.

Orinyay opened the message and gasped. "That can't be right."

"What?"

"Amaya has been removed from active service."

URUSHALON

"You're joking." Vadin looked over her shoulder.

"What for?" Nurinyan leaned on the wall and watched the screen. "What's happened?"

Orinyay hit the reply. "I don't know. All Talin says is that I have to relieve Amaya from active service." She typed a message back to Talin. "Please advise on necessary action." She clicked the "Send" button.

Nurinyan looked back toward the hangar. "I think I know."

Vadin spun around. "Tell."

"Think about it. Cold hands. Pretty much a permanent tremor. The incident with her coming back from Las Palomas this afternoon. Several times in the last couple weeks, she's slipped and called me Essien. How does that add up to you?"

Jevon groaned. "I hope your guess is wrong."

"I hope it's not too late."

The computer signaled new incoming mail.

Orinyay opened the message. "It's from Talin. He says he won't release Amaya for duty until the blank in her personnel file is filled in." She opened the personnel database and scrolled through the list to find Amaya's file. "You don't see me doing this."

Vadin reached over the turned off the monitor. "You're breaching protocol."

Orinyay shook her head. "Not exactly. I have to know what the problem is so I can tell whether I need to request a temporary replacement."

"That's an awfully thin thread to hang a two-ton brick from."

She turned the monitor on. "I know. I think Nurinyan is correct, but I need to know for sure."

After clicking on Amaya's name, the file opened. Orinyay scrolled through to the section listing Rites of Final Memorial.

LIKE HERDING THE WIND

A handful of family members were listed, including four grandparents and a sibling. Someone with her surname had been the guide for each of them. Then a husband and son were listed, and the name Essien Kitonu appeared for the guide. The next line showed Essien as the deceased, but no guide was mentioned.

Nurinyan leaned closer and checked the date. "She's out of time."

"That explains a lot, actually." Orinyay sighed and logged out of the database. "All right. I'll handle the calls until morning. If she isn't released by then, we'll have to call in a replacement. Who wants to talk to Amaya?"

Jevon snorted. "Not me. I've been a guide before and don't want to do that again."

Vadin shook his head. "I wouldn't know how to be a guide."

Nurinyan shrugged. "I am her partner, at least until I graduate. I'll do it, but someone will have to take over dispatch until I'm finished."

"I'll take it for you." Vadin raised one hand.

Nurinyan walked through the light rain to his house where he slipped on his jacket before heading back outside. His target sat on the roof of her house, staring at the nighttime clouds.

He sighed. *The messes I get myself into.*

There was no way out, so he walked up to the house. In an easy jump, he caught the eaves, pulled himself up, and made his way to where Amaya sat. Did she know why he'd come?

He looked up at the clouds. "You know, it's raining out here."

She nodded. "Your training progresses well."

"Umhm. I'm a quick learner."

URUSHALON

She sighed. "I'm afraid I'm no good for conversation tonight."

"That's not why I came out here." *Here goes.* He drew a deep breath. "We know why you moved to Woran Oldue."

Any spark of humor in her eyes sputtered and died. "Why do you bring it up?"

"Orinyay received a message from the new *kiand* of your old station declaring you unfit for service."

"Thank you, Talin." She snorted and shook her head.

"Yeah, well, naturally, we wondered what heinous crime you had committed to make that happen, so we asked. The *kiand* up there indicated that until the blank space in your personnel file is filled in, he will not release you for service. More curious than ever, we opened your file and there it was, larger than the sky itself. There is no name for the one who guided you through the Rite of Final Memorial for–"

She glared at him. "I have thirty-three days from the event to take care of that."

"Umhm." He tapped his watch. "And day thirty-three ended seventeen minutes ago. Fifteen minutes ago, Orinyay got the word."

She growled. "I don't have time for this right now! Someone is trying to kill one whom I love. I can't afford to become an emotional wreck for even eight hours."

"Amaya, you already are. You tremble almost constantly. A person can get frostbite by touching you. You told Ishe you were cold because the air cooler in the avi wouldn't regulate properly. You were flying the cargo hauler. Its air cooler doesn't function at all above half throttle. It's the courier that won't regulate."

"I wasn't flying that fast." She glared.

"Yeah, well, maybe not, but when Orinyay contacted you, she was on the roof with me." He pointed to his house. "I had my telescope aimed right at you. I don't know who was flying

LIKE HERDING THE WIND

that avi, but it wasn't you."

"Of course it was me. I was alone."

"Oh, you were sitting at the controls, but you were mentally somewhere far away and talking to someone. And you weren't using your comm." He tapped his own dark blue crystals. "The lights were dark."

She shook her head.

He twisted to face her directly. "Amaya, you're already in emotional danger, and it won't get better if you ignore it. I volunteered to bring this to your attention. My brother is a professional guide. He sees people at any time day or night because, as he says, people aren't always ready to deal with their grief during daylight hours."

Amaya's jaw set in a hard line, and her eyes narrowed.

Nurinyan sighed. "Well, Orinyay will handle all the emergencies for the rest of the night, but come morning, she will have to call in a reserve if you're not released for duty. So which is it? Are you talking to me or to one of the others, or am I taking you to Ed's house, or are we going to my brother's place?"

"I scared a whole century off Ed's life when he insisted on hearing about why I still wear a wedding bracelet. I wouldn't want to frighten him so badly again."

He winced. "So not him."

She rubbed her eyes. "I hate this rite."

"I don't think anyone likes it. It must be done, though. A wound won't heal if there's poison in it. More to the point, if you're not constantly trying to dodge your grief, you'll be able to think more clearly, which will protect Ed much better."

Amaya nodded. "Are you sure you know what you're getting into?"

"Specifically, no. I could've done the research, but it's already past midnight, and Orinyay will need you to take over

URUSHALON

in the morning. Generally, yes. I watched my older brother help a friend of mine."

She blew out a sigh, trudged to the edge of the roof, and then jumped down. He followed her and sat next to her on the porch. Her whole body shivered.

LIKE HERDING THE WIND

Chapter Ten

Nurinyan settled next to Amaya on the porch. The shivers settled until just her hands shook. He'd be in for a long wait before she started on the tale of Essien's death. If the matter had been easy to deal with, she wouldn't have let it sit for so long. After a couple minutes of listening to the rain, he shifted. Should he prompt her or not?

Well, we can't sit here until daybreak. "'Confess to one another.' You'll feel a lot better once it's in the open."

"Maybe, but you may wish you hadn't volunteered." Amaya rubbed her forehead. "I, uh, I threw a punch at my last guide."

Oh, no. You're one of those. He'd have to restrain her if she started tensing up. "That wasn't Ed, was it?"

"No. Essien."

He ran his fingers through his short hair. *Going hand-to-hand with my supervisor was not what I had in mind.* "Well, I'm a combat specialist, and I out-mass you. Now, tell me what happened."

"Fine, but you've been warned." She took a deep breath. "Essien and I were partners for most of the time I was stationed up north. Even before I was *kiand* there. He was at my wedding and celebrated the birth of my son with us. When I really needed his support a few years later, he helped me through the grief."

Nurinyan nodded. *That confirms your record. Enough background. Get to the point.*

"Because of our long friendship, I was surprised a couple years ago when–" She paused as the tremor spread from her arms to her whole upper body. "–when he began insisting that the time had come for me to stop wearing the bracelet. He was adamant and wasted no opportunity to bring the matter up."

Some friend. "That is odd. And you were still at the same station? Did he have someone else in mind for you?"

"No, he was interested for himself." Amaya snarled at her tremulous hands. "The others at the station noticed that, too, and tried to talk to him, but he heard none of them."

"I'm sure that got irritating."

"Yes, it did. Then a little over a month ago, a tunnel collapsed in a nearby copper mine, trapping twelve miners. After five days, the humans asked the *kiandarai* for help, and the *kiat* dispatched my station. We were nearly there when Essien brought up the whole issue of the bracelet again. I'd heard all I could tolerate after two years."

Nurinyan nodded. "After a while, persistence becomes harassment."

She grew more tense and stopped shaking.

Oh, don't tighten up, or I really am going to wish I hadn't volunteered. He put his arm around her shoulders. "Relax. You're going to get jittery. That's normal. We don't need you hurting yourself."

The tension faded as her whole body quivered an order of magnitude worse than before. No wonder her *urushalon* had been terrified. Nurinyan drew Amaya closer to him.

Amaya clutched his arm in a firm grip. "As we landed, I

LIKE HERDING THE WIND

gave him an ultimatum. 'If you bring this up again, I will transfer you.' With that, I told everyone to set up camp and went to coordinate with the humans. When I returned after dawn, there was no sign of Essien. The others had thought he was with me. He often was."

The chill cut through his jacket.

He shivered. *Should've grabbed my heavier coat.*

She stuttered a few useless syllables. "A human ran into my camp and told me to come quickly. He took us to the mine's one remaining vertical shaft and down an elevator to the bottom of a one-hundred-fifty-stride hole. We–we found Essien. His whole body was twisted around. Compound fractures. Deathly pale. As still as stone. It looked like he hadn't secured his climbing rope correctly, and the knot had failed."

"He climbed down when there was an elevator?" Nurinyan asked.

"I still don't understand that myself, but when I saw him, I felt nothing. For the death of this friend of over fifty years, I felt nothing! I should have felt something. Grief, revulsion, sadness, something."

Nurinyan shook his head. "That's not unusual. My brother says sometimes the shock of an unexpected death takes a while to get past. It obviously affected you, though. Have the courts ruled on who is responsible for Essien's death?"

Her head bobbed. "By the time we'd finished the rescue, our courts had ruled his death had been caused by his own error. Shortly after, I heard about the new station here and applied for the transfer."

"Amaya, this is hitting you too hard for that to be all of it. What aren't you saying?"

Both arms twitched hard, smacking tense fists into her collarbone with dull thud. "His death was my fault. If I hadn't been so harsh with him, then he wouldn't have gone off alone."

URUSHALON

Nurinyan shook his head. "His demands breached all protocol, common sense, and basic decency. Even I know it's not unusual for a widow to continue to wear the bracelet for decades. Didn't you have the right to tell him to stop harassing you?"

Her jaw clenched.

"Well? Didn't you?"

"That's not the point."

"Did he listen to you or to the others who spoke on your behalf?"

"No, but that doesn't make him wrong." She tried to push away from him.

He held her more firmly. "Whose fault was it that he didn't listen?"

She tensed again, and the tremor abated.

Uh-oh. He grabbed both of her freezing cold wrists in one hand. If she couldn't get enough of a back swing, she couldn't take much of a shot at him.

"What if he was right?" she asked.

"Fine. Let's say he was right. You told him to quit. The other *kiandarai* at the station told him to quit. He didn't. Whose fault is that?"

"Mine. I outranked him."

"Wrong. You can issue orders. You can't make him obey."

She jerked a hand free and banged her wrist on her holster. He should've disarmed her before they'd started. She still outclassed him in weaponry. He'd have to make sure she couldn't get to any.

He snatched her hand in a firm grip. "Did you send him down that mineshaft in the dark?"

"No, but–" She strained against his hold and almost tore loose again.

LIKE HERDING THE WIND

Stronger than I thought. He rose up into a crouch to gain some leverage. "No. He decided that on his own, no matter what else happened between you. He's the one who chose to descend into a dark hole at night. Maybe he wanted to prove something. Maybe he was deliberately reckless as a way of committing suicide without shaming his family. 'Died in the line of duty' sounds a lot better than 'Suicide by ingesting poison' or whatever."

"Nurinyan, you never knew him! You don't know why he did anything!" she screamed as she pushed away from him.

He lost his grip on one hand. She pushed off from the ground and wrenched her other hand free. As she went for her pistol, he launched himself at her. He tackled her and twisted to make sure he hit the ground first. Continuing the momentum, he rolled and pinned her face down on the wet grass. She threw her weight to try tossing him off. He extended his leg to one side.

"You're right. I don't know his motivations, and neither do you. You weren't responsible for what he chose to do. You can't control what someone else does. Even God lets us make our own choices."

She stayed tense, but her efforts to break free dwindled until she went still. Tears welled in her eyes.

He blew out a deep breath. *Almost there.* "Bring it in the open, Amaya, so I can help you."

She sobbed. "He was my friend, and I loved him, but you're right. He did it to himself. I can bear no blame on his behalf."

The tension bled away. He released his hold on her. How could his brother do this day after day? He helped her up, but her legs buckled.

Gathering her up in his arms, he stood. "Door, open."

The front door slid open, and Nurinyan carried Amaya inside. Halfway down the hall to her bedroom, he stopped. *Wait. No opposite gender* kiandarai *in the bedrooms.*

URUSHALON

The cobbled-together bench with its motley cushions here in the front room would have to do well enough until one of the women could move her. He set her on the couch and covered her with the blanket draped over the back. She sniffled and brushed her eyes with her hand.

"You'll never have to speak of this event again. Rest in the grace of our Lord, and you'll feel better when you awaken."

She nodded.

Okay, so that's the end of the Rite. Now what do I do?

He could leave, but should he? What if she still needed to talk? He sat in a nearby chair and stretched out all the strain of the last few minutes. Once she became still, the sniffles ceased. Her eyes drifted closed. He turned off the light and left.

***

Mark Hollis pulled into the driveway and turned off the car. He went around to open Ruth's door and give her a hand up. After a night full of drizzle, the humidity rivaled the air temperature. Breathing without scuba gear was going to be an effort today.

He sighed. "That was rough."

Ruth rubbed his back. "Jane really appreciated you taking the kids to get ice cream. She needed that hour to talk without putting on the brave face for the kids."

"Yeah, but those kids had some hard questions about Sumner's death."

"They'll all need time, dear."

"I know, but what are you supposed to tell a six-year-old who wants to know why some stranger killed her daddy?"

"I don't know what the right answer is, but I'm sure you did fine. You'd better get ready. I'll get Laura."

Hollis nodded and went inside. A thin, shadowy form

LIKE HERDING THE WIND

crouched at the corner of the bedroom hallway. An Eshuvani pistol whined. He ducked as a dart buzzed past his ear and struck the wall behind him. Mark drew his gun as a gray-clad figure bolted out the kitchen door. Mark raced after him. The Eshuvani jumped over the back fence. Hollis tucked his gun into his belt and pulled himself up. He dropped down into the greenbelt behind his house.

The mottled green avicopter and the suspect in it readied for takeoff. Symbols imprinted on the side of the avi near the tail were a brighter green than the surrounding sun-faded paint. Hollis studied the marks, attaching names to the couple he recognized and committing them all to memory. He ran back inside and took Ruth's shopping list notepad from the refrigerator door. He sketched out what he'd seen, tore the paper off, and put it in his pocket. Now to find Ruth and have her use the neighbor's phone to call the police and request the *kiandarai*.

He dashed outside. His wife stood on the porch across the street. Mrs. Andrews held onto Laura inside the screen door.

He jogged across to meet Ruth. "It's all right. He was waiting for me, but all he hit was the wall."

She collided with him for a hug. "When I saw the avi lift off, I asked Mrs. Andrews to call the police. They're sending a car and *kiandarai*."

"Now will you take Laura and go to your mother's until this is all over? They've got doctors and hospitals in Austin if your time comes."

"I really want you to be there."

He kissed her forehead. "I really want to be there, but I'd rather you and our children live through this, and that might not happen if you stay here. If you go to your mother's, you'll be safer. I'll come get you once this mess is over."

She twisted around to see Laura and then turned back to him and rubbed her belly. "Once the police are finished, I'll pull a few things together."

URUSHALON

"And I'll talk to Ed about getting the day off."

An avicopter rumbled overhead. He shielded his eyes and grinned at the gray and silver courier belonging to Hawk's Nest.

He kissed Ruth's cheek. "Stay with Mrs. Andrews while I deal with this."

Hollis raced back through the house to the backyard. Jevon vaulted over the fence while Orinyay hoisted herself up and over.

I'm sure they're competent, but waiting for her to translate for Jevon wears me out. He painted on a smile.

"You look beat." Hollis fell in step with Orinyay.

She squinted at him. "I haven't been in any fights."

Hollis smiled. "No, I mean, you look tired."

"Oh, yes. Last night was very long. I had many calls."

Something wrong with Amaya? He escorted them into the house.

The doorbell rang. He motioned for them to come along as he let in two officers from the western division station covering his address.

"What happened?" one of them asked.

Hollis walked the officers and *kiandarai* through the last quarter hour. When he got to the part about the faint markings, he slid the paper from his pocket.

Orinyay took the paper. "Most of de avi's ID numbers. You have good eyes and a strong memory, to recall five of seven in a language you don't read."

She showed the paper to Jevon and gave him instructions. He stepped aside and started talking to someone over his comm system.

Orinyay handed the paper to the two officers. "Dere should be two more numbers at de front or at de end."

Like Herding the Wind

"At the front. There was no more space at the end," Hollis said.

After the officers had collected all their information, Hollis signed the report and called Osborn to fill him in, finishing with, "Anyway, we're all fine, but I want to take today off so I can get Ruth and Laura to my mother-in-law's place in Austin until this blows over."

"I understand, really. I wish I could get Esther to go to her sister's in Houston. She agreed to send the kids, but she won't be scared out of her own house, as she says. With Gale out on leave and Tucker still nursing cracked ribs, I'm down two already."

"Yeah, but Kirby can fly solo, can't he?"

"I don't like it, not with that nut still out there. I can try to pull a guy in for overtime or maybe get someone to swap a shift with you, but don't get your hopes up."

Long, spindly fingers tapped on his shoulder, and he looked back at Orinyay.

"I can take your family to Austin," she said.

"Hold on, Ed." Hollis covered the mouthpiece. "It's a long way from here."

"I have business in Woran Kishay, a little sout'west of Austin. It would be easy to detour, settle your wife and child in Austin, den handle my business on de return."

"If you're sure it's no problem."

Orinyay shook her head. "We will be a little cramped until I drop off Jevon at Hawk's Nest, but den, easy."

"Thank you."

Orinyay smiled and backed away.

Hollis returned to the phone. "Ed? Problem solved. Orinyay will take care of Ruth and Laura."

"Okay, good. I'm glad it'll work out."

"I'll be headed in soon, but I'll probably miss part of roll

URUSHALON

call."

"Understood. I'll see you when you get here."

He hung up. Jevon crouched in the hallway right where the shooter had been. He pointed toward the dart in the wall while Orinyay stood by the dart and directed him.

Mark waited for them to pause. "I'm going to get Ruth from the neighbor's. Thanks for your help."

"T'ank you for de opportunity to serve." Orinyay nodded once. "We will finish shortly and wait until she is ready."

Mark nodded and headed across the street. At least Ruth, Laura, and the baby would be out of reach.

***

Wylin dialed the payphone and pulled a piece of paper out of his pocket. Pinning the phone's receiver between his ear and shoulder, he unfolded the paper and rehearsed the script one of his allies had written out for him. The English words meant nothing to him, but below them, he'd written the text phonetically in the Eshuvani alphabet.

A woman's voice came through over the top part of the phone's receiver. Her words were gibberish, so he waited out her greeting.

He read his paper and spoke carefully. "Dere are a group of kids causing a disturbance. We are afraid dey will get violent. Send a car to–" He turned to the nearest building and read the numbers of the address, changing the last by one. "–four-eight-one-two Oak, please.

The woman spoke again, but Wylin hung up. He crumbled the paper and crammed it into his pocket. Checking both ways down the street, he darted out of the phone booth and into an alley across the street. He launched off from the ground toward one of the walls and kicked off, zig-zagging his way up to the roof where he had a good view of the entire street, and especially the vacant lot where the human *kiandarai* would get what they deserved.

LIKE HERDING THE WIND

"For you, Maran." In spite of the heat and humidity, a bitter chill shook Wylin.

***

Amaya entered the station.

Vadin came out of the storeroom and walked with her. "Good afternoon."

Amaya smiled. "It is, isn't it? You guys let me sleep too long."

"We've had a light call volume this morning, so Orinyay said to let you sleep until noon if possible. How are you?"

She arched her back and grimaced. "Stiff, sore, but much clearer in the head."

Her collar chimed. Amaya tapped a dark blue crystal. "Amaya."

"Ishe."

Her voice came from Amaya's collar and from the dispatch desk five strides away.

Amaya severed the connection. "I'm right here, Ishe. Behind you. What did you need?"

She swiveled the dispatch chair and waved. "Oh, hi! Las Palomas dispatched Mark and Robert on a public disturbance call. The caller had an Eshuvani accent. Las Palomas requests backup."

"Have Nurinyan meet me in the hangar."

"You think it's the guy?" Vadin asked.

"I don't know, but I don't like the smell of it." Amaya ran for the hangar and powered up the avicopter.

***

Hollis stopped the car on the street next to the vacant lot. A second patrol car rolled to a stop further down the block.

Kirby frowned. "Awfully quiet for a public disturbance call."

URUSHALON

"You're telling me." Hollis tapped the steering wheel a few times. "I don't like it. Verify the address while I check the office building over there. If the address works out, join me."

"Right."

As Kirby picked up the radio mic and identified himself, Hollis stepped out. He signaled his backup to check the north side of the street. With a loud crack, the windshield sported a new, small spider web crack with a thin, metal tube stuck in the glass. Half a heartbeat later, something pinged off metal. Pain exploded above Hollis's right eyebrow. He stumbled back and covered his eye with his shaky hand. He fell flat, sucked in a breath, and stayed still.

"Shots fired! Officer down! Probable Eshuvani shooter!" Kirby exclaimed into the mic.

Four more darts hit the windshield.

Hollis flinched when someone pulled on his shoulder.

"It's me." Kirby slipped an arm around Hollis' shoulders. "Come on. It won't take him long to reload. Car Nine's going to try to work their way around behind the shooter."

Hollis sat up and accepted Kirby's help. They retreated toward the rear of their car. The shooter started up again, and the hood of the car took a few more hits as they passed. Blood poured down the side of Hollis' face.

With Kirby's help, Hollis eased down to the ground behind the car. Kirby produced a handkerchief from his back pocket and dabbed at the blood from the wound. Each contact brought a new spear of pain.

Hollis winced. "Easy there, partner."

"The dart is lodged under your skin like a splinter, but it looks barbed. If I pull it out, I'm afraid it'll tear your scalp wide open."

Hollis took the handkerchief and used it to keep the blood out of his eyes. "Leave it for now, and see what you can do to discourage our friend out there. Be careful."

LIKE HERDING THE WIND

Kirby drew his gun and knelt, leaning on the back of the car. Hollis crouched and tried to trace the trajectory to where the shots came from. A dart blasted through the front windshield.

"I don't see him." Kirby ducked back down. "Do *kiandarai* pistols have a muzzle flash?"

"No. They work on some kind of magnetic system, I think."

The front, passenger side window cracked as a dart blew through the glass and stuck to the headrest.

"He's on the move," Kirby said.

"Yeah, and it looks like there's a power control on that thing." Hollis groaned as he started to rise. "Let's not wait for him to find a new spot."

Another dart sped through the top of the car and pierced the rear driver's side window.

He scooted around to the rear driver's side wheel and took cover. An Eshuvani avicopter flapped overhead.

Hollis tapped his partner's shoulder and pointed. "Reinforcements."

"Good. Maybe they'll see more from the air," Kirby said.

The avicopter hovered over a building. Nurinyan somersaulted out and landed on the roof.

Hollis sat down by the wheel. "That'll keep the shooter busy."

Kirby holstered his gun. "Let's hope Amaya knows a trick for getting that thing out of your head."

Looking at the soaked handkerchief, Hollis nodded.

URUSHALON

Chapter Eleven

Blood from the drenched handkerchief dripped down Hollis' arm as Kirby waved Amaya over.

Hollis managed a smile. *I'm glad it's you.*

She joined them and knelt. "Mark, other than the dart, are you hurt?"

"No, but for a little dart, it hurts like the devil."

"We'll take care of that. Are you hurt, Robert?"

Kirby shook his head. "The suspect missed me altogether."

"Good. The other two officers made it to the roof as Nurinyan jumped. They appeared to be fine."

She pulled out her test kit and drew a small amount of blood into a capillary tube.

"I think the dart's barbed." Kirby took the thin tube from her and held it in a loose fist.

She nodded. "You did the right thing. Mark, when I retract the barbs, you'll feel and hear a click."

"Ready when you are."

He cringed as Amaya pressed on the dart. The fletching

161

and barbs snapped, and the tube slid out from under his skin. The speed of the drip from the kerchief doubled.

Kirby stared, slack-jawed. "I know scalp injuries bleed more, but–"

Amaya pulled a plastic packet from her backpack. "The tranquilizer decomposed to an anticoagulant."

She took the capillary tube from Kirby and held it up to the light. A bright green stripe floated above the edge of the blood column.

Amaya shook her head. "You'll have to heal the old-fashioned way."

Hollis snorted. "That figures."

She cut the plastic packet open. "This is sterilized water. I'll irrigate the injury, then put a bandage on it."

Amaya poured water over the wound, which stung like a swarm of fire ants. He winced as she applied the bandage.

"How do you feel?" She sat back.

"I'll make it." Leaning on the bumper and trunk, Hollis stood. He surveyed the darts stuck in the car like spines on a porcupine. "I guess we're pretty lucky the assailant was a lousy shot."

Amaya rose. "He may not be a lousy shot."

Hollis arched an eyebrow. "Really? He had to have fired thirty or more rounds at us, and we were pretty exposed a couple of times."

"Oh, I don't dispute that he spent an impressive amount of ammunition and made only one hit. His beneficial lack of success may be less about his pathetic aim and more about the equipment."

"The guns you had back then were that inaccurate?"

Amaya shook her head. "Over time, a misalignment develops. If our suspect has not done proper maintenance on his gun, he could aim for your nose and hit the dirt five strides

URUSHALON

away." She took a few steps in the direction Nurinyan had gone. "He should have reported in by now. If you're both all right, I'm going to try to find him."

"Could you use a couple extra pairs of eyes?" Kirby asked.

"Certainly. Once we've found him, I'll take you to your station."

After Amaya collected her equipment, Hollis followed her to the avicopter.

***

Nurinyan closed with his target as the chase went on. The suspect turned a corner. When Nurinyan got there and saw no sign of his quarry, he slowed and panted. Plenty of parked cars lined both sides of the street, and across from him, flowering shrubbery formed a perimeter for the park.

Civilians. If the suspect had run that way, he'd find civilians to harm.

He checked the nearest half-dozen cars and crossed the street. The suspect bolted from behind a car and went straight into the park. Nurinyan took off after him, ignoring the ache in his muscles.

They came to a high bridge over a shallow, wet-weather creek. A man, a woman, and two children, all human, rode bicycles on the other side of the bridge.

"Stay clear!" Nurinyan called, but his raspy voice didn't carry.

The suspect changed direction on a dust particle. He grabbed one of the children and pitched her over the edge of the bridge. The bike she'd been riding toppled as the woman screamed. Nurinyan's comm beeped a second before he dove off the bridge, kicking off from the railing to propel himself toward the child. He caught the girl midair and rotated around to land on his feet in the creek bed. A damp rock slipped under his foot, and a sharp pain raced up the side of his leg.

LIKE HERDING THE WIND

The girl clung to him and wailed as he hobbled to the dry ground.

Nurinyan sat, keeping the child in his arms, and panted hard to try to regain his breath. Someone on the bridge above hollered in English, but he couldn't make the translation. The comm crystals on his collar glowed indicating that whoever was calling had activated the tracking circuit.

Sorry, Amaya, but I'm a little occupied. "Are you hurt?" Nurinyan asked in between gasps.

The sandy-haired child rubbed her eyes with the bottom edge of her pink dress and sobbed too heavily to answer.

He gave her a quick visual check. No blood. Nothing out of alignment. *Thank you, God, for protecting the girl.*

On the bridge, the mother leaned over the hip-high rail.

He drew a breath and shouted in English, "She is all right."

"My husband is on his way down," the woman yelled.

Nurinyan waved an acknowledgment and tapped out the code on the comm system that would connect him to Amaya.

"Amaya."

He raised his eyebrows. Could she have been that calm three days ago? Would she have even allowed him to attempt the pursuit alone?

"Nurinyan. I lost him. He threw a girl over a bridge. I had to do an inverted descent midair rescue."

"Are either of you hurt?" Amaya asked.

"The child is frightened, but uninjured." He rubbed his leg. "I landed badly and turned my ankle. I don't think anything broke, but whatever I did, I did it well."

"If you're in a safe location, stay still. I'll find somewhere to set down, then we'll come to you."

"I'm sorry, Amaya. I nearly caught him."

URUSHALON

"You made the correct choice, Nurinyan. You have no cause for shame."

"Message received."

The connection broke. Nurinyan checked his pockets and frowned. Where was his nutrition bar? It must have fallen out while he was running or when he dove after the child.

Footsteps pounded across the rocks behind him, and he twisted around. The man from the bridge was coming.

"Daddy!" the girl cried.

The man leaned over, picked up the girl, and hugged her to his chest. "What was that about?"

Nurinyan took a couple breaths before trying to answer in English. "I was chasing a suspect, and he used your little one for his diversion. I am sorry. I did not want anyone to be hurt."

"You took a huge risk diving off that bridge."

"Dere was no ot'er way. I am pleased to serve." Everything in Nurinyan's vision took a hard spin toward the left. He put his hand down on the rocky dirt to steady himself.

A firm hand gripped his shoulder. "Whoa, pal, you all right?"

"I ran too hard for too long. Now it is time to pay for dat."

"What can I do?"

"Not'ing, but t'ank you. Help is coming, my *kiand,* um, captain?"

"I'll stay with you until he arrives."

"T'ank you."

"Least I could do, pal." The man pointed across the river. "There, the Eshuvani woman coming across with the police officers."

Through the persistent blur, Nurinyan picked out the gray of a *kiandarai* uniform. "Yes."

As they came closer, Amaya's face came into focus.

LIKE HERDING THE WIND

Robert and Mark, sporting a white bandage that stood out against his black hair, trailed her. Amaya crouched nearby.

"He looked a little unsteady, and I think he hurt his leg." The man stood up. "I have a water bottle on my bike if he could use it."

Amaya pulled a nutrition bar out of her backpack and opened it. "You're kind to offer, but for Eshuvani, food must precede fluids by an hour after heavy exertion, or hyponatremia may develop."

"Hypo–whatever you said?"

"Forgive me. Hyponatremia is a sodium imbalance causing swelling in the brain cells."

Nurinyan took a bite of the nutrition bar.

"Once I have Nurinyan stabilized, I can attend to your child, if you wish. I'm knowledgeable of human medicine as well."

"Thank you, but I don't think she's hurt. Your man did a first-rate job."

Mark stepped forward. "Sir, we'd like to ask you and your wife some questions about this incident."

"Sure, sure. There's a path back up to the bridge over here."

The humans left. Nurinyan finished the nutrition bar and shoved the wrapper into his pocket.

"There's another one when you're ready for it," Amaya said in their native language.

Nurinyan wiped the sweat from his face. "Let the first one settle."

"Fair enough. How do you feel? Can you see at all?"

"I'm dizzy. My vision is cloudy at a distance, but clear up close. And my right leg. The pain starts below the ankle and travels all the way up to my knee."

Amaya pulled out her transdermal viewer and turned it

URUSHALON

on. "What's your best diagnosis?"

You want to quiz me on diagnosing injuries now? Fine. "Um, torn lateral ligament."

"Differential diagnoses?"

"Could be a fracture, but I don't think anything broke. I could have pulled the muscle, I suppose, but it feels worse than that."

"Let's check."

The viewer chimed.

She scanned up and down his shin, changing the viewing depth with each pass.

"You were half right. You did tear the ligament, and you strained several tendons."

Nurinyan sighed. "I was such a klutz."

She gripped his shoulder. "Riverbeds are treacherous landing places. These rocks are big enough to put weight on and small enough to slide when you do. With the silt and algae on the wet ones, you would have needed divine intervention to make a good landing. You kept the civilian safe and did the least possible harm to yourself. There is no failure here, *Kiala*."

He nodded. Easy for her to say. If he'd been that much faster, he could've caught the suspect before the girl had been endangered.

She unsnapped the outside seam of his pants to expose his wounded leg, untied his boot, and slipped it off. She withdrew a regenerative salve tube from her backpack.

He took it from her. "No unnecessary risk."

Amaya backed away while he applied the gel. It sank through his skin. A few moments later, a wave of dizziness slammed into him again. Amaya's arm across his shoulders steadied him.

He pressed a hand to his forehead. "That other nutrition

LIKE HERDING THE WIND

bar. You wouldn't happen to have a berry one, would you?"

"I might. Those are too salty for me, but I grab one by mistake now and again." She pulled four bars out of her pack, sorted through them, and then peeled the wrapper on one. "You're in luck. I'll have to start keeping a couple on hand. You, Ishe, and Vadin all prefer them."

"Thank you." He ate the nutrition bar and put the second wrapper in his pocket with the first. "Do you think you can land the avicopter in this ravine?"

"Me? No." Amaya pointed at the overhanging trees. "Those are too close for me. I can carry you out unless you weigh over two hundred twenty pounds."

He chuckled. "No, not even in full gear."

"We may have to stop a couple times for a short rest, but we'll be okay." She looked past him. "Mark and Robert are on their way back."

"Good. I hope the parents could tell them something. I never saw the fellow's face. Every suspect I've chased before this one looked back from time to time to see if I had gotten closer, but not this one. Never even a glance. And his endurance was better than average."

"He may have been an athlete at some point, or military."

"How's the patient?" Mark asked as he and Robert arrived.

Nurinyan switched to English. "I need real food, some water, and some rest, but I will be okay."

"The girl's okay, too. She's pretty rattled, and there's a scratch on her neck, probably from the guy grabbing her, but she's all right."

"Good," Amaya said.

"The mother was no help." Mark rolled his eyes. "All Eshuvani look the same to her. She was upset about the whole thing. Says it all happened too fast."

URUSHALON

"The older brother and the father agree on most points, though." Robert consulted a little notepad. "The suspect is over six feet tall. Salt-and-pepper hair."

Nurinyan tilted his head to one side. "What?"

"Was black, now going gray," Amaya translated.

Robert read his notes. "Athletic build. The boy said dark eyes, but the father said blue."

Nurinyan nodded. "So, probably blue or could be green like mine."

Mark pulled out his own notepad and jotted something. "You mean, in Eshuvani–"

"Blue eyes are much darker. Gray is the only light color." Amaya pointed to her own eyes.

"Interesting." Mark flipped his notepad closed. "So they didn't necessarily contradict."

Robert slid his notepad back in its pocket and retracted the ink of his pen with a click of the top button. "After he threw the girl over the rail, he continued in the same direction he'd been going, but no one saw where he went after leaving the bridge."

Amaya slid her backpack onto her shoulders. "Well, let's get you two to your station so you can present yourselves whole to Ed, and then I can take Nurinyan home."

Nurinyan looped an arm over Amaya's shoulder as she lifted him.

***

Amaya sat at the dispatch desk, allocating her meager budget to cover costs for the next six months. Footsteps padded nearer through the hangar hallway.

She scooted the chair back and waved to Orinyay. "Good morning."

Orinyay entered the foyer. "Didn't we get calls last night?"

LIKE HERDING THE WIND

"Just a few. I took care of them. You looked exhausted when you got in. How was the trip to Woran Kishay and Austin?"

"Mark's family is safe at their relative's house." Orinyay handed her a folded paper. "In Woran Kishay, I found the old *kiat* who has the personnel files we need about the dead *kiandarai* of forty-five years ago."

"Excellent. How long will the record search take?"

"I don't know. He won't do business with anyone ranked lower than *kiand* and will only do business in person. Otherwise, he says, he'd spend all his time chasing trivia for the curious."

Amaya smiled and shook her head. "We do get eccentric in our old age, do we not?" She unfolded the paper and found the *kiat*'s name and a map to the Woran Kishay enclave. "All right. Take charge of things here while I go present our request. If you must send two *kialai* together on a call, pair Nurinyan and Jevon and take Vadin with you."

Orinyay nodded. "Be safe."

"Always." Amaya grabbed her medical kit and the small case containing her evidence of their attacker.

A couple hours into the flight, she found the place. Woran Kishay consisted of twenty buildings in the middle of a grassy area punctuated by clusters of junipers and oaks. Austin was visible in the distance. The typical semicircle of houses were arranged around the main building of the *kiandarai* station, which sat in the center of the town.

She landed, took her gear, and walked in. The station's stone walls and warm, brown wood trim gave the place a professional demeanor. The man at the dispatch desk wore the silver collar tabs of a *kiandara*.

Amaya stopped at the desk. "Grace be unto you."

"And peace from God, the Father of our Lord." He looked up from the computer. "How may I serve?"

URUSHALON

"I am Amaya Ulonya *Kiand* from Woran Oldue's Hawk's Nest Station. I am seeking Calwin Iviro *Kiat*."

"Oh, yes. Your data analyst came by yesterday. Come with me."

She followed him past the briefing room and hangar to a room marked "Data Storage." The *kiandara* ushered her in and left. A gray-haired man stood straight but shuffled forward.

I hope I can still serve when I reach his age. Better the more formal greeting for one so venerable. "May the–"

The old man scrunched up his face and held up a hand. "Yes, yes, yes, and stay on the path and all that. Who would you be, and what would you want?"

"I am Amaya Ulonya *Kiand*. My data analyst was here yesterday. She has given me your instructions."

"Yes, yes, I remember now. She had some fool request about *kiandarai* whose gear weren't recovered after death forty-odd years ago."

"Between forty-five and forty-eight years ago."

He glared at her. "What could you possibly need that for?"

"The Las Palomas Police Station and the Hawk's Nest Station of Woran Oldue are under attack by someone who has gear that old but doesn't know how to take care of it."

"And how can you narrow it to such a tight range?"

Amaya pulled a small case out of her backpack, flipped the lid up, and handed the whole thing to the old man. "I was a *kiandara* at the time in question, and I recognized the equipment."

He picked up the paralytic canister. "Did you check the numbers on it?"

Amaya nodded. "It's one of the two that were never accounted for. I anticipate finding the other in the possession

LIKE HERDING THE WIND

of the same man."

"That'll narrow the dates for you. And that record didn't say who was issued which, I know. I was a *kiand* at the time, and we told the Council of the *Kiati* these might come into criminal hands. Would they listen to us? Hardly." Careful to handle only the fletching, he picked up the dart she had recovered from Robert and Mark's car. "Model Four. How many shots has your boy fired?"

"Approximately sixty. For his effort, he has achieved only two glancing blows against targets who were exposed enough a novice could hit them."

He set the case on the counter. "And what good will the data you're wanting do?"

She numbered off points as she spoke. "With the information I've requested, I can look for living family members who have knowledge of designing and assembling obscure equipment and probable athletic or military background."

"Sounds like quite the character you've got there." He chuckled.

"I would agree."

His good humor faded and the apparently permanent grimace returned. "You have certainly done your part. This search will take time, but I'll see to it and have one of the lads here send the results to Hawk's Nest in Woran Oldue."

"Thank you, *Kiat*. I appreciate your diligence."

"Yes, yes, yes. Now let me work." He wobbled back into the files.

Amaya closed the case and slid it into her backpack before leaving for home.

She came at Woran Oldue from the northwest and crossed over into the Buffer Zone. Checking for air traffic, she spotted a green avicopter to the south and turned toward it, trying to catch a glimpse of the cockpit. Did the pilot match their

URUSHALON

suspect? All she could make out was gray clothing, but the shade was right. In any case, the pilot had gotten around the border guard and into the Buffer Zone. He needed to be turned around.

She tapped Ishe's code on a comm crystal.

"Ishe."

"Amaya. Did we ever get an identification on the partial registration Mark gave us?"

"Yep. Reported stolen two months ago. Why?"

"I think I'm looking at it." Amaya squinted at the ship. *Naturally, I can't see the tail properly.* "Is Orinyay available?"

"No. She and Jevon are out helping Las Palomas, West Division."

"Have Dispatch send me help from Wolf's Teeth."

"Message received. Be careful."

"Always." Amaya set the avi's radio to the universal frequency. "Green avicopter west of Las Palomas. You are in restricted space. Turn due west and proceed to Woran Oldue. Noncompliance will be deemed willful defiance of *kiandarai* directive."

The avi continued southeast toward the city.

"Green avicopter west of Las Palomas. You are in a restricted area. Turn due west and proceed to Woran Oldue. Refusal will result in a charge of willful disobedience of *kiandarai* directive, which is punishable by time in prison or a fine or both."

He maintained his course. Amaya shut off the air cooling systems and other non-essentials and opened up the courier to full throttle. She interposed herself between the avi and the city and pulled alongside. A metal tube the diameter of her fist poked out the other ship's side window. Amaya hauled the courier to the left. The canopy imploded, spraying her with glass fragments.

LIKE HERDING THE WIND

A canister struck a passenger seat and ruptured, spewing vile smoke that burned her eyes, mouth, and nose and irritated her lungs. She flipped the switch to engage the ventilation fans, but the indicator light stayed dark, and the fans stayed silent. Almost as a distant echo, glass fragments stung the right side of her face and body. Coughing, Amaya guided the avi straight down as fast as she dared.

The landing gear hit with a solid jolt that rattled every bone Amaya had. She groped for the door handle, threw open the door, and stumbled out, gagging.

Urushalon

Chapter Twelve

Once clear of the smoke, Amaya collapsed to her knees in the shin-high grass. A dart pistol whined, but blood and tears obscured her vision. Through her left eye, she could make out a large green blob for the other avicopter and a smaller, dark gray blob for the pilot.

A police siren crescendoed, but wasn't near enough to support her yet.

"Who will help you now?" the man asked.

Amaya grabbed her left collar tab, pressing and holding as many crystals as she could.

"They'll be too late."

She struggled to draw an even, slow breath, but hacked up and spat out a ball of phlegm. "What is this vendetta about?"

"Your lies killed my brother!"

"You mean the fellow from the park, Maran Leonan?" Her raw throat burned with every effort.

The pistol fired, and the dart struck her right shoulder, injecting an all but useless load of a mild anticoagulant. The sirens were loud enough to be almost on top of her. She had to keep Maran's brother focused on her and let the officers get in position to take him.

She turned her head, keeping him in her diminishing field of vision. "I testified in court to exactly what I saw. Your brother held a human police officer hostage and drove a shellfish knife into his chest."

"Liar! Maran was unarmed!"

The pistol fired again, and the dart whistled past her left ear.

"He had a knife and nearly killed the officer."

His footsteps rustled the dry grass. "He'd already surrendered when you shot him!"

"That's not what happened at all." Amaya drew her gun. She aimed, relying on his footsteps in the dry grass and the last memory she had of his location and direction of travel.

***

Mark Hollis braced himself as the patrol car bounced across the open field. If there were any ditches or unexpected rocks, they'd tear up the undercarriage of the car, but he and Kirby had to reach Amaya before her assailant did.

Ahead, a dark gray and silver avicopter spewed gray-green smoke from the cockpit via a hole in the canopy and an open door. The wings, still extended, slowly lifted and fell. Some twenty feet away, a mottled green avicopter sat waiting, wings tucked in. Between them were two gray-clad Eshuvani.

Amaya knelt in the grass. Her face, right hand, and much of the right side of her uniform were stained with blood. A man wearing a faded *kiandarai* uniform took a one-handed stance and sighted his pistol on Amaya as he crept toward her. A short-bladed knife in the other hand glinted in the sunlight.

Hollis gripped the steering wheel, still too far away to help. *We're going to get there in time for him to slit her throat with that knife.*

No. He couldn't think like that. They'd get there. With a

URUSHALON

little divine help, they'd reach her before it was too late.

Amaya drew her own pistol left-handed. The man staggered back a step and a trickle of blood welled on his cheek. He dodged to one side and drew down on her. She winced.

"Get ready," Hollis said.

Kirby unhitched the shotgun from its carrier under the seat.

The man brought his gun to bear, but a moment later, he glowered at his gun.

As Hollis stopped the car, Kirby bailed out and targeted Amaya's attacker.

Hollis switched the radio to public address and grabbed the mic. "Police! Drop your weapon, and put your hands in the air."

Amaya dropped flat on the ground. The man sprinted for the far side of his avi. Kirby led the suspect and fired. The man dove into a roll and came up limping before he swung himself into the cockpit. Kirby aimed for the avi and fired. The shot made a score of scratches on the canopy. Hollis fired pistol rounds, making neat, little spiderwebs, but he couldn't break through. The green avi lifted off.

Hollis ran toward Amaya. "Amaya? Amaya, it's Hollis. Kirby is with me."

Kirby pointed to her avi. "I'll see if there's a chance I can get to her kit."

Hollis nodded.

With a trembling arm, Amaya pushed herself up, but collapsed and rolled to her back.

Hollis knelt beside her. Her eyes were swollen. Her face had multiple lacerations and her uniform had myriad holes. Blood still ran from the wounds, and glass fragments glittered. Darts stuck out of her right shoulder and left thigh, and her collar was lit up like the emergency vehicles at a four-alarm

LIKE HERDING THE WIND

fire.

"Mark?" Her voice rasped.

"I'm here. We saw your avi take the shot. We couldn't get here fast enough."

She coughed hard. "You were just in time."

"Anything I can do?"

"Do you remember how to retract barbs on a dart?" She coughed again and winced.

"Yeah, the tail's a switch." He pinched the fletching until it clicked, pulled out the dart, and gave the one in her leg the same treatment. "Okay. What else? Remove the glass?"

"No. That will have to be left for the hospital. The bleeding will increase and the glass may damage other tissues as you remove it."

Kirby came around the back of the avi, coughing. "Couldn't reach her backpack. What is that stuff?"

"Tear g–" Amaya broke into another rough fit of coughing.

"Tear gas?" Hollis asked.

"Yes. Very concentrated form." She drew a raspy breath. "Old gear. Solvent leaked out."

"How did you ever land that thing?" Hollis glanced back at the avi. "Don't tell me they teach you to fly and shoot blind."

"Fly blind, no. Land, yes." Her words slurred together. "The other was my own bit of insanity."

"You did actually hit him. Once in the cheek."

"Incredible. I was jus' hoping to back him off until you 'rived." She squeezed her eyes closed.

Light reflected off another avicopter.

Hollis squinted. "There's an avi coming across Las Palomas."

URUSHALON

"Las Palomas?" She frowned. "Th'neares' available was that far 'way? Then I'm doubly blessed you're nearby. I don't think I could've backed him down mush longer."

"The lights on your collar. That's a call for help?"

"Emergency beacon," she whispered, barely loud enough to hear.

The incoming avicopter set up for a landing.

He gripped her left arm. "Stay with me, Amaya."

"Tryin' to." She wilted like a flower in a dry vase.

Kirby's eyes begged for a suggestion.

Hollis shrugged. *I'm at the same loss you are, partner.*

Orinyay and Jevon hopped out of the avicopter.

Hollis met them halfway and briefed Orinyay on the situation.

Orinyay ran over to Amaya as Jevon put on a bulky gas mask and grabbed a small fan.

Squatting nearby, Orinyay rummaged through her pack. "Robert, if you will press and hold any t'ree crystals on her collar for five seconds, please. Amaya, how do you feel?"

"Wretched. Dizzy. Hurt all over. Eyes're burning. Hurts t'breathe."

Kirby pressed a red and two blue crystals until all the lights went out.

Orinyay laid out two foil packets, an aerosol can, and a plastic-wrapped syringe. "I am going to use a spray styptic to slow de blood loss, give you a hemogenesis injection to restore your blood count, and irrigate your eyes. Agreed?"

Amaya nodded.

Orinyay unsnapped seams on the right side of Amaya's uniform. "Help me roll her onto her left side."

Hollis reached for Amaya and stopped. Where could he put his hands where he wouldn't interfere with injuries?

LIKE HERDING THE WIND

Amaya turned on her own. There weren't many injuries on her back.

Orinyay snatched the aerosol can and sprayed a fine mist. The bleeding injuries clotted. Hollis supported Amaya's shoulders and back as she lay flat again.

Orinyay dropped the can on her backpack, unwrapped the pre-loaded syringe, and picked up a small foil envelope. She tore open the packet and pulled out a wet piece of gauze smelling of alcohol.

Amaya fumbled with the cuff of her left sleeve.

"Quit dat." Orinyay tapped Amaya's hand. "You are a patient."

Amaya managed a smile. "Ol' habits and so on."

Hollis unbuttoned her sleeve and pushed it up.

Orinyay used the gauze to wipe a patch of Amaya's forearm and then uncapped the needle and slid the point under Amaya's skin and emptied the vial. Removing the syringe and securing it, she grabbed the larger, fluid-filled packet.

Amaya's muscles all tensed at once and her breath caught.

Hollis grabbed the *kiandara*'s arm. "Orinyay!"

"Peace. Dat is a normal reaction."

Moments later, Amaya relaxed and breathed again.

Orinyay cut the corner off the packet and eased open Amaya's right eye. She poured water on her eye, then did the same on the other side. "You mentioned she was hit by old tranquilizer darts."

Hollis smoothed out the material on her shoulder and leg, searching for the round holes. "There and there."

Orinyay used shears to cut an opening in Amaya's clothes near the site, then poured water over the small wounds.

"We can't bind the wounds, can we?" Hollis asked.

Orinyay shook her head. "Dat would drive de glass deeper

URUSHALON

into her body. De styptic will slow de blood loss and de injection is already making new blood cells."

Amaya reached her hand toward Hollis, and he caught it in both of his.

"Thank you," she said.

He managed a smile. "You said we might have to watch over you some day."

"I wish we could have done more," Kirby said.

"You both did fine." Amaya's grip tightened. "Your help was timely."

Jevon came over and took off the breathing mask. The avicopter was shut down and the fan had ejected most of the smoke from the cockpit.

Orinyay spoke to Jevon for a few moments, and whatever she said brought a scowl to his face. She slid her arms under Amaya's shoulders and knees.

"Careful. I may have glass in the folds and seams of my clothes," Amaya said.

"Cannot be helped. You certainly are not going to be walking." She stood, bearing Amaya in her arms.

Hollis rose with them and kept Orinyay steady. He followed them back and opened the rear door of the cargo hauler.

Orinyay stepped up into the avicopter and laid Amaya on the floor. "I will contact your dispatcher and have him relay de prognosis once we are finished at de hospital."

"Thanks." Hollis closed and secured the door, then backed out of the way.

***

Pain shrieked from the tiny bullet holes in Wylin's leg. The human *kiandarai* and the injured *kiand* were well behind him. With any luck, her wounds were mortal, and one more of Maran's killers would be gone. A shiver rattled his body.

LIKE HERDING THE WIND

"You all right, Wylin?" Maran asked.

Wylin turned, searching the cockpit. The pain in his leg spiked. "Maran? Maran, where are you?"

"I'm right here. Are you going to come get me out of this place soon?"

"What place? Where are you?" He looked down at his collar tabs. The crystals were dark.

"I'll be waiting. Just don't make it too long, okay. This isn't an amusement park, y'know."

"Just tell me where you are."

"The courthouse, dummy. Are you coming to get me out of here or not?"

"Of course I am. Soon as I get my leg fixed up." He pressed and held a blue crystal on his collar tab.

"See you soon, then."

"What do you need, Wylin?" His contact yawned.

"Medical help. I've been shot." He looked at the blood stains on the leg of his pants and winced.

"It'll wear off."

"It's not a dart. A handful of small bullets from a human gun hit me in the leg."

"Go to the medical center." Her tone had a built-in eyeroll.

He scowled and bared his teeth. "And tell them what when they ask how I got shot? That I was hired by–"

"Look, you've gone off on your own. Why should we continue to help you?"

"You hired me to acquire the equipment for your team. You got all of what you asked for, and there's another set just like it at my camp. Even if I have gone after my own targets, my efforts still benefit you. They're your targets, too."

She huffed. "Standby. I'll ask him." The line went silent

URUSHALON

for what seemed like eternity. "He says he'll meet you at the drop point. Land with the trees between you and Hawk's Nest."

"You really think they can't see that far?" he asked.

"Just do it!" she screamed.

The line clicked and went dead.

Wylin glared in the direction of his contact's headquarters, and looped around toward the drop point.

***

Osborn leaned forward barely aware of the song on the radio. He'd turned it on as a distraction from his worry, but he couldn't get Hollis and Kirby's report out of his head. Amaya was in the hospital after some maniac had shot her down with some kind of toxin-spewing canister. He tried to remember a time when she'd survived worse, but he drew a blank.

As the song ended, an announcer came on. "In a press conference today, President Johnson..."

He twirled the dial and turned off the car radio. Osborn had heard the report about President Johnson's speech as he'd started off on the highway headed north toward Woran Oldue. He joined a line of cars at the first checkpoint for the Eshuvani border. A border guard with an electronic notepad walked up to the car as Osborn rolled down his window.

"Good morning," the guard said in English. "What is your intention?"

"Grace be unto you," Osborn said in Eshuvani. "My *urushalon* is in the hospital. I wish to visit her and bring blessings of comfort and peace."

"Do you have your access card?"

"In my wallet." Osborn pulled his wallet out of his back pocket and sorted through business cards and slips of paper until he came to his Eshuvani ID.

The border guard checked over the ID. His eyes widened.

LIKE HERDING THE WIND

"Kin by adoption and nearest available?"

"Her natural family is overseas."

The guard handed the ID back and annotated his notepad. "Very good. You may park your vehicle in that lot and use the public transportation to get to the hospital. From here, the blue avicopters will be the most direct. On the return, yellow will be the swiftest choice. They run every quarter hour."

Osborn slipped his card in his shirt pocket to keep it accessible. "I appreciate your diligent service."

He pulled into the almost empty lot, locked his car, and walked to the empty public transit depot.

A few minutes later, a brilliant blue avicopter the size of a city bus landed and tucked in the wings. The door opened. Osborn stepped into the avi and presented his ID to the driver.

"Destination?" the driver asked.

"Hospital."

"Be seated."

Four Eshuvani were scattered around the other seats. Osborn took the nearest seat behind the driver. They passed through a commercial sector. Businesses and shops, arrayed around central parking lots, sported signs that glittered and changed with the names of the businesses and ads for various goods and services. Moving sidewalks carted people from one business to the next.

The transit avicopter landed at a business. One person disembarked and three others got on.

Two stops later, the driver turned around. "This is as near as we get to the hospital. Take the moving sidewalk north from here."

"Thank you." Osborn stood up and stepped into the aisle. "I appreciate your service."

He hopped off and walked alongside the moving sidewalk for a few strides before stepping up. Crepe myrtles had been

URUSHALON

planted alongside the walkway at regular intervals. Many still sported blooms, but a few bore the brown, spherical seed capsules, subdivided like orange sections.

The sidewalk ended in sight of a multilevel building constructed of natural stone. Osborn dodged avicopters in the parking lot to reach the front door. He entered the hospital and bee-lined to the chest-high information desk. A woman in the red uniform of hospital staff scrolled through a computer screen.

"Grace be unto you." Osborn leaned on the desk.

"And peace from God, the Father of our Lord." The woman looked up from her screen and smiled.

"I'm looking for Amaya Ulonya *Kiand*. She was brought in yesterday afternoon."

The woman consulted an electronic notepad. "Here she is. Go to the third floor and then to the traumatic injury ward."

"Thanks." Osborn took the escalators up two flights. A sign directed him to the desk on his right.

"In what way may I serve?" the lady at the desk asked.

"I'm looking for Amaya Ulonya *Kiand*."

"I'm sorry, but the doctor has not agreed to visitors yet." The receptionist offered a sympathetic look. "Only family is permitted."

Osborn produced his ID card. "I'm kin-by-adoption and the nearest available."

She looked between him and the card a few times. "Oh, well, that will solve it. You want the second door on the right."

"Thank you."

He hesitated outside the door. Would he enter and find Amaya hovering a step away from death, or would she be sitting up in bed, laughing and swapping tales with whoever was with her? He'd never know standing outside the door.

LIKE HERDING THE WIND

Painting on the serene but concerned "Everything's under control" look he reserved for the wives of wounded officers, Osborn stepped into the room.

The nurse assigned to watch over Amaya set a book aside. "Oh, you have a visitor, Amaya."

Amaya lay in bed with her head elevated. Her eyes were bandaged, and the visible part of the right side of her body was covered with white gauze and tape. A breathing mask full of a pinkish cloud that roiled as she breathed covered her mouth and nose, and an IV needle pierced her left arm. As she stretched her left hand toward him, a pain gripped his heart.

Osborn crossed to her and pressed her hand between his. "Amaya, I came as soon as I could."

Her hand tightened around his, and she rubbed the back of his hand with her fingers. He'd come to comfort her, and yet she was trying to reassure him?

"She is unable to speak at this time," the nurse said.

"Can you tell me how she is?" Osborn asked.

"Do you know what happened?"

Osborn nodded. "I'm a sergeant with the Las Palomas police. The two officers who helped drive off her attacker are in my command."

"The lacerations, for the most part, were superficial. A couple were more serious and needed to be sutured, but none are life threatening, and we expect those wounds to fully heal." The nurse turned to Amaya. "The smoke from the canister is the real issue. She breathed quite a bit of it, and her eyes and lungs in particular took some damage."

"And with her sensitivity, you can't use regenerative salve to heal the injuries," Osborn said.

"No, but when those canisters were first made, regenerative salve was new. There are older protocols that do not use it, and she is responding well to those. Proper recovery may take a full week, but we expect no lasting effects or

URUSHALON

complications."

"I'm glad for that." He sighed. "If their avis had been blessed with modern equipment, this wouldn't have happened. She could have forced him down from a kilometer away."

"So the *kiandara* who brought her in said." The nurse shook her head. "Strange that a new station has outmoded gear."

"It's political." Osborn let go of Amaya's hand.

He spoke to her, and she answered in the sign language she'd helped him learn for a merit badge decades ago. They spoke of how she felt and how Esther and the kids were doing then went on to whatever other benign things he could come up with.

At some length, the doctor came in to check the progress of Amaya's recovery.

Osborn kissed Amaya's forehead. "I won't get off duty in time to see you tonight, but I'll be back in the morning."

She gave him a thumbs-up.

Osborn paused at the door and looked back at her one last time, then waited in the hall to talk to the doctor.

***

Wylin landed the avicopter in the open area behind the fence of Sergeant Ed Osborn's house. He retracted the wings but left the engine in standby mode. This little errand shouldn't take long.

"Are you going to come get me or not?" Maran asked.

"I have a better idea, Maran. I'm going to make them give you back." Wylin grabbed the paralytic cylinder sitting on the passenger seat and slipped it into his pocket.

"You think that'll work?"

"It'll work or they won't get the girl back." He hopped out of the avicopter and headed for the fence. "Now quiet so I can work."

LIKE HERDING THE WIND

Wylin darted to the fence and hauled himself up and over easily. The kitchen curtains were drawn back for both the small window and the larger glass door. Inside, a small, blonde, human woman was moving around.

The human *kiandara* shouldn't be here yet, but if he had gotten home already, Wylin was ready for him.

"I'll watch for him. You worry about the girl." Maran sounded almost giddy.

Wylin scowled at the ephemeral image his brother was somehow producing from his jail cell. What technology was that, anyway? "You stay out of this. I don't want you getting hurt." He shivered and hugged himself to chase the chill away.

Darting to the glass door, he pressed his back against the wall and pushed the handle. The door stayed firmly in place. There was no lock to pick from this side, and a chunk of metal lay in the track for the sliding half of the door.

Kicking in that thin a piece of glass would be no problem, but why risk injury? A walkway edged in stones bigger than his head provided a much safer way to get into the place. He peeked into the smaller window. The woman stood at the stove stirring some brilliant red concoction.

Wylin darted to the nearest stone in the path and picked it up. A small, brown scorpion scurried away. He returned to his place by the sliding door and crouched. No reason not to make this the warning message for the *kiandarai*, Eshuvani and otherwise. He tugged the red and gray ribbons out of his pocket. Wylin wrapped them around the rock like a big present and tied them off, making sure the text on the tail of one ribbon was visible.

He picked up the rock again, feeling the strain across his shoulders, and pitched it through the non-moving side of the sliding door. Glass shattered, spraying across the kitchen. The stone came to rest against the legs of the table and chairs.

Wylin darted through the opening to the sound of the blonde screaming. She started for the door into the rest of the

URUSHALON

house, but he leapt over the table and blocked the path. Glass crunched under his boots. She slid to a stop and headed for the opening he'd created in the glass, and he jumped over the table again and caught her by the back of the dress. Wylin shoved her against the intact side of the door and pulled the paralytic canister from his pocket. Holding it close to her face, he turned his own head away and triggered the release with his thumb, spraying the vile-smelling compound at her nose.

She coughed and gagged, then went rigid. He picked her up and headed back for the avicopter. In a few hours, he'd either have his brother back with him, or the humans would be mourning the death of one of their own.

***

Ed parked the car in his garage. He checked his watch and smiled.

On time for a change. First time since we rotated to day watch.

He entered the house. *Trailmaster* played on the TV. Odd. Esther often left the TV on for "background noise," but she didn't usually care for westerns. Too much gun violence for her tastes.

He shrugged and continued on through the living room. The smell of tomatoes and spices gave away their dinner as something Italian. He smiled. His favorite, especially the way Esther cooked.

"Dinner smells great, honey." He dropped his briefcase on the couch. "Esther?"

Kids played tag in the greenbelt behind the house. Every giggle, every shout came through far too clearly.

He frowned. *She promised me she'd keep the house secured.* "Esther? Honey?"

He quickened his pace and entered the kitchen. Glass shards from half of the sliding door littered the floor and kitchen table. A ribbon-bound rock the size of his head sat by

LIKE HERDING THE WIND

the legs of a chair. Purple dots glittered on the intact side of the glass door. He stepped around the debris. As he neared the broken door, the distinct, rotten garlic and skunk odor of the old Eshuvani paralytic wrinkled his nose. Spaghetti sauce bubbled over a low flame on the stove, and noodles on the counter awaited cooking. The pot designated for that purpose had boiled dry.

He shook his head. "Oh, no."

Urushalon

Chapter Thirteen

The courier landed at Hawk's Nest. Amaya stepped out and waved to the pilot. The main door of the station slid open. Ishe stood there beaming.

"Amaya!" She zipped over and crushed Amaya with an exuberant hug.

Pain reporting from her arm and side made Amaya wince. "Gentle. I'm not fully recovered yet."

Ishe backed away. "I'm sorry! Did I hurt you?"

"I'll be fine. How are you?"

"Oh, much better now that you're back." Ishe ushered Amaya inside to escape the heat. "We were so worried about you when the dispatcher called and said that your emergency beacon switched on, and the *kiat* wouldn't let Wolf's Teeth go help you because he said there were humans involved." She spun toward Amaya and frowned. "I'm not sure how he knew that, but anyway, I thought Vadin was going to explode when he heard that." She drew a mushroom cloud in the air with a wide circling motion of both arms. "And then Jevon brought our courier avi back, and oh did it smell! Ugh! We had to let it air out for two whole days before we could even try to repair the canopy, and your replacement, oh, I could kill him! He makes Jevon seem like a perpetual spring of joy." She paused a moment and grinned. "I am so glad you're home again."

Amaya waited. *Finished?* "It's good to see you, too. I've been cleared to resume my duties. Can you bring me up to the current situation?"

"Sure. Jevon found another avi like our courier in a junk yard, so our courier is repaired now." Ishe counted off the points on her fingers. "Nurinyan postponed his last two mastery tests because he wanted some more class time next week. What else?" She squinted toward the corner of the room. "Oh! Jevon passed his test on basic Eshuvani medicine. Two more to go, one tonight. The *kiat* at Woran Kishay sent the information you requested, and Orinyay is sorting through it. No more attempts by that wacko in the green avi. Orinyay says to expect him to change tactics pretty soon. We checked the wacko's claim that he's the brother of the guy who tried to kill Robert, and did you know Maran Leonan actually had four brothers? None of them are exactly wholesome characters, so that didn't tell us much, but we're tracking down where they are. Is that it?" She counted on her fingers. "Yeah, I think so."

Glad it was a slow week. Amaya nodded. "Excellent. Thank you. Where did my trauma kit end up?"

"It's on the couch in your quarters. Wow, did it reek! Whatever was in that canister was foul! We washed your backpack and cleaned your gear as well as we could then put it all back together according to the protocol. I hope that was okay."

"Perfect. And my relief?"

"Oh, him. Mr. Midnight-on-a-Sunny-Day? He's on a call with Nurinyan. Oh, and Orinyay and Vadin are on another call while Jevon is studying for his test. Data analysis. His favorite." She grinned.

Amaya smiled. "I think Jevon likes data analysis as much as you enjoy marksmanship."

URUSHALON

Ishe rolled her eyes. "Ugh. Don't remind me. I have to try to qualify again next week. Can you help me get ready for it? I can schedule class time, I guess, but the instructor at the training center yells at me when I ask a question."

"No problem. Give me some time to get the kit from my quarters and see what I have that will pass for food."

"Oh, not much." She shuddered and leaned closer. "We, uh, cleaned the unprocessed penicillin out of your fridge last night."

Amaya chuckled. "Thank you. Please let me know when Nurinyan returns."

"You got it!"

Amaya was halfway down the hall to the back door when the hangar doors rolled up.

Her collar chimed. She pushed two dark blue crystals. "Amaya."

"Ishe. They're back."

"Thank you. I'll be right there."

"Complete waste of time," a man's high tenor voice said. "Why they couldn't handle that without our help, I'll never know."

Nurinyan sighed. "Look, Soren, they're still being equipped and trained. Be glad it was an easy call. Some are much harder."

"Maybe, but I could do with something worthy of my time." Soren's voice distorted around a mouthful of food. "And you people really need to see about replacing that avi."

"We're accepting donations."

"This whole station needs rebuilding."

"So you've said. Repeatedly."

Amaya leaned on the corner where the hallway met the foyer and crossed her arms. Nurinyan walked in with an average height, unusually stout fellow with brown hair and

LIKE HERDING THE WIND

dark blue eyes, presumably Soren. A wrapper left his hand and skidded across the floor, ending up next to Ishe's chair. Amaya cleared her throat. He stepped over quickly and snapped up the wrapper, tucking it into a pocket.

Respectful to my face and rude to my back. Is that the way? Any wonder you don't have a permanent post?

"I appreciate your concern about the state of Hawk's Nest." Amaya stalked toward them. *Let him wonder about my intentions.* "Since it would be a waste of valuable time to lament about things you don't intend to fix, shall I arrange with the dispatcher for you to remain on hand for a few more days to help with repairs and rebuilding?"

Soren swallowed. "Um, *Kiand*. Welcome back. No, I'm afraid I'm–I'm scheduled to work at another station."

"In that case, I appreciate your service in my absence, *Kiandara*. You are released."

"I, um, thank you. I'll collect my things and be on my way." He darted down the back hallway.

Nurinyan smiled and kept a light touch as he hugged Amaya.

"Gentle!" Ishe rushed a few steps closer. "She's not entirely better yet."

Nurinyan shook his head and whispered in Amaya's ear, "She bear-hugged you. Didn't she?"

Amaya nodded. "Umhm."

He stepped back. "How are you?"

"Much better." She ran a hand along her right arm, still tender in a few places. "A couple cuts still need a day or two, but I was declared fit for duty."

"Good. It was horrible knowing you were calling for immediate aid, Orinyay was ten minutes away, and we could do nothing but wait."

She led him to the back door while they talked. "I'll do

URUSHALON

my best to avoid getting into that kind of situation again."

"Please. If we ever get Soren as a replacement again, Ishe will have a live test subject for her medical training. At least when Jevon complains he follows it by doing something useful. But really, you can see and breathe okay again?" He stepped in front of her and turned to walk backwards while he looked her over.

"Yes, I'm fine." Amaya smiled.

He ran his hand down his right arm. "Except for those few last cuts that need to heal."

"Except for that." As Amaya opened the door, hot Texas air blasted her.

Bare footpaths in the yellowing grass were starting to show between the station and each of the houses. She'd have to consider some way to make rock or concrete sidewalks. Surely Texas got significant precipitation at some point in the year. Amaya followed the path that led to her house and abandoned the oppressive heat for the cool air in her living room.

Her trauma kit sat on the edge of the park bench serving for her couch.

Nurinyan leaned against the inside of the door. "Maybe, after I get my instructor's credentials, I can help you improve your aerial combat rating. Then, if there is a next time–"

Amaya's collar tab chimed. She pressed two of the dark blue crystals. "Amaya."

"Ishe. You have a call, Amaya. It's Ed's address."

Amaya froze. Had their attacker gone after him? Perhaps, but there could be all sorts of reasons Ed would need her help. Not all of them were disasters. She shrugged on her backpack and followed Nurinyan to the hangar while Ishe gave them the rest of the details.

***

Amaya landed the avicopter in Ed's front yard.

LIKE HERDING THE WIND

Nurinyan gave her a light push on the shoulder. "Go on. I'll power down and meet you inside."

She grabbed her trauma kit, jogged to the front door, and knocked.

"It's open," Ed called from inside.

She frowned at the empty tone in his voice.

Amaya walked in. The air was full of cooked herbs and vegetables, a burnt metal sort of tang, and a faint hint of decay. Ed sat on the edge of an armchair, rocking back and forth.

She crouched in front of him. "Ed?"

"I should've made her go to her sister's with the kids. She didn't want to leave. Wouldn't be scared out of her own house, and I couldn't convince her. I should've bodily picked her up and took her to Houston kicking and screaming the whole way."

Sympathetic pain grabbed her heart. Was Esther dead? Had she been killed in the crossfire between Maran Leonan's brother and the *kiandarai* and police? She knew that grief too well.

Nurinyan came in but stood back against the wall.

Amaya held Ed's hand and ran her fingers through his short, red hair. "What happened, dear one?"

He kept a grip on her hand as he stood and tugged her toward the kitchen. She glanced back at Nurinyan and gestured for him to follow.

Ed stopped inside the kitchen door. "Aside from turning off the stove, I've touched nothing."

She took in the whole room in a panoramic gaze. From Ed's demeanor, she'd expected to find Esther's mangled body.

Amaya stepped over to the intact side of the sliding door to look at the purple spots. She couldn't mistake the putrid odor of the old paralytic. "Esther's been abducted, but I don't

URUSHALON

think he'll kill her."

Ed pointed to the remembrance token made from ribbons and a huge rock on the floor. "He will if I can't figure out this cryptic message."

Nurinyan crouched next to the large stone and read the ribbon. "If you want her back, meet me at the Gull before sunset."

Ed leaned on the counter. "Does that mean something to you?"

Amaya shook her head. "Not to me. I only know 'gull' as a type of sea bird. Nurinyan, is there a land formation or a location around here known as the Gull?"

"I'm not native to this area. Vadin grew up here, though. Orinyay, too, I think. Maybe they know something."

"Fortunately, it's summer. The days are longer. Sunset is what, eight o'clock or eight-thirty?"

Ed stared at the floor.

Nurinyan stood. "About that."

She checked her watch. "It's four-twenty. We have time."

Ed rubbed the back of his neck and sighed.

Amaya pulled him into a one-armed embrace. Ed would need to do something to stave off despair and anxiety. He had to think straight, for Esther's sake.

Amaya returned to the broken window. "Do you have boards or sheet metal we can use to secure your house?"

Ed nodded. "I keep plywood in the garage in case we have to board up for hurricanes."

"Good." She looked at the phone on the wall. "Have you contacted Mark, Harry, and Robert? They or their families may be next."

Ed shook his head. "After Sumner's funeral, Gale swapped vacation days with someone and took some additional days off. He went out west to get his head screwed

LIKE HERDING THE WIND

back on. Mark already moved his wife and kid to Austin. Robert isn't married."

"He has plans to marry soon, doesn't he? The suspect may know of it."

Ed smacked his forehead. "I forgot about Susan."

"I'll call Mark and Robert to warn them and offer Susan the safe room in Hawk's Nest." She pointed at Ed and Nurinyan. "You and Nurinyan get the hardware we'll need to board up the broken window. We'll collect everyone and go back to Hawk's Nest. I have a skilled analyst who might make sense of that remembrance token."

Ed nodded. "Right."

He tapped Nurinyan on the shoulder and the two of them jogged to the garage. Amaya picked up the phone and opened the nearest cabinet door. As his parents had done, Ed kept important numbers taped to the inside. Mark was listed halfway down.

***

Mark Hollis hung up his phone. Esther? Kidnapped? Quite a change from the snipe-and-run tactics the suspect was known for, and what was this business about meeting gulls? This guy was starting to sound a half-bubble off plumb.

After tucking his keys and wallet in his pocket, Hollis secured the house and jogged to the back fence. He pulled himself up and over. The boards swayed under his weight. One of these days, he'd install a gate and quit this ridiculous fence-hopping.

Hollis paced until the roasting sun drove him to the shade of an ancient, sprawling oak tree. The space between the lower hanging branches didn't give him room to walk, so he spent his restless energy seeing how far he could throw acorns.

He'd landed a couple in his backyard when the wingbeats of an avicopter heralded the *kiandarai*'s approach. Hawk's Nest's behemoth cargo hauler settled in the greenbelt.

Nurinyan, in the pilot's seat, hopped out and jogged to the fence. Amaya slid over into his place.

Hollis hustled out of the shade. "Nurinyan!"

Nurinyan slid to a stop within arm's reach of the fence and ran back. Hollis hurried to the avi's side door as Amaya vacated the pilot's seat for Nurinyan.

Hollis climbed into the avicopter and settled in the open seat next to Osborn. He was staring out the window and fidgeting with the clasp on his watch.

We'll find her, pal. Alive, I hope. Hollis patted Osborn's shoulder.

Osborn glanced back then returned to the window as the avi lifted off.

Amaya twisted around in the shotgun seat and pressed her *urushalon's* hand between both of hers. While the two of them spoke in Eshuvani, Hollis stared out the window. From the air, houses were like gray and brown polygons on fields of green among black and white intersecting stripes.

Osborn squeezed Amaya's hand and took a deep breath.

She let him go. "Mark, do you know what 'the Gull' is?"

"Just an obnoxious sea bird that makes a mess everywhere it goes." He smirked.

Osborn frowned. "That's what everyone else has come up with, too."

Nurinyan hovered over an apartment complex with units facing into a central courtyard. "Vadin's family has been in de area for centuries. If 'Gull' means anyt'ing, he will know." He landed the avi and put it in standby mode. "Room t'ree-twelve?"

Hollis nodded. "Right. It's in the south wing."

Nurinyan slid out, and Amaya took his place. He bolted up the concrete and iron steps three at a time to the top floor.

Hollis leaned over to watch for his partner. After a few

LIKE HERDING THE WIND

moments, Nurinyan, pistol in hand, hustled down the balcony ahead of Kirby and Susan, Kirby's charming, Japanese bride-to-be. Susan carried her own floral-print suitcase. The two men constantly checked every direction for signs of their attacker. When they came near, Hollis opened the door and took Susan's suitcase as Kirby helped her up. Amaya vacated the pilot's seat, and Nurinyan climbed in and took over as the pilot. Kirby accepted Amaya's hand up and sat in the remaining seat. The avi's wings extended with a hydraulic whine, and the ship lifted off.

Kirby leaned toward Hollis and whispered, "How's Sarge holding up?"

"Better than I would be."

Kirby nodded.

Hawk's Nest appeared on the horizon and grew larger as Las Palomas passed by below. When they arrived, Nurinyan brought the avi in for a perfect landing, but didn't retract the wings and power down until the hangar door had closed again. Kirby disembarked and helped Susan down. Hollis grabbed her suitcase and stepped out.

Kirby kissed Susan's cheek. "These are good people. You'll be safe here."

Tears glittered in her eyes. "Be careful."

"I'll keep him out of trouble." Hollis gripped her shoulder.

Ishe ran over, hooked Susan in a one-armed embrace, and took the bag. "Hi, I am Ishe. Come wit' me, and I will show you to your room." She chattered like a gaggle of girls at a slumber party all the way down the hall.

Hollis shook his head. "Either that'll be just what Susan needs to keep her mind off worrying for you, or she'll be ready for a jacket with wraparound sleeves by the time we get back."

Kirby chuckled. "Susan's pretty adaptable."

URUSHALON

They jogged to the briefing room. Inside, Vadin arranged a half-dozen chairs in a ring. When Hollis sat, the chair wobbled. He extended his arms to check his balance, but stayed steady.

Rather than draw another chair into the ring, Amaya perched on the makeshift table near one wall. "Orinyay, Ishe tells me we received the information requested from Woran Kishay."

"Yes, *Kiand*. Dere are eleven *kiandarai* who died, but de relatives kept de equipment." She handed Amaya a paper. "I contacted de nearest relative for ten of dem and dey say everyt'ing was neutralized. I could not reach de last. De *kiandarai* of dat city agreed to track him down and find out what became of his dad's equipment, but I t'ink I know. De last relative is a cousin of Maran Leonan. T'ree of Maran Leonan's brot'ers are confirmed overseas, either in jail or on parole. De last is Wylin Leonan, ex-military. He and Maran were last known to be here in Woran Oldue. Dey worked on a fishing boat until dey were fired a mont' and a half ago."

"So, Wylin Leonan is our boy." Osborn paced away from the group then turned back and looked at Amaya. "Any way we can find out if he's dealt with his grief?"

"Why would that matter?" Hollis asked.

"If he hasn't, then he will be even more unstable and possibly more violent."

Nurinyan shrugged. "I could contact my brot'er. He has access to a database dat tells him which clients have been to see which professional guides."

Amaya nodded. "That's a start. It wouldn't tell us if he used a friend for a guide."

"He's been on the run since before Maran's death." Osborn shook his head. "I doubt he's keeping contact with sympathetic friends."

Hollis leaned his elbow on his knee and his chin on his palm for a moment then sat up straight again. "Are there signs

LIKE HERDING THE WIND

we can pick up on from a distance?"

Amaya looked at her hand. "Constant tremor and chill are the only ones that are consistent. Other than that, inconsistent behavior, talking to people who aren't there, paranoia, things of that sort."

Hollis couldn't remember Amaya's hands being so rock-steady as they were now. Had she been grieving for someone?

"So, we need to find where he's keeping Esther." Amaya retrieved a huge map from a stack in the corner. "We have two clues about her location. We've seen Wylin flying in from the coast or back toward it, but the border guard has never seen him cross into Woran Oldue. Second, Wylin left a remembrance token at Ed's house. 'If you want her back, meet me at the Gull before sunset.' What is the significance of 'Gull?'"

She spread the map out on the floor in the middle of the room and knelt, using her knee to hold one corner. Hollis squatted and pinned down another corner. Vadin crouched next nearby.

"He came in from de coast, and he retreated to de coast." Vadin pointed to a barrier island. "It has to be Woran Juvay."

Hollis looked closer at the map but saw nothing written on the long, thin island paralleling the coast. "'Juvay' has something to do with seagulls?"

Amaya nodded. "Woran Juvay means Seagull Enclave."

"It's here." Vadin pointed to the same barrier island that had nothing marked on it. "When I was young–"

Nurinyan snorted. "You still are."

"Ishe is younger. Anyway, my grandparents told me stories of deir first home. It was on a barrier island." Vadin pointed to the map. "Here. A hurricane destroyed de city. Few survived. Instead of rebuilding on de island, dey formed Woran Oldue."

Osborn looked closer at the map. "I wondered why it was

URUSHALON

called 'Second Enclave.'"

Vadin nodded. "Now Woran Juvay is only sand, grass, and ruins."

"Is there any way to come in undetected?"

"I do not t'ink so. It is very flat."

Amaya sat back on her heels. "We need to be quick. We'll run out of daylight in a few hours." She rolled up the map. "Orinyay, do the best you can with the call volume. If it gets too busy, see if Falcon's Wing or Wolf's Teeth can take some calls on the Woran Oldue side of the Buffer Zone. Contact them directly. Do not go through the dispatch center."

Hollis followed her back to the hangar. He climbed up into the avicopter and took a seat. Kirby settled next to him and Osborn sat behind him. Nurinyan, in the pilot's chair, flipped labeled switches. The avicopter groaned through start-up while Amaya spoke to Orinyay before hopping into the shotgun seat.

The hangar door rumbled up, the avi's wings extended, and the craft lifted off.

Nurinyan spoke Eshuvani to someone over his comm system, and Hollis stared out the window at the grassland zooming by. Grasses and juniper shrubs gave way to a sandy beach which in turn gave way to the bay.

Nurinyan glanced back. "My brot'er says dere is no record dat Wylin ever used a professional guide."

Osborn leaned forward between the seats. "So we don't know if he's dealt with his grief."

"You are correct."

Nurinyan brought the avi around to the northern tip of the island and flew down the center. Hollis watched out his side of the avi, scanning for a camp or some sign of Wylin.

"There." Kirby pointed. "That guy up ahead."

Nurinyan nodded. "I see him."

LIKE HERDING THE WIND

He brought the avicopter down on the beach.

Wylin stood on the top of a dune with the old dart pistol in one hand and a bare-toothed grin on his face. He wore a gray leather jacket in spite of the sweltering heat, and his hands were shaking.

URUSHALON

Chapter Fourteen

Osborn opened the avi's door before Nurinyan settled the ship on the beach.

Hollis caught his arm. "Easy, Ed. You go charging in there like your own marine platoon, and you're likely to get us all killed."

Osborn sighed. "Yeah, you're right. Sorry."

He stepped out onto a flat stretch of beach above the line of driftwood and bivalve shells marking the high tide line. The barrier island paralleled the mainland coast and stretched northeast and southwest from where they stood. Dunes rippled the landscape, and tufts of knee-high grass broke up the monotony. A hundred yards away stood a ragged-edged arc of concrete, the first reminder of Woran Juvay.

Amaya exited the avi and set her backpack next to the landing strut.

Osborn stepped past Amaya and said in Eshuvani. "We're here, Wylin. Where is Esther?"

"Safe enough. For now."

Some answer. Ed frowned. "What exactly do you want?"

"I want Maran back."

"Maran is dead." *Which you know because that's why you killed Sumner, took Esther, and put Amaya in the hospital.*

Wylin scowled and fingered the trigger on his pistol. "You wanted me to think that! Even down to faking a news report of the execution. All lies!"

"What's the story?" Hollis asked.

Amaya translated.

Wylin's ears went red. "You're hiding him somewhere. I've heard him. Seen him!"

Kirby whistled. "This guy's on the express train to Loonyville."

Nurinyan tilted his head to one side. "Where is dat?"

Amaya smiled. "He means Wylin's star is running out of hydrogen."

"Oh, definitely. Listen, dere are five of us and only one of him. Why can we not rush him?"

Amaya shook her head. "Don't be too–"

"Stop it!" Wylin bared his teeth and aimed the pistol at them. "Shut up! None of your human talk. You're trying to trick me again."

Osborn's pulse raced. He held up both hands and spoke in Eshuvani. "All right. All right. Take it easy, but we can't turn Maran over to you. He's dead."

"No!" He aimed the pistol at Amaya. "She shot him after he surrendered, and he's being held prisoner even now."

Nurinyan edged his way around to the left.

"Don't!" Wylin spun toward the *kiala*. "Get back with the others. Only I know where Esther is. Either you cooperate, or she'll die before you find her."

Osborn, wide-eyed, glanced at Amaya, and indicated Nurinyan with a nod.

URUSHALON

"You will take no action without my orders, *Kiala.*" Amaya frowned at Nurinyan.

Nurinyan nodded and rejoined them.

Osborn bit his upper lip. He refocused on the lunatic in front of him. "Why do you think we're holding Maran prisoner?"

"He told me so. Every time I see him, he tells me."

"Where did you see him?"

The tremor accelerated in both frequency and amplitude, making the barrel of the gun dance around and fail to keep a bead on any of them. "Here! Right here! I saw him right here! As close as you are now. You're holding him prisoner. He said so."

Oh yeah, you're grieving all right. "If you're right, and we have him in jail, how could he have been here?"

"You're trying to trick me again. It won't work."

Ed took a step forward, showing both hands empty. "Wylin, your brother was executed for attempting to kill a peace officer."

Amaya nodded. "I provided the testimony and heard the sentence pronounced."

The tremor quit as Wylin tensed.

"Get ready," Nurinyan said in English. "He will attack soon."

Wylin sighted his pistol on Nurinyan. "I told you, no human talk if you want the woman back. You took my brother away. I want him released here. Now."

Osborn shook his head. "He's gone, Wylin. You–"

Amaya gripped his shoulder and stepped past, whispering, "This sparring is getting us nowhere." She drew a deeper breath. "Hear me, Wylin. Maybe we do have your brother, but that's hardly our fault. You left him alone."

"I did not!"

LIKE HERDING THE WIND

She edged nearer. "You did. He left the car to escape on foot, and you went on without him. You could hardly expect us to leave the lad alone in the world. You were supposed to take care of him."

What are you doing? He's too unstable to goad like that. Osborn reached for her as she took another step toward Wylin.

Wylin growled. "I did! I did take care of him!"

She shook her head and continued on toward him. "You left him. You were more concerned about protecting yourself than taking care of your little brother. He counted on you, Wylin. You let him down. If Maran isn't with you now, it's your own fault."

"Shut up! Shut up!" He pulled the trigger four times.

The first dart whistled past them and embedded in the nose of the avicopter.

Osborn dropped into a crouch and shielded his head with his arms while the other three darts whizzed by. Wylin growled and pulled the trigger again, but the gun clicked, and he tried twice more before he opened a pouch on his belt. Bearing his teeth, he shoved the gun into its holster. Wylin shrieked and charged at Amaya.

She kicked his leg out from under him and sent him sprawling face down in the sand. Amaya spun and grabbed one of Wylin's arms, but he whirled around, tossed her onto her back, and drew a shellfish knife, raising it over his head.

Osborn gasped and charged forward, but Kirby passed him and caught Wylin's wrist. Wylin twisted loose a moment before Osborn caught a handful of Wylin's shirt. When, the suspect swung the knife, Osborn jumped back. Wylin turned and ran inland.

Amaya rolled onto her shoulders and pushed off, landing on her feet. She ran after him, closing the distance.

Osborn followed, but she and Wylin outdistanced him, disappearing over the crest of a dune. Within seconds,

URUSHALON

Nurinyan passed Osborn in full pursuit.

Ahead, an avicopter hummed through start up.

Not this time! Osborn ran faster.

He reached the top of the dune, where the green avi sat in a depression, its wings extended; its doors hanging open. Amaya yanked Wylin out of the avi and sent him sprawling in the sand. She stood between him and the avicopter, as Osborn ran down the dune.

Wylin charged at Amaya. The shellfish knife in Wylin's hand glinted in the sunlight.

Amaya stepped aside and caught Wylin's hand, but he wrenched it free and kicked her in the gut. She reeled back, slammed into the extended wing and then fell flat.

Osborn's chest tightened in sympathy. Nurinyan reached the bottom of the depression and drew his pistol.

"Wait!" Osborn reached for Nurinyan.

Three darts hit Wylin's leg as he climbed into the avicopter, causing him to collapse and fall backward into the sand.

Nurinyan smiled, powered down his gun, and holstered it. "Got him!"

He ran to Wylin and secured him with the figure eight plastic loops of Eshuvani handcuffs.

Osborn squatted next to Amaya. "Are you okay?"

She rolled onto her back and sat up, breathing hard. "I think so." She rubbed her abdomen. "He is particularly strong. A charging bull might not hit so hard."

Nurinyan grinned. "Well, don't worry. He's out."

"What do you mean?" Amaya twisted around to face him, glaring. "Tell me, *Kiala*. Exactly how do we convince Wylin to tell us where he's hidden Esther if you've driven him into unconsciousness?"

Nurinyan struck his forehead with his fist. "I didn't think

about that."

"I recall instructing you to take no action without orders." She bolted to her feet. "Do you suppose I might have had a reason for that?"

"I'm sorry, Amaya. I-I just..."

She wobbled and threw a hand to the side to check her balance.

Osborn caught her and helped her sit back down. "You wait here. I'll get your kit."

He took two steps toward their own avi before Hollis and Kirby crested the dune at a jog. Kirby had Amaya's backpack on.

Osborn met them and took two nutrition bars from a pouch on the side of the backpack. On the way back, he checked the wrappers. One apple and one berry. Amaya preferred the apple kind, so Nurinyan would have to deal with the berry. He tossed the berry nutrition bar at Nurinyan and crouched next to Amaya.

Peeling off the foil wrapper, he handed her the bar. "Here you go."

Kirby and Hollis joined them.

Hollis indicated Wylin with a nod. "He say where he stashed her?"

"No," Osborn answered in English, then glared at Nurinyan.

Nurinyan pressed a fist to his forehead. "I am sorry. I did not t'ink."

"Umhm. You're young." Amaya finished the nutrition bar. "You have potential. Until you have experience, follow orders. For now, watch him. Once you have rested, take the prisoner to the avi. If he comes back to himself, contact me."

Nurinyan looked at Wylin and frowned. "Why don't we just—"

URUSHALON

Amaya glared at him.

He sighed. "Right. I will watch de prisoner."

Osborn wiped his face with his handkerchief. "Now what do we do? We can't wait for those darts to wear off."

Hollis leaned on the side of the avi, pushed back off, and rubbed his arm. "Man, that thing's hot. Can you give Wylin a stimulant or something?"

Amaya shook her head. "That would make him alert, but cloud his thinking even more than it already is. We'll have to start searching the island." She tapped a code on her comm crystal.

"Orinyay."

"Amaya. Are you on a call?"

"Yes. An avicopter crashed in Woran Oldue on de highway nort' from Las Palomas. Huge mess. You have Esther?"

"No. Wylin is in custody, and we're beginning the search. I'll contact you when we're finished."

"Message received."

Amaya rubbed her forehead. "We know he's not settled north of us. We came in from that direction and saw nothing."

Kirby shrugged. "Camouflage."

"Possibly, but if you're in a spaceship and a drop of water hits your nose, your first thought shouldn't be 'thunderstorm.'"

"Sorry, what?"

Osborn looked up at Kirby. "Check the obvious solution first."

"Oh."

"Why don't Hollis, Kirby, and I get going?" Osborn looked off to the south. "You can catch up once you're rested."

LIKE HERDING THE WIND

Amaya drew a deep breath and blew it out. "If we can avoid any more flat-out sprints and hand-to-hand combat, I can go now."

"You're sure you're ready?"

"I'm fine now, dear one."

"You need some water."

"When the time comes, the sterile water in my backpack will do." Amaya stood and took her pack from Kirby.

"How 'bout we use an avicopter to speed our search?" Hollis pointed to Wylin's stolen avi.

"No good," Nurinyan shook his head. "Our insane friend here parked dis far away for a reason."

Kirby shrugged. "For all we know, he thinks his brother is sleeping in the camp and parked out here so he wouldn't wake him."

Amaya grimaced and studied Nurinyan for a moment. "You think there are noise-triggered traps?"

"We know he has training wit' de military." Nurinyan nodded. "Dey have such t'ings."

"Then we're on foot," Osborn said.

"Let's go." Amaya walked backwards for a few steps. "We'll form a line and start searching. Watch where you walk."

Osborn looked at the sun and then at his watch. *Still a couple more hours of daylight.*

They dispersed along a line and kept a slow pace toward the first of the ruins. Osborn stopped, rubbed his chin, and turned to look the way they came. He used the sun to get a general compass direction and studied the terrain.

Hollis came over. "Whaddya got, Ed?"

Osborn shielded his eyes with his hand. "When he took off, he was running pretty much due south. It's not as flat this way. If he'd meant to escape, wouldn't he have gone where

URUSHALON

the ground was more level?"

Kirby nodded. "Path of least resistance."

"Right. I think there's something he wanted to get to."

Amaya turned one hand upward. "Possibly, but he may have run this way because he was hallucinating."

"Maybe."

"Continue the search pattern. I'll strike off to the south and see if there's anything of note."

"Watch yourself."

"Always, dear one." Amaya got a bearing from the sun and walked away from them.

Osborn gestured for Kirby and Hollis to extend the line a little further, then started forward.

He walked slowly, checking the ground and the horizon, for what seemed like eternity. Osborn checked his watch. *Only ten minutes?* He groaned.

A gray form to his right caught his attention, Amaya passing one of the ruins. As she did, a huge, spatula-shaped contraption sprang out of the sand, staying rooted on the handle end. It hurled cedar spikes as long as his forearm, and one of them drove through Amaya's arm and kept going as she dove into the sand.

Osborn's guts turned to lead. He ran, skidding to a stop when he reached Amaya. Kirby and Hollis were right behind him. She pushed herself up, but didn't move like she was hurt, and he didn't see any blood.

He grabbed her by both shoulders. "Are you all right?"

She poked her finger through two broomstick-diameter holes in her sleeve. "He installed a new cooling system in my shirt, but he missed me."

He sighed. *Too close. Way too close. Please, God, don't let her get hurt by this lunatic.*

Hollis leaned closer to examine the hole. "Wow. From

LIKE HERDING THE WIND

where I stood, that hunk of wood looked like it went through you."

Amaya stood and brushed herself off. "I was fairly sure it would."

Osborn accepted her hand up. "Did you find anything?"

Amaya nodded. "His camp. This way."

They moved inland and came across another crumbling wall of concrete. Traces of splotchy, blue paint decorated the ten-foot-long, knee-high wall.

Something clicked.

A solid pull on Osborn's arm threw him sideways. He landed with a thud and rolled downhill a short ways. He rose up onto his side and spat sand.

"Are you two okay?" Amaya asked.

"Yeah, I'm fine," Kirby said.

"Mark?"

"Okay, I think. Where'd we lose Ed?"

"Over here." Osborn pushed himself up. A twinge in his right shoulder urged caution. He stretched and moved it through the range of motion. *That'll be sore in the morning.*

"There he is." Hollis jogged over. "Ed, you okay?"

"Yeah, I'm all right. What happened?"

Hollis offered a hand up. "I found a tripwire. It launched some sticks at us."

Osborn took Hollis' hand, stood, and dusted himself off. "Who gave me the flight lesson?"

Amaya smiled. "That was my doing. I was a little overzealous, I think."

"A little, but thanks." He stretched out his shoulder again. "We should stay away from the ruins."

"Yes, and be more careful. The closer we get, the more dense the traps may become." She jogged to the top of a dune

URUSHALON

and pointed.

He joined her and sighted along her arm. They overlooked a shallow depression. Five brown canvas tents had been pitched in a neat arc to the south. A pile of driftwood and cedar sat next to a fire pit built of blue-flecked stones.

Osborn nodded toward the tents. "Anything in those?"

Amaya shook her head. "I don't know. Given our friend's penchant for surprises, I didn't want to go down there without someone to keep watch."

He put a hand on Hollis' shoulder. "You two check around the right edge of the rim. Amaya and I will head left."

Osborn followed Amaya until they were even with the corner of the first tent. He turned sideways to slide down the embankment. A firm grip on his arm hauled him back.

"Don't be too hasty." She walked a few feet away to a half-height, blue-speckled wall and picked up a twelve-inch-square, six-inch-deep rock. Her whole upper body shook from the effort.

He rushed to her and took it from her arms. "You're supposed to be resting."

"When Esther is safe, I'll rest." She pushed her wedding bracelet into her sleeve.

This scenario is nothing like how you lost your family, but I think I'm finally starting to understand. "What'd you have in mind for this rock?"

She nodded toward the tent. "Better for it to find the traps before we do."

Osborn led the way back. He set the rock on the edge and gave it a shove, but it only slid a couple of feet before it stopped.

Amaya chuckled. "Another brilliant idea fails upon contact with reality."

Keeping a hold on Amaya's hand, Osborn went down to

LIKE HERDING THE WIND

one knee and gave the rock a kick. It slid another couple of feet.

He accepted Amaya's help back up. "We'll follow it down."

Across the depression, Hollis and Kirby reached the bottom and headed for the tent.

Osborn frowned. "With a nut like Wylin, I can't tell if I'm being cautious or paranoid."

"If you're going to be wrong about something, it's always better to expect danger than to expect safety."

He side-stepped down the dune, following the path the rock took.

That was safe enough.

Amaya wobbled.

Osborn caught her as her legs buckled and sat her down on the rock. "It's okay. I gotcha."

She leaned against him. "I'm sorry, Ed."

I knew you should have rested longer. He hugged her. "Hey, in this heat, not even humans have unlimited stamina." He slid her backpack off and fished out another nutrition bar. "Eat this. Get some rest. It'll take us a few minutes to search the tents. We'll see how you feel then."

She accepted the bar and nodded. Once she had the foil open, Ed went to the first tent and tugged the zipper upward. He drew back the flap and peeked in. The air in the tent was hotter, more humid, and smelled of plastic. Camping gear, still in its packaging, made neat floor-to-ceiling stacks. Osborn counted eight kerosene stoves, an even dozen lanterns, two more tents, and several coils of rope.

"You planning on company or on staying awhile?" He went to the next tent and found more of the same. He turned to go and found Hollis standing in the entry.

"We found the one he was living in." Hollis stepped back

URUSHALON

and pointed. "The other two were fishing tackle."

Osborn followed Hollis to the middle tent. It had a camp cot with a few flat mattresses and a sleeping bag, a pile of camouflage green and brown clothes, and a few storage boxes. A silver *kiandara* collar tab with the blue comm crystals, a couple of knives, and underwater breathing gear were arranged on the cot. Kirby crouched next to one of the storage boxes.

Osborn picked up the collar tabs. "Where did you find this?"

Kirby glanced back over his shoulder. "On top of this crate. Where's Amaya?"

"Resting."

"She okay?" Hollis asked.

Osborn nodded. "Pushed herself too hard. She's not going to like it, but she's got to rest. Those nutrition bars are only short-term fixes otherwise." He turned the silver collar tabs over in his hand then looked at the rest of the gear on the bed. The knives showed specks of rust near the hilt and decaying tape on the grips. The underwater gear was bulkier than the current models, and the plastic had yellowed and cracked.

He returned a critical eye to the collar tabs. "What were these doing in Wylin's possession?"

Hollis leaned closer. "What's the matter?"

"These shouldn't be here." Osborn stepped closer to the door flap and tilted the tabs toward the sun. The underside had numbers stamped onto the metal.

"Why not? He seems to have everything else Amaya mentioned as *kiandarai* gear."

"Yeah. That's the problem. These are new technology. I was just out of college when Amaya got her first set. If all of his other gear is so old, where'd this come from?"

Kirby twisted toward them. "Sarge, I found something." He held up a cardboard-bound notepad.

LIKE HERDING THE WIND

Osborn slipped the anachronistic collar tabs into his shirt pocket then took the notepad from Kirby and flipped through it. Dates were scrawled across the tops of the pages. The handwriting remained strong and steady until a few weeks ago, but then it degenerated until the most recent entry looked no better than a kid's scribble. "A journal of some kind. From about the time we came under siege." He handed Kirby the notebook and collar tabs. "Take these to Amaya. Tell her we need to know where these tabs came from and what the journal has to say. Don't let her follow us. She needs the rest."

Kirby nodded. "I'll keep an eye on her."

Osborn patted the young officer's shoulder. "Thanks."

He led Hollis around to the tents Osborn hadn't seen, then up the trail Hollis and Kirby had taken to get down into the depression. They walked along the ridge and stopped at the southern edge. Twenty yards away, a small, gray canvas tent stood between the flotsam marking the high tide and the leading edge of the lapping waves a foot past the Gulf-side of the tent.

Hollis shielded his eyes with his hand. "He wouldn't be that obvious, would he?"

"It can't be that easy," Osborn said. "There must be traps or something. Watch where you step."

"Yeah, but if she's in there, we may not have time to go slow. Tide's coming in."

Osborn slid down the windward face of the ridge. Hollis joined him, and they walked toward the gray tent. A stiff breeze blew in from the Gulf. A heavy petroleum smell wrinkled his nose. The odor took Osborn back decades to his father's workshop, well away from the house. An old camping lantern had needed a few adjustments.

"Kerosene," Osborn said.

Hollis nodded. "Which makes me think he's set up something incendiary."

URUSHALON

"Yeah, it's like the lady or the tiger gag." Osborn blew out a breath.

Hollis snorted. "'Cept all the doors are booby-trapped."

"Right. Follow in my footsteps but stay well back." Osborn stepped forward.

Hollis caught his arm. "And why do you get to play minesweeper?"

"I've met both of my kids. Have you?"

Hollis frowned. "Just be careful."

Osborn's gut tightened. His skin tingled. *All right, Wylin, what did you do?*

He threaded his way forward, stepping gingerly. At any moment, the ground would give way, or some tripwire would launch cedar spikes out of the sand, or some cobbled-together Bouncing Betty would send what was left of him flying. Well, maybe that last was paranoia. Anti-personnel mines were not the usual way of Eshuvani, but, then again, neither was Wylin.

Faint rake marks marred the sand to his left. He knelt and used his pocket comb to scoop away some of the disturbed sand. The comb's teeth caught. A high-pitched whirring ripped the comb from his hand and tossed a straight-line plume of sand two feet in the air.

Osborn jerked his hand back and inspected the thin scrapes left by the teeth of the comb. "Whoa."

Hollis leaned over him. "You okay?"

"Yeah, sure. Watch for places where the sand's been raked." He stood.

"Right." Hollis nodded toward the tent. "Water's getting closer."

Osborn glanced that way. A wave came within a hand-length of the back of the tent. "I wish we could know for sure if she's even in there."

"I don't think he'd trap sand for no reason."

LIKE HERDING THE WIND

"Maybe." Osborn stood.

After studying the immediate terrain, he avoided another disturbed patch of beach and placed his heel first. When nothing jumped up at him, he transferred his weight.

Behind him, another loud whir preceded a thud. Hollis cried out in surprise, and Osborn whirled around. Hollis lay on his back, his right leg stretched out and the left bent at the knee.

"What'd you do?" Osborn asked.

"You must have stepped over one I stepped in." He sat up, pulled out his pocket knife, and cut a thin fishing line near his ankle.

"You hurt?"

"Nah. If that's the worst of what he's throwing at us..." He picked himself up and dusted off.

Osborn wove his way forward, expecting each step to launch some kind of surprise at him. Each uneventful moment ratcheted up the acidic churning in his stomach. Far too easy. They'd reach the tent in a handful of steps. Was the tent a decoy, after all? Was Esther in mortal peril somewhere else while they wasted time here? He'd never forgive himself if he let Esther die while–

Wood cracked beneath his foot, and the ground gave way. He landed with a soupy plop, wrapped in rough, dark material. Cold water flooded in. He flailed, but couldn't find the edge of the cloth wrapped around him. His lungs ached.

A fierce grip seized his arm. Osborn wrenched away. His thrashing muscles burned and became sluggish. The material snaring him felt weighted. The firm hold on his arm returned. Osborn pulled to get away but his captor held fast. Cloth like sandpaper raked past him then came away from his head. Osborn coughed and spat gritty water until the fit subsided. Sand crunched in his teeth.

"Take it easy, Ed." Hollis steadied him. "Take it easy.

URUSHALON

You all right?"

"Yeah." He tried to clear the rasp from his throat. "Yeah. I think so. What happened?"

Hollis pointed overhead. "Ground moved. I heard a crack, you stepped aside, and then the ground kinda caved in. I got to the edge and found you wrapped in this tarp, fighting half of Satan's army trying to get loose, so I came in after you. We need to find a way out. Each wave coming in adds to the swamp."

Osborn accepted Hollis' help up. "Let's make sure Esther's not down here."

Hollis pointed. "This moat leads around both ways from here."

Osborn led the way through knee-high water. The shoulder-height ditch lined with blue-flecked bricks made a wide arc around the tent. Tarps buried in shallow sand were supported with thin pieces of wood dug into the edges of the pit.

When he reached the end, incoming waves eroded the end of the arc, bringing in water and soggy sand.

Osborn followed Hollis back around the other way and found the same thing on that side. They returned to the middle.

"Now what?" Hollis asked. "If we try climbing out, the wall will just come apart."

Osborn nodded. "Yeah, but we can make stairs or a ramp from these bricks. Leave a few feet of wall on each side and start gathering stones. We'll pile them here."

He went a few feet to his right and started moving the rocks over while Hollis worked from the other direction. When they had enough for the next step down from the top, they started building a makeshift stairway. The murky water had risen to his knees.

"Whatever you do, don't light a cigarette," Osborn said.

"Don't worry. I gave that up right after the first baby."

LIKE HERDING THE WIND

The water level grew with the approaching tide. Sand from the sections now missing their support walls make murky grit out of the water. Osborn stepped up onto the first step. It seemed steady enough. So did the next two, but when the fourth one wobbled, Osborn crouched slightly and extended his hands. Hollis held onto him. The bricks stopped moving, and Osborn hustled the rest of the way up.

He blew out a breath. "Made it." He knelt in the sand and stretched out his hand. "Your turn."

Hollis climbed up the stairs. The fourth step wobbled and Hollis tried to check his balance. Osborn reached for Hollis as the younger officer pitched over sideways into the water. He surfaced and wiped water and sand from his face.

"When the fire won't light, get another match," Osborn said.

Hollis raised an eyebrow. "Eshuvani idiom?"

"Umhm."

Hollis started up again and skipped the missing step. Osborn caught Hollis' hand and leaned back. Hollis ran up the rest of the way and stumbled to a stop. He fell flat next to Osborn. "That was fun."

Osborn smiled. "I could toss you back in if you want to try again."

Hollis shook his head. "Pass. My question is, how'd Wylin get out?"

"Jumped."

"That high?"

"Yep. You saw Amaya jump, kick off from a car's roof, then go another handful of feet higher. Think how well she might do if she had more time to prepare?"

Hollis shrugged. "I guess."

Osborn stood and pulled Hollis with him. A couple of easy steps later, and they were at the door of a six-foot by six-

URUSHALON

foot tent with a peaked roof, not terribly different from the ones in the campsite.

Osborn grimaced and tried waving his hand to clear the air. "Wow, that kerosene's potent."

"Ed? Ed, is that you?" Esther called.

"Esther, honey? It's me. Mark's with me. Where are you?"

"In a hole under the tent." She coughed. "It smells like gas down here."

"Hang on, honey. We'll get you out of there." Osborn reached for the zipper pull.

Hollis tugged his hand away and whispered, "Wait. He threatened we couldn't get to her in time." He drew his pocketknife and pushed the point through the canvas. After peeking in, he frowned, and backed away. "Have a look."

Osborn leaned closer and pulled the damp canvas apart. Light filtering through the canvas was no brighter than a moonlit night, but the shaft of light from the slit Hollis cut lit a stripe on the back of the tent and a stack of canisters marked "kerosene" piled next to boxes of shotgun shells.

He frowned, grabbed Hollis' arm, and whispered, "He's rigged it to blow or at least catch fire."

Hollis nodded. "Probably some sort of trigger mechanism attached to the zipper."

"Something that would generate a spark."

"Right."

Osborn ran his fingers through his damp hair. "So if we do nothing, the tide comes in and she drowns. If we try to go in there, the zipper generates a spark, which probably lights a fuse."

"Exactly. So, we make a new opening."

"Just big enough to see the whole picture."

Hollis nodded.

LIKE HERDING THE WIND

"Ed? Are you there?" Esther asked.

Osborn crouched. "We're here, honey. Hang on, okay?"

Hollis cut a larger hole with his blade. "Esther, above you, is there a hard surface like a piece of wood or metal?"

"I don't know what's above me. I can't see anything, and I can't reach, but the walls feel like rock."

Hollis widened the new opening He leaned in. "Take a look."

Osborn lay prone and looked at the interior. A pair of matches were taped to the inside of the tent above the zipper pull, which had a striker panel attached to it. A long, thin piece of cord ran from there to the pile of kerosene and shells. Osborn reached in and ripped out the matches. He handed them back to Hollis.

Osborn shook his head. "Nice guy, Wylin."

Hollis set the matches well away from the tent. He expanded the new opening from floor to ceiling. "Esther, how big is that hole?"

"Um, about two feet square, and deep enough I can't reach the top. Water's coming in."

Osborn leaned through the opening and pressed several places as far as he could reach. The floor wasn't solid enough for wood or metal under the canvas, but it wasn't hollow either. His head swam with the odor of the kerosene.

He backed out and stepped away from the tent for some cleaner air.

"Anything?" Hollis asked.

"Not yet. I need a stick. Arms aren't long enough." Osborn returned to the moat and tugged a broken piece of one-by-two from the flotsam at the edge.

The board was longer than he was tall, but it'd do. After a deep breath, he returned to the tent and prodded the ground wherever it was clear of kerosene and boxes of shotgun cartridges.

In the center of the tent he pushed on the canvas. Instead of the slight squish of sand, he got a loud tap of wood on rock. When he tapped harder, the stick vibrated. He smiled and reached a little further, the canvas dented downward with a dull pop.

"What's that?" Esther asked.

"That's me. I found your hiding place. Have you out in a jiffy." Osborn tapped the ground between the side of the tent and the hole then backed away. "Found it." He tossed the stick aside. "Hand me your knife."

When he held out his hand, Hollis slapped the hilt of the pocketknife into Osborn's hand.

He slid through the opening, crawled to the edge of the hole, and knocked the stone all the way around the square hole to find the perimeter. Osborn cut the canvas three sides around, and the flap fell downward. Esther stood in the bottom of a waterlogged hole lined with blue-flecked bricks. She leaned against the stone wall and pressed one hand to the side of her head.

Osborn reached toward her. "Take my hand honey. Walk up the side of the wall while I pull, okay?"

She stretched upward and wrapped her thin fingers around his wrist. As tiny as she was, his arm and shoulder muscles strained to pull her up. Hollis came in behind him and caught Esther by the arms as she came up high enough. Once she was clear, Osborn escorted her outside and pulled her into a tight embrace. She fell against him.

"Are you okay, honey?" He adjusted his hold on her. "Did that lunatic hurt you?"

"He pushed me around a lot and was none too gentle about it. I have a headache, and I'm pretty dizzy."

"Amaya's at Wylin's camp. Let's get you there."

LIKE HERDING THE WIND

Chapter Fifteen

Amaya drew a deep breath and opened her eyes. Robert sat nearby on the rock she and Ed had used to check for traps.

She sat up and brushed the sand off of her clothes. "I hadn't meant to sleep."

Robert shook his head. "You've only been out ten minutes. Osborn and Hollis went on."

"Without you?" She started to stand up.

He caught her arm. "It's not safe to leave anyone alone, and you weren't up for travel. They'll be all right."

"I suppose." She settled again, pulled a sterile water pouch from her backpack, cut off the corner, and drank half of it before passing the rest to Robert.

He handed her a book and a set of silver collar tabs. "We found these in one of Wylin's tents."

"What's he doing with a comm system?" The silver tabs were *kiandara* issue based on the configuration of the swirls, but the only crystals were the four dark blues for the comm. She turned the tabs over and found the ID number. "Not standard gear of forty-five years ago."

"They're not available to the public?"

She shook her head. "No more than your badge would be."

He picked up one and turned it in his hand. "Sarge asked if you would find out where those are from."

"Is this just a ruse to keep me from following him?" She smiled.

Robert laughed. "Not going to answer that."

"Mmhm. Well, I'll play along with your conspiracy. For now." Amaya started tapping Orinyay's code on the blue crystals but stopped. Orinyay was sorting out the highway accident. She'd be on that for a while yet. Pavwin would have a data analyst at Falcon's Wing. What was his code?

Amaya held two of her dark crystals and mentally switched to Eshuvani.

"Dispatch."

"Amaya Ulonya *Kiand*. Connect me to Pavwin Vueltu *Kiand* of *Vueltiya Ens Kiandarai* please."

"Standby." A relay clicked.

"Pavwin."

"Amaya. I'm involved in a rescue operation and found something incongruous. Can I borrow your data analyst? Mine is engaged in a call."

"I'm the analyst, Amaya. What do you have?"

"Our adversary with the old gear has a set of silver collar tabs." She turned the collar tabs over in her hand.

"Odd. Do you have the number?"

Amaya found the number stamped into the back. "Yes."

"Let me log into the database, and we'll look it up. Standby." His comm system relayed rapid fire typing. "All right, I'm in. Let me have the number."

Amaya read the number to him then listened as he read it

back to her. "That's it."

The keyboard clicked as he typed commands into his terminal then paused. Pavwin mumbled something, then drew a breath. "Amaya, I have two positive matches. One in the disabled database and one in the active."

She frowned. "Recycled number?"

"Maybe." Keys clicked. "The active database lists Ianolin Simiala. There are a few such names here, all listed within the last few months." More keys clicked. "The number on your incongruous set was once registered to Orinyay Midorin."

Amaya's eyes went wide. "She has a set already."

"She's one of yours?"

"My analyst."

"The spare you're holding is listed as lost or stolen. In fact, there appears to be a rash of such losses within the same time frame."

"Standby, Pavwin." Amaya looked at Robert and switched to English. "Do you recall when the Eshuvani attacks on the police started?"

Robert blew out a breath and looked past her. "Yeah, yeah, March twelfth."

Amaya arched an eyebrow. "Good memory."

He chuckled. "It was the day before Susan's birthday. I had to change our date when I was volunteered to cover part of the injured officer's shift."

She nodded and spoke Eshuvani. "Pavwin, that timespan matches up well with the assault on Las Palomas Police."

"Hmm. I don't like the odor this produces. Let me look into it further."

"All right, Pavwin. Thank you for chasing that down."

"The curiosity would get the better of me otherwise. Amaya, Orinyay may be innocent of all wrongdoing, but..."

URUSHALON

Amaya frowned. *No, she can't be involved, but better to assume she is and be wrong...* "I'll keep an eye on her."

"Good. I'll see you in the morning."

"Message received."

The connection severed with a click.

Amaya stared at the sand in front of her and leaned her chin on her steepled fingers. This had to be some sort of elaborate frame. A new set of collar tabs could have been dubbed with the number of her lost set, but then how had the tabs been assigned to this Ianolin Simiala? Was that even a real person? How had the tabs ended up in Wylin's possession? As an analyst, Orinyay had the right to access and modify the database, but that didn't make her guilty. Who belonged to the other unrealistic names?

"Amaya, what's wrong?" Robert asked.

She shook her head to dispel her mental meandering. "Forgive me."

How much could she tell him without unfairly placing blame or suspicion? He was a professional. Perhaps she should trust that he wouldn't rush to declare Orinyay a traitor without evidence. She tossed the tabs a couple of inches into the air and caught them, then relayed Pavwin's findings to Robert.

"That's weird." Robert squinted into the distance. "Maybe Orinyay or this Ianolin Simiala guy can shed light on this."

"If he exists." Amaya frowned. "Ianolin Simiala is the Eshuvani equivalent of 'John Smith.'"

"That would mean..." Robert paused, his brow furrowed. "...that there's someone inside the system with access to the records who's equipping nuts like Wylin."

Amaya sighed. "I'd hoped Wylin was a weird outlier." Her collar chimed, and she pushed one of the crystals. "Amaya."

"Nurinyan. Wylin is coming around. Should I interrogate

LIKE HERDING THE WIND

him or bring him to you?"

"Standby." She slung her backpack over her shoulder and stood. "Robert, would you know which way Ed and Mark went?"

He hopped to his feet and led the way out of the depression. "This way."

She followed. At the top of the dune, he turned south and pointed. Amaya followed his hand. A gray canvas tent ringed by a semicircular moat sat at the edge of the water. A line of footprints went from the camp all the way to the moat.

Were they still in the tent? Caught in the flooding moat? Had they followed the exact path back that they'd taken to go out? A sudden chill raced through Amaya, but she shrugged it off and darted past Robert. "I don't see them."

He came even with her. "Wait up."

She reached the southern edge and stopped. Ed carried Esther up the dune with Mark supporting Ed from behind. Esther rested in her husband's arms, but other than an egg-sized knot on her forehead, she had no obvious injuries.

Amaya smiled. "Nurinyan, we have Esther. Keep the prisoner contained. We'll be on our way back shortly. Consider ways to get everyone where they belong safely without exposing the victim to the kidnapper again."

"Message received." The comm clicked off.

She met Ed at the top of the dune and lifted Esther from his arms. "What happened?"

"She took a whack on the head and some rough handling. A little woozy, too, but I suspect that's from the kerosene dousing that tent."

Amaya nodded. "I'll assess and treat what I can out here. Talk to Robert about the collar tabs."

She carried Esther to the nearest tent and set her on the camp cot she found there.

URUSHALON

***

Amaya walked out of the Woran Oldue courthouse. Everyone's depositions were properly recorded and filed. That would keep Wylin in prison until his trial and probable execution in a few days. In the meantime, a grief counselor was on the way to be his guide if it wasn't already too late.

As Amaya left the courthouse, she scanned the area for the others. Ed's voice drew her attention to a few benches near a stone sculpture of a trio of unarmed, smiling Eshuvani who greeted armed, scowling humans. As usual, the artist had depicted humans as puny and paranoid toward the peaceable Eshuvani. The truth, although less flattering, would have been more interesting.

Esther sat on a bench flanked by Ed and Nurinyan, who kept a close eye on her. The jumpsuit the court had given her to change into was a drab brown and it hung on her small frame like a tent, but at least it didn't smell of kerosene. Robert and Mark stood nearer to the statue as Ed spoke. Amaya headed toward them and listened.

"My history classes suggested the Eshuvani landing party was armed for battle and aggressive." Esther gestured to the statues. "This looks exactly the opposite."

"And neither account is accurate. When I was in middle school, Amaya took me to an Eshuvani museum that had won some awards for being totally honest. The humans were armed and scared, true enough, but—"

"Oh, no doubt about that. Even today, I'm pretty sure I'd panic if some building-sized ship crashed in my backyard," Mark said.

"Yes, but the Eshuvani were also armed." Amaya joined them. She walked up to the statue and pointed to the hip of one of the Eshuvani. "Pistol-like weapons were hidden here under their tunics. A few managed to slip their guns out but kept them concealed until they were sure of the humans' intentions."

LIKE HERDING THE WIND

"So how'd that not end up a Medieval version of the OK Corral?" Robert asked.

"A clergyman of some sort." Ed looked at the humans in the statue and shook his head. "Not shown here. Monk, priest, we're not sure what he was, but he talked the humans down and when they backed off, the Eshuvani also stood down."

Esther blinked hard and rubbed her forehead before she smiled, a little strained, up at Ed.

"So, I'm guessing they didn't kidnap the priest." Mark said.

Nurinyan hopped up onto a bench and perched on the back. He rested the arm closest to Esther on his knee, but placed no weight on it. "No, not'ing like dat."

"The record isn't clear, but that's unlikely." Ed shook his head. "He probably came back voluntarily to teach them how to find food, how to speak the local language, things like that."

"It is said he was de first *urushalon*." When Ed drew a breath to speak, Nurinyan held up one hand. "Speculation, yes, but it would explain much."

"Is that museum still there?" Esther clasped Ed's hand.

Ed turned to Amaya.

She smiled. "Oh yes, and they have been gradually adding to the timeline since our visit."

"We'll bring the kids there when we go." Ed stepped closer to Amaya. "Are we all set here?"

"Yes. Your depositions are all properly filed. I will have to return on the trial date to represent them, but the rest of you are finished."

Nurinyan hopped down from the bench. "We should discuss history later. I t'ink it is best to get Esther home to rest."

When Ed helped her up, she clutched his arm tighter but only for a moment.

URUSHALON

"Yes, then you can drop off Mark. He's only a few blocks away." Ed slipped his wife's hand in the crook of his elbow and picked up the plastic bag containing her own clothes.

"Then we'll get Susan, and you'll take us home?" Robert suggested.

"That will work fine," Amaya said.

As they headed toward the cargo avicopter, Nurinyan hung back and caught Amaya's arm.

He waited until the others were several paces ahead and whispered in Eshuvani. "She seems a little unsteady. More than kerosene fumes, I think."

"She has a concussion, not a severe one, but she will be a little unsteady for a while. Ed knows what to do, and she'll see her regular physician in the morning."

Nurinyan blew out a breath. "Good. I was afraid it was something worse, but when you didn't do anything, I wasn't sure how to react."

They hustled and caught up a moment after the others arrived at the avicopter. After dropping off Ed and Esther and staying long enough to make sure she was situated, they left Mark in his backyard.

On the way back to Hawk's nest, Amaya turned her thoughts to confronting Orinyay. The issue of lost collar tabs in the possession of a criminal needed resolution. Questioning Orinyay could be a simple matter of curiosity. Perhaps Pavwin's research would settle the matter.

Another possibility nagged at her. Emyrin had assigned all of her staff before her arrival. He made no secret of how much he hated humans. What if he had sabotaged her personnel more than she already thought? Paranoia, almost certainly, but given the elaborate arrangements to hobble the station, was it unreasonable to think he had done more to her staff than load her with misfit kids?

Nurinyan brought the cargo hauler in for a landing in

LIKE HERDING THE WIND

front of the building. Amaya stepped out as Robert opened the rear door. He passed her the trauma kit then climbed down.

The station's main door opened. Ishe ran out and grabbed Amaya by both arms. "Where's Mark?"

"At home. Why?" Nurinyan asked.

Ishe whirled to face Nurinyan. "Las Palomas dispatch called here looking for him. His wife was attacked."

"Attacked?" Robert tensed and drew a sharp breath. "By who?"

"A bird of some kind. She is in de hospital."

"A bird?" Robert turned to Amaya. "Is there some idiom I'm not getting?"

Amaya looked past them and tried to come up with some kind of bird that would attack a person in a city. "All right, Ishe, slow down. Relay the message word for word as you received it."

Ishe blew out a breath. "A dispatcher called and asked for Mark."

"When?" Robert asked.

Ishe looked at her watch and counted on her fingers. "Fifteen minutes ago. I told de dispatcher Mark was wit' de rest of you going after Esther. De dispatcher said if I saw him, tell him to call his mot'er-in-law at de hospital in Austin. A stork visited his wife."

Robert laughed.

"What?" Ishe looked at Nurinyan. "If dey took her to de hospital, dis dumb stork hurt her, right?"

Amaya smiled and suppressed her own chuckle. "Not exactly. In some old human fiction, storks brought babies to expectant mothers."

Ishe put her hand on her hip. "Do you mean de dispatcher was trying to say dat Mark's wife delivered her baby?"

"That's right."

URUSHALON

Ishe groaned, rolled her eyes, and walked away. "I t'ought she was hurt by dis dumb stork."

"I'll call him when I get home," Robert said.

"Let's get you and Susan on the way." Nurinyan nodded toward the building.

Amaya followed them in. Ishe, sitting at the dispatch desk again, beckoned her over, then watched Nurinyan and Robert disappear down the hall.

Amaya perched on the edge of the dispatch desk. "What's wrong?"

Ishe spoke in Eshuvani. "Vadin and Orinyay got back from that huge wreck a little while ago."

Amaya waited for the rest of the story.

Tugging her closer, Ishe looked around. "He's not talking about it, but the wreck seems to have, you know, bothered him a lot."

Amaya nodded, recalling some of her more emotionally trying calls. "They do that sometimes. I'll talk to him."

Ishe pointed toward the briefing room. "He's in there."

"Thank you. And Orinyay? How's she?"

"I don't know." Ishe turned one hand toward the ceiling. "She went straight to her house without checking in."

Amaya looked toward the larger house at the end of the arc. "Her husband's home?"

"Yeah, I think so." Ishe glanced that way.

"All calls route to me for the rest of the night." Amaya started for the briefing room.

Ishe caught her arm. "You mean she's upset, too?"

Amaya nodded. "Most likely. I'll check on her later."

"Wow. Okay."

Amaya walked into the briefing room and secured the door. Vadin had lined several chairs up side by side and lain

LIKE HERDING THE WIND

across them. A clipboard sat on his chest. A damp track glistened from the corner of his eye to his ear. The smell of smoke lingered around him.

Amaya crouched next to him and rested a hand on his shoulder. "Vadin?"

He started and shrank away from her.

"I'm sorry." She brought a chair closer and sat. "I hear your last call was difficult. Tell me about it."

Vadin sat up and dried his eyes. "An avicopter crashed into the human highway through the enclave. It hit two cars directly and four others crashed with each other or barriers on the road's edge. Orinyay and I were assigned to help the paramedics extract and treat the injured humans."

Amaya nodded. "That's reasonable."

"Yes, and two of the cars had just the driver. One was only rattled, no injuries. He'd almost stopped when he hit the barrier. The other banged his head on the steering wheel and his knee on the control panel."

Dashboard, but we'll worry about vocabulary some other time.

"Three other cars had a couple people each. Various injuries, but nothing they won't recover from." Vadin's hands shook.

"And the last?"

"It–it caught fire, Amaya, and by the time–by the time fire suppression put it out, ev-ev-every—" He clenched his jaw and squeezed his eyes closed. The tremor spread.

She sat next to him and wrapped her arm around his shoulders. "Bring it into the open."

He nodded. "There were two adults and two kids pinned in the car. And they were all-all dead. We couldn't do anything for them." Vadin sobbed on her shoulder for minutes while the tremor faded.

URUSHALON

When he'd calmed, he pulled away from her and slumped in his chair, rubbing his eyes. His eyelids hung half-closed. "I'm going to have to resign from active service, aren't I?"

"Why?" She moved back to her previous seat, facing him.

He snorted. "I'm grieving for people I never even knew."

She turned one hand toward the ceiling. "That means you have compassion. That's a prerequisite for this job, not a deterrent."

"Orinyay didn't come apart at the welds like this. Neither did the other *kiandarai*."

"Ishe tells me Orinyay went straight to her house without checking in." Amaya leaned her elbows on her knees. "Why do you suppose she breached protocol? She has her husband for a guide, Vadin. With practice, you'll learn how to hide what you feel until you get somewhere safe with a suitable guide."

"Then you never get used to this?"

She shook her head. "You learn to persevere and live past it, but if you ever get to the point where death, particularly violent death, has no effect on you, then it's time for you to leave active service." She stood and offered her hand. "Let's get you to your hammock. You need to rest."

"I'm supposed to relieve Ishe."

"Not tonight."

"All right." He yielded to her guiding arm.

***

Amaya stood on the crest of the dune overlooking the site of Wylin's camp. Footprints traced paths down into the depression and all around the area. Avicopter landing struts had made impressions in a variety of places.

The tents, the equipment, and even all the stacked driftwood was gone. Such a thorough job might have been done by random looters or opportunistic thieves, but more

LIKE HERDING THE WIND

than likely, Wylin had allies. Pavwin had mentioned other silver collar tabs reported missing and reassigned to convenient-sounding names. That couldn't be a coincidence.

She returned to her avicopter and headed for home.

URUSHALON

Epilogue

Osborn stepped back and surveyed his living room. Everyone had a lemonade in hand, but one remained on his tray. He counted each of the men on his watch, their families, and the members of Hawk's Nest and came up one short. Amaya had wandered off somewhere.

Crowd got to be too much for you, huh?

He slipped into the kitchen as his, Gale's, and Hollis' kids blazed through the door. The girls had flower wreaths made of yellow and pink wildflowers on their heads, and the boys wore wreaths of oak leaves.

"Dad! Dad! Look what Amaya made for us!" Gale's boy called. "She said Greek athletes used to make these."

"And look, she made flower headbands for us," Hollis' girl added.

That answers the question of where Amaya disappeared to.

"Dinner will be ready soon, dear," Esther said.

Osborn inhaled a deep breath of tomato sauce and spices. "Okay, honey. Smells great."

He stepped out the back door and turned left. Amaya perched on the patio table, staring at the sunset.

He joined her. "Almost time to eat."

"I'll go in with you shortly."

"I don't think you can. You're taller than I am."

Amaya smiled. "Not if you stand on the table."

Ed looked back at the table and grinned. "That'd do it, all right." He turned southward toward the ruins of Woran Juvay. "So, what'd Emyrin have to say about the cleared-out campsite?"

She nudged him with her elbow. "We're supposed to be celebrating, not looking toward the next challenge."

"Yeah, I know, but…"

"Emyrin thinks looters got there before we got back."

Ed snorted. "Convenient. You buying any of that?"

"Are you?"

"I'm not as dumb as he thinks I am."

Amaya nodded once. "Good. Neither am I, but let's suspend our worries about that until tomorrow. Your wife is safe, and Wylin will be no further harm."

"Sounds like a plan." After a few easy moments of silence, he glanced back toward the house then wrapped an arm around her shoulders. "I know it's crowded in there, but it's more than the crowd this time, isn't it, *Urushalon*?"

"Umhm. I needed to think."

"Care to think in the open?"

"That might be best." Amaya paused and rubbed her eyes. "When you asked me about why I came to Las Palomas, I only told you part of the truth."

Osborn nodded. "I know. Who was it?"

"Essien."

Osborn sighed. *I wish you could've told me. Maybe I*

URUSHALON

could've helped.

She slipped an arm around his back. "I felt haunted up north. I came down here in part to start over, to get away from the pain, the grief, and the constant doubt. Then I found that I had brought it all with me like an extra, ten-ton suitcase. I have been slowly destroying myself ever since I lost my family. Yes, I finished my Rites of Final Memorial as required, but I never let the past go."

Amaya folded something metallic and segmented into Osborn's hand. Her hand was warm and rock steady. He opened his hand. In his palm lay her wedding bracelet.

"I have no nearby kin but you, *Urushalon*. You may do with that as you choose. I don't need it any more. I have grieved too long and uselessly questioned my actions too many times."

"Will you remarry?"

She turned one hand skyward. "I've left that decision with God. I am content either way."

He smiled. "I may have some success at herding the wind now. I've been very concerned about you many times over the years, Amaya. I knew something wasn't right, but I was at a loss to do anything to help."

"I'm sorry I worried you, dear one. You've been exceptionally patient with me."

He shrugged. "Could I do differently? Some lessons take longer than others."

The sun faded below the horizon.

Hollis leaned his head out the door. "It's soup!"

Amaya glanced that way as the door closed again. "I thought it was lasagna."

Osborn smiled. "All I know for certain is Esther is a fabulous cook, and it smells too good to be garden mulch."

He pocketed the bracelet and followed Amaya inside.

LIKE HERDING THE WIND

Time-line
Years given in Earth Calendar

1612 – The Eshuvani generation ship makes a controlled crash landing in the Saxony region of the Holy Roman Empire in a farmer's recently harvested field. They make contact with the local humans, particularly a clergyman who teaches them about the local environment, Christianity, and other cultural information.

1613 – The 2,000 survivors of the crash establish enclaves on six of seven continents and keep to themselves to protect human civilization. In the same year, a small pox epidemic in Brazil, inadvertently caused by the enclave there, is stopped by the Eshuvani.

1614 – Japanese leadership bans Christianity in an unsuccessful attempt to drive the Eshuvani out.

1616 – Eshuvani efforts to prevent the spread of small pox and other diseases by their own settlements and European settlements in the New World are not entirely successful. In New England, 95% of the local indigenous population is wiped out.

1618 – Thirty Year War begins. The French army attacks an Eshuvani enclave, but the Eshuvani repel the attack without harming anyone and refuse to retaliate. The defeat is so decisive that the European enclaves are feared and avoided.

1619 – A Russian envoy, on the way to the Chinese court, tries to establish relations with an Eshuvani enclave. They ignore the envoy.

1629 – Brazilian slavers attack Jesuit missions. The Jesuits seek help from the Eshuvani, who protect them without causing harm to the slavers.

1630 – When a famine strikes India, the Eshuvani attempt to airlift supplies in, but the locals do not trust the Eshuvani and refuse help.

1631 – Prior to an eruption of Mt. Vesuvius, the Eshuvani move their enclave and try to warn the humans, who do not heed the warning.

1637 – After failing to convince the European settlers to refrain from enslaving Pequod Indians, the Eshuvani rescue the Indians and relocate them.

1641 – In another attempt to force the Eshuvani from Japan, all foreigners are banned. This is also unsuccessful.

1644 – The Ming Dynasty ends in China. The Eshuvani keep a close eye on the change in power but do not interfere.

1647 – In response to an earthquake in Santiago de Chile, the Eshuvani mobilize to help the locals rebuild but only within the then current human technology level.

1648 – Following an Eshuvani expedition, Russian explorer Semyon Dezhnev discovers the Bering Strait. The same year, an Eshuvani enclave provides protection for Russian Jews during an attempted massacre, then relocates them in the Holy Roman Empire.

1652 – The Eshuvani encourage the Dutch settlement at Cape of Good Hope in South Africa, but then become upset by the way the Dutch settlers treat the locals. Attempts at negotiation are not successful.

1658 – When the new ruler of India comes to power and establishes Islam, the Eshuvani become even more reclusive in their enclaves and prepare to ward off attacks. Although threats are made by the new ruler, no attack comes.

1674 – Pressured by the Eshuvani, Spain ends the Chilean slave trade.

1675 – An Eshuvani-negotiated treaty between local Indians and New England settlers was breached resulting in a brutal war called King Philip's War.

1676 – At the urging of an Eshuvani negotiator, Governor Berkeley of Jamestown refuses to grant permission for a raid on a local Indian population. The Jamestown residents, led by Nathan Bacon, go on a rampage.

1686 – The Eshuvani serve as a mediator for a peace treaty between Russia and Poland, becoming very frustrated with both sides in the process.

1689 – A border treaty between Russia and China results in Outer Mongolia being declared neutral. The Eshuvani enclave there enforces the treaty.

1690 – Woran Juvay is destroyed by a hurricane. The enclave is rebuilt as Woran Oldue on the coast of the mainland in what later becomes Texas.

1697 – The Eshuvani mourn the end of the Mayan civilization by making careful records and preserving whatever artifacts they can find.

1701 – With the advice of the Eshuvani, Russia founds the School of Mathematics and Navigation.

1702 – Another famine hits parts of India. The Eshuvani fly in supplies, which are better received this time.

1705 – Eshuvani try to discourage the slave trade on the Gold Coast, but have only marginal, short-lived success.

1707 – Sweden invades Russia and attacks an enclave. The Eshuvani effortlessly repel the attack without harming anyone and refuse to retaliate. In the same year, Mount Fuji erupts. The Eshuvani rescue several Japanese living in the path of the eruption.

1717 – A Russian expedition is attacked in Khiva, Central Asia. Eshuvani attempt a rescue but they're too late to prevent the massacre.

1718 – Using falsified rumors about the Eshuvani as a diversion, Russia thwarts a Khazak invasion.

1732 – On an expedition to an Eshuvani enclave, Russian explorers get lost and find Alaska instead.

1740 – Appalled by the slave trade from Africa to the western hemisphere, the Eshuvani begin interfering by rescuing slaves and sinking empty slave ships.

1750 – During civil war in Persia, the Eshuvani secure themselves in the enclave and defend against attacks without harming the attackers.

1755 – Major earthquake in Portugal results in the deaths of 60,000 humans. Eshuvani offer their medical assistance.

1762 – Amadeus Mozart becomes the *urushalon* of an aging Eshuvani musician. Mozart writes his first symphony two years later after his *urushalon* dies.

1768 – During a massacre of Jews in Poland, Eshuvani rescue teams save as many as they can and relocate them to the Holy Roman Empire.

1769 – Eshuvani attempt to airlift supplies to relieve a famine in Bengal, but the supplies are intercepted and destroyed.

1775 – During the American Revolution, Eshuvani secretly assist the colonists.

1780 – Eshuvani begin a campaign in many parts of the world to end the slave trade.

1791 – Russia permits Jewish settlers in some areas, so Eshuvani relocate some of the Jews from the Holy Roman Empire, at the settlers' request.

1805 – Eshuvani attempt to prevent a massacre of Jews in Algeria but arrive too late.

1810 – A peasant revolt led by Father Miguel Hidalgo in Mexico is squashed. A grieving Eshuvani, whose *urushalon* was killed in the revolt, seeks revenge, killing her *urushalon*'s murderer before the *kiandarai* catch up and put her under arrest.

1811 – Eshuvani negotiators argue for the release of Father Miguel Hidalgo, but are unsuccessful.

1821 – An Eshuvani helps his *urushalon*, Moses Austin, secure colonization rights in Texas.

1828 – After failing at diplomatic measures for ten years, the Eshuvani encourage the assassination of Shaka, a Zulu king, to stop his attacks on settlements and villages.

1829 – The Eshuvani negotiate a treaty between Persia and Russia.

1830 – In response to the Indian Removal Act in the United States, the Eshuvani offer to establish safe zones around their cities where Indians can live, but very few take them up on it. When some of those groups use the safe zones as staging areas to attack American settlements, the Eshuvani rescind their offer.

1831 – During a cholera epidemic in Russia, the Eshuvani offer medical assistance.

1832 – After years of negotiation and Eshuvani encouragement, Britain ends slavery.

1835 – Samuel Morse observes Eshuvani communicating by tapping on a handheld device. That gives him the idea for Morse Code and a telegraph, which takes him a couple years to perfect.

1836 – During the Runaway Scrape, Woran Oldue, an Eshuvani enclave, protects humans fleeing across Texas by slowing the Mexican army down to allow them time to escape.

1838 – Eshuvani interference in the Brazilian slave trade frees thousands of slaves.

1839 – Following the Trail of Tears, the forced removal of Cherokee from Georgia to Oklahoma, the Eshuvani offer to assist with further removals to prevent the huge numbers of deaths. The United States does not trust the Eshuvani to honor that agreement and refuses the offer.

1840 – The Eshuvani attempt to interfere with the slave trade again, but rather than risk an Eshuvani victory, the slavers kill most of the slaves before the Eshuvani rescue effort arrives. Distraught over the failure, the Eshuvani decide not to interfere so openly.

1844 – As Texas debates joining the United States, the Eshuvani attempt to dissuade them, suggesting that if they wait a while longer, tension with Mexico will cool off. Texas leadership isn't interested in the advice.

1845 – Disgusted by slavery in the United States, the Eshuvani help humans organize the Underground Railroad. In the same year, the Eshuvani suggest that the United States refrain from annexing Texas until tensions with Mexico are significantly lower. United States leadership resents the advice and annexes Texas anyway.

1846 – During the famine in Ireland, Eshuvani airlift food supplies under cover of darkness.

1850 – Amaya Ulonya is born.

1852 – When an assassination of the Iranian shah fails, Iran massacres the group responsible. The Eshuvani argue for forgiveness, resulting in an attack against the enclave that is easily repelled.

1855 – With Eshuvani encouragement, Russia and Japan enter diplomatic talks.

1858 – The Eshuvani negotiate another border treaty between Russia and China.

1865 – Eshuvani rescuers are too late to prevent the assassination of Abraham Lincoln.

1867 – The Eshuvani encourage the United States to buy Alaska from Russia but will not explain why.

1869 – When the Japanese government encourages colonization of Hokkaido, the Eshuvani enclave there sets up and maintains a perimeter.

1870 – The Eshuvani attempt to provide aid for a famine in Iran, but the Iranians do not trust them and refuse help.

1873 – The Japanese ban on Christianity is lifted at the

insistence of the Eshuvani.

1875 – The Eshuvani attempt to convince colonizing powers in Africa to back off. They are not successful.

1876 – Alexander Bell invents the telephone to try to reproduce an Eshuvani communication system.

1877 – Eshuvani help Sitting Bull and a few hundred of his people escape into Canada.

1881 – Due to massacres of Jews, the Eshuvani relocate as many as they can to the United States and the area that will later become Israel.

1891 – During a famine in Russia, Eshuvani airlift supplies.

1896 – With Eshuvani guidance, Ethiopia and Liberia block European invasions.

1897 – An Eshuvani helps her *urushalon*, Torakusu Yamaha, found a company that makes musical instruments.

1899 – The Eshuvani negotiate a business deal between a United States company, Western Electric, and a Japanese company, Nippon Electric Corporation.

1900 – During the Boxer Rebellion, Chinese forces attempt to drive out the Eshuvani. With only a few casualties on either side, the Eshuvani ward off attacks.

1902 – Eshuvani negotiators convince France to give up its claim on Benin in Africa.

1903 – Trying to emulate an Eshuvani avicopter, Orville and Wilbur Wright fly the first plane at Kitty Hawk.

1914 – World War I begins. The Eshuvani keep a non-interference policy.

1915 – With a few subtle hints from his *urushalon*, Albert Einstein develops the General Theory of Relativity.

1919 – China invades Mongolia in an effort to get at the Eshuvani enclave there. The enclave repels the attack, but accidentally kills several dozen attackers. In the same year, the

Treaty of Versailles ends World War I. Eshuvani encourage forgiveness, but the winning nations punish Germany with harsh requirements.

1920 – At the urging of his *urushalon*, Mahatma Gandhi begins a non-violent protest.

1921 – Edward Osborn is born.

1922 – Gandhi is imprisoned, but his *urushalon* rescues him and provides a home for him in the enclave.

1923 – A sniper aiming for Amaya Ulonya kills her husband and son instead.

1925 – While on a camping trip, Eddie Osborn wanders off in the middle of the night to chase a rabbit. Amaya Ulonya tracks him down. He finds her so fascinating that he adopts her, becoming her *urushalon*.

1930 – Upon the death of his *urushalon*, Gandhi returns to human civilization to protest British rule.

1937 – Amelia Earhart runs into trouble on her Pacific flight. Eshuvani attempt a rescue from a Japanese enclave, but they're too late.

1939 – World War II begins. Eshuvani leadership insist on continuing the policy of non-involvement.

1941 – Eshuvani warnings about the possible attack on Pearl Harbor are too vague and not deciphered in time. Japanese forces bomb Pearl Harbor, drawing the United States into World War II.

1942 – Disgusted by the Nazi concentration camps, Eshuvani rescue teams defy the non-involvement orders of their government and begin rescue missions.

1945 – United States bombers on the way to Hiroshima are intercepted by Eshuvani military and held at bay while an enclave in the intended blast area is evacuated. The Eshuvani warn Japan that they need to surrender or make peace with the United States before the enclave is empty or else the atomic bombs will wipe out the cities of Hiroshima and Nagasaki.

Japanese officials do not take the warning seriously. Once the enclave is clear, the Eshuvani issue their warning again then release the United States aircraft. Japanese forces deflect the attack on Hiroshima, but Nagasaki is destroyed. Japan surrenders shortly after that.

1946 – Upon learning of Russian efforts to develop biological warfare, the Eshuvani step in and force an end to the project.

1947 – Eshuvani help with negotiations to free India and Pakistan from British rule.

1950 – When China invades Tibet, Eshuvani help refugees escape, resettling them in India.

1956 – The British are not impressed with Eshuvani interference in the matter of India and Pakistan, so they resist further attempts in other areas, resulting in an independence war in Kenya and a defeat of the Kenyan forces.

1961 – Eshuvani cause an interruption in the space race, insisting that humans are not prepared for what's out there. They provide just enough information about one of the more violent races out there as proof. Space programs are aborted until defensive and offensive technology can catch up.

1963 – Basing the programs partially on Eshuvani *kiandarai*, the first human paramedic programs start.

1965 – Eshuvani criminals begin devastating attacks against the human police force of Las Palomas, Texas. Amaya Ulonya's partner dies. She moves to south Texas to be closer to her *urushalon* and takes command of the Buffer Zone *kiandarai* station to help Ed Osborn and his department get to the bottom of the attacks.

Timeline Sources Retrieved May 1, 2014:

http://www.thelatinlibrary.com/imperialism/notes/nativeamericanchron.html

http://www.scaruffi.com/politics/history.html

Glossary of Eshuvani Words

Eshuvani: eh-shoo-VAH-nee – one or more members of an alien race that crash landed on Earth in 1612 when their generation ship developed a critical system failure. Initially from a world with less gravity, Eshuvani are tall and wiry and naturally thinner than humans. Like an ambush predator, they are capable of extreme bursts of speed or strength, but only for a very short amount of time. They are more emotional than humans as a rule.

kiala (pl. *kialai*): kee-AHL-uh (pl. KEE-uh-LIE) – a journeyman who has finished basic training for becoming a member of the *kiandarai* but has not completed specialization. Training and field experience are needed to complete this level. The comm system collar tabs are black enameled metal like an apprentice but endowed with a tracking circuit.

kiand (pl. *kiandai*): kee-AHND (pl. kee-AHND-eye) – the captain of a *kiandarai* station. The *kiand* is well-experienced in police work and trained in medicine to the level of a nurse-practitioner. A *kiand* is certified to teach at least two skills: the *kiand's* specialization and one other that is chosen through training. The comm system collar tabs are gold.

kiandara (pl. *kiandarai*): kee-ahn-DAH-ruh (pl. kee-ahn-duh-RYE) – 1. A typical officer trained as a paramedic and experienced in police work. A *kiandara* must be able to teach in the chosen specialization. The comm system collar tabs are silver.

2. the general name for the job, equivalent to using "police" or "EMS" in the human system. All members of the *kiandarai* can be referred to collectively by this title.

kiat (pl. *kiati*): kee-AHT (pl. kee-AH-tee) – a chief in charge of an entire enclaves' *kiandarai*, experienced in police work and trained as a physician or surgeon. A *kiat* must be able to teach the chosen specialization and at least two other skills chosen through training. The comm system collar tabs are copper.

Uloniya Varoosht: oo-low-NYE-uh vah-ROOSHT – Literally translated "Hawk House," but more commonly understood "Hawk's Nest." *Kiandarai* stations are typically named after the current *kiand*. *Uloniya Varoosht* is the *kiandarai* station dedicated to protecting the Buffer Zone between Woran Oldue and Las Palomas. This station is also tasked with helping the police force of Las Palomas get the proper training and equipment to handle the crime wave caused by Eshuvani criminals.

urushalon: oo-ROO-shah-lawn – Literally translates "beloved" and refers to a special adoption between a human and an Eshuvani. They regard each other as family members, usually in a parent-child relationship.

Vueltiya Ens: voo-el-TIE-uh ENS – Literally translated "Falcon Fingers," but more commonly understood "Falcon's Wing." Vueltiya Ens is located in Woran Oldue. It is the closest station to Uloniya Varoosht.

Woran Juvay: WAR-on JOO-vay – "Enclave of the Seagull" or "Seagull Enclave," sometimes referred to simply as "The Gull." This Eshuvani enclave located on a barrier island was wiped out by a hurricane. The survivors decided that the mainland would be safer, so they chose not rebuild on the island. Woran Juvay is in ruins.

Woran Kishay: WAR-on KEE-shay – "Enclave in the Middle" or "Middle Enclave" was built near the middle of Texas. The human city of Austin, Texas was built nearby. Woran Kishay's main *kiandarai* station houses an old *kiat* historian and record-keeper in addition to their regular staff.

Woran Oldue: WAR-on AWL-dway – "Enclave the Second" or "Second Enclave" was built after the destruction of Woran Juvay. Woran Oldue provided protection for human settlers during the Texas Revolution by slowing down the Mexican army, which allowed the settlers to escape. After the revolution, the city of Las Palomas was built nearby to take advantage of Eshuvani protection. Over time, as both cities expanded, Woran Oldue ended up forming an almost complete loop around Las Palomas, open on the coastal side. At the time, the humans didn't mind that, perceiving the Eshuvani as a shield. Traffic on the roads through the enclave and Buffer Zone is carefully monitored. The Buffer Zone between the cities prevents any further encroachment. Uloniya Varoosht monitors and supports the area.

ABOUT THE AUTHOR

After a long run of teaching 4-footers (that's height, not leg count), Cindy Koepp took a job mangling and wrangling glasses for a major retailer while she worked on her Master's in adult education. With that safely out of the way, she has returned to pursuits more interesting than reading dry academic texts, such as whistling with Masika D. Greyt, African Grey extraordinaire. Masika makes a valiant effort to keep an eye on her human and provides entertainment in return for oatmeal boxes to destroy.

When not writing whatever stories come to mind, Cindy quilts, sews, does beadwork and embroidery, and comes up with all kinds of wild crafty things to do. Naturally, this means no horizontal surface is safe from collecting partially completed projects and unattached mysterious parts.

The author invites you to his website for exclusive behind-the-scenes information about the writing of *Like Herding the Wind*. If you have enjoyed this novel, please be sure write a review or post it on your social media and share it with others!

www.ckoepp.com
Facebook: KoeppC
Twitter: cckoepp
Linkedin: cckoepp
Wordpress: cindykoepp @ wordpress

CPSIA information can be obtained at www.ICGtesting.com
Printed in the USA
BVOW06s1501290116

434469BV00008B/114/P